"Just for the record, you are the most inconvenient woman I've ever known."

She made him want things he couldn't have—made him want to be a man he couldn't be.

He would try if he had the chance, would spend the rest of his life trying...but that chance could come only with the truth. With her trust and understanding. Even then...

It was too damn big a risk.

She rewarded him with a teasing smile. "Thank you. My goal in life is to be inconvenient." Rising onto her toes, she kissed his cheek, then pulled away.

The reminder renewed the ache, the longing in his soul.

Dear Reader,

Who hasn't wished at some time that she could make a fresh start—pull up roots, move to a new place where she doesn't anyone (and no one knows her!) and become the person she wants to be, in the life she wants to live?

We were lucky enough during my husband's navy career to move to a number of new places. I still remember the optimism that greeted me with each new town. No matter how good things had been in the last town, they could always be better in the new place. At the least, they would be different, and even that was exciting.

Some of that optimism was with me while writing this book—and nostalgia, because while Sweetwater was brand-new to Jayne, it was a trip down memory lane for me. I created the town in *Somebody's Baby* and revisited it in *Somebody's Lady*. It was like coming home again.

I hope you enjoy it, too!

Marilyn Pappano

MARILYN PAPPANO
SOMEBODY'S HERO

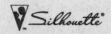

INTIMATE MOMENTS™

Published by Silhouette Books

America's Publisher of Contemporary Romance

 SILHOUETTE BOOKS

ISBN-13: 978-0-373-27497-0
ISBN-10: 0-373-27497-1

SOMEBODY'S HERO

This edition published by arrangement with Harlequin Books S.A.

® and TM are trademarks of Harlequin Books S.A., used under license.
Trademarks indicated with ® are registered in the United States Patent
and Trademark Office, the Canadian Trade Marks Office and in other
countries.

Visit Silhouette Books at www.eHarlequin.com

Printed in U.S.A.

Books by Marilyn Pappano

MARILYN PAPPANO

has been a daydreamer and a storyteller all her life. After traveling across the country in the course of her husband's career, she's now back home in Oklahoma, living high on a hill overlooking her hometown. With woods, a pond and a small orchard, she keeps busy outside and has learned such skills as operating a chain saw and building flower beds and steps with the rocks that are her most abundant crop. She and her husband have one son, who's following his own military career through places like Italy, Korea, Iraq and Afghanistan, and a houseful of dogs who are fully convinced they're children, too. You can visit her Web site at: www.marilyn-pappano.com.

To my own hero, Bob.
I love you.

Chapter 1

Fat, wet snow collected on the windshield, obscuring the view ahead. Jayne Miller nudged the intermittent action of the wipers up a notch, and the blades swept across the glass, but the view didn't improve. She wanted desperately to believe that she was at the wrong house, but the directions she'd gotten from the man at the gas station left little room for doubt. This was not only the last house on the left, it was the *only* house on the left for the past two miles.

The wooden sign hanging next to the front door, clearly visible with each swipe of the wipers, left even less room for doubt. Miller, it announced in rough letters carved in a half moon around a flower.

It was a great old house, Greg had told her when the news had come that he'd inherited it. Big, with high ceilings, hardwood floors and a banister just made for sliding down. It was too big for their little family of three, with its huge yard, gardens and orchard.

The wipers cleared the window once more and she stared at the house. It looked about the size of a two-bedroom apartment. There was no second story and, therefore, no banister. And the yard, if it had ever existed, had long ago returned to the wild. High ceilings? Hardwood floors? Gardens? She doubted it.

At some point in its existence, the house had been painted white—at least, that was the shade the few chips that remained took on in the headlights' glare. The shutters at one front window hung askew and were missing completely from the other. The porch appeared crooked from where she sat—or maybe it was straight and the house was tilted. Or, hell, maybe both porch and house were level and *she* was the one off balance.

She choked back a laugh for fear it would turn into a sob, then twisted in her seat to check her daughter. Five-year-old Lucy was asleep in the backseat, snoring softly, a quilt pulled over her and a teddy bear serving as a pillow. Their adventure, as she'd insisted on calling their move from Chicago to the southeast Tennessee mountains, had worn her out. Jayne was starting to feel pretty worn out, too.

She tucked the quilt closer around her daughter, then pulled on her coat, a hat and gloves. With the house key clenched tightly in one fist, she left the SUV's warmth for the wet snow that was rapidly accumulating and tramped across uneven ground to the porch. The first step sagged precariously under her weight, and she climbed the others with more caution. The last thing she needed was a broken ankle or neck out here in the middle of nowhere.

It took some effort to work the key into the lock, then a jiggle and a jerk to get it to turn. When she swung open the door, she could see little inside. It was only four in the afternoon, but the late-March snowstorm that had led them here turned the day dark. Groping blindly, she found a light switch and flipped it, but nothing happened. Of course not. She hadn't called ahead and arranged to have the power turned on…if there even was power. What if Greg's grandmother had lived by candlelight?

She shuddered, then gave herself a mental shake. The darkness was her own fault, and she could remedy it first thing in the morning.

With a glance back at the truck, she eased into the house. The lumpy shadows were furniture, draped in heavy dust cloths. There was one sofa-size, two chair-size. A fireplace of native stone filled most of one wall, so heat was a possibility—*if* there happened to be some firewood lying around somewhere—and the oil lamp on the mantel sloshed when she picked it up. Let there be light, she thought gratefully.

She did a quick tour of the house: a kitchen with a tiny corner set aside for the dining room, a decent-size bedroom, a bathroom—thank you, God—and a second bedroom about the size of a closet. There were beds in the bedrooms and mattresses on the beds. She had plenty of linens in the truck, along with enough blankets to warm an igloo for a night or two. Now if she could just find some dry wood, they would be in business.

She was returning to the living room when a shadow appeared in the open doorway. It stretched from the floor all the way to the top of the door frame and pretty much filled it side to side, as well. A startled cry escaped before she could stop it, and her heart leaped into her throat.

The shadow was a snow-dusted man. He wore jeans, a heavy coat and thick-soled boots, and a knitted cap covered his head and much of his face. Likely he lived in the house where the road ended its meandering journey. That didn't make her feel any safer or any less worried about her daughter.

Before she could find her voice to speak, he did. "What are you doing here?"

He was a neighbor, she counseled herself, and out here a neighbor was A Good Thing. Taking a deep breath, she started across the room toward him. "I'm moving in. I'm Jayne Miller. Edna Miller was my grandmother-in-law. My husband's grandmother. Actually, my ex-husband now. We're divorced, but he gave me the house. Well, he didn't exactly give it to me. He took everything we owned of any value and left me the deed to this place in exchange." Abruptly she caught her breath. "That's too much information, isn't it?" She offered her hand, remembered she still wore her gloves, stripped the right one off, then stuck out her hand again. "I'm Jayne Miller. Your new neighbor. And you are?"

His gaze dropped to her hand—she felt it as much as saw it—but he made no effort to shake it. Instead he looked at her again. "You're not planning to live here, are you?"

She felt foolish standing there with her hand out. She tugged the glove on again, slid her hands into her coat pockets, then pulled them out and folded her arms across her chest. "Yes. Probably. That *was* the plan, at least." And still was, she told herself. She needed a change of scene. Lucy would be better off growing up in Smalltown, Tennessee, than in Chicago. And Jayne's writing career, barely alive the past few years, desperately needed the boost that time, inspiration and isolation could give it.

"Yes. We're going to live here."

"We?"

"My daughter and me—I—we. Lucy and me." She dragged in a cold, musty breath. "I didn't get your name."

He scowled harder and said, "Lewis."

"Lewis," she repeated. He didn't look like a Lewis. Naming characters was important in her work; sometimes it took longer to find just the right name for a character than it had to name Lucy. A Lewis should be older, heavier, less brooding. *This* Lewis was tall, lean though broad-shouldered, scowling and somewhat handsome. Not knock-your-socks-off gorgeous but attractive in a dark, brooding sort of way.

Dark and brooding always appealed to a romance author.

But at the moment she was in mother/woman mode, not romance author. "Well, Lewis, it's nice meeting you, but I've got to see if Gran left any firewood around here or head back into town and get a motel room for the night. I, uh, forgot to make arrangements to have the power turned on."

Though she took a step forward, he didn't move. "The nearest motel is thirty miles back north, not that it matters. You're not getting off the mountain today. The road's impassable. My truck's stuck at the bottom of the last hill."

That explained the snow that coated his shoulders. She glanced past him and saw that her SUV was shrouded in the stuff. "Well, then, that makes the firewood more important. If you'll excuse me…"

Still he didn't move. "Wouldn't matter if you had called ahead. The power's off. And there's not any firewood here. I'll bring some over."

Jayne swallowed hard. "You don't have to do that. I mean, I appreciate the offer, but if you'll just tell me where it is, I can bring it over myself. You probably want to get out of the cold." Probably almost as much as *she* wanted out of it. Lord, this had been a stupid move on her part—Greg-stupid, which was about as irresponsible as it got. But it had been seventy degrees that morning. How could she possibly have known they'd be in a snowstorm by midafternoon?

Lewis looked as if he wanted to take her up on her offer, but his mouth tightened and instead he said, "Go ahead and get what you need out of the truck. You did bring food and blankets, didn't you?"

I'm not stupid, she wanted to say, but hadn't she just admitted that sometimes she was? "Yes." She'd stocked up when they'd stopped for lunch—chips, peanut butter and crackers, cookies, canned soup, bottled water and chocolate. She and Lucy could live for days on that.

Finally he moved out of the doorway, but instead of leaving, he came inside. He took something from the table pushed against one wall, then went to the fireplace and removed the globe from the lamp there. There was a strike, a flare of sulfur, then the odor of burning oil as the flame caught the lamp wick. A moment later the second lamp was also burning. "You might clean those globes before you put them back on," he said shortly, then left before he could hear her faint "I will."

Jayne went to the door to watch him. He moved with long strides, paying no attention to the snow that crept halfway up his calves. She hadn't really given any thought to neighbors when she'd decided to move here; she'd just assumed there would be more than enough. After all, in Chicago, neighbors were in plentiful supply. Lewis had the potential to be a good one—not too friendly, so he wouldn't interrupt her work the way Greg had, but willing to help when needed. She and Lucy wouldn't be alone up here on the mountain, but they could feel as if they were. That was a big plus.

Then she turned back and looked at the drab, dusty room that was even more depressing with the lamplight shining on its shortcomings and sighed. She really *needed* a big plus right about now.

The last thing Tyler Lewis wanted in his life was a neighbor—no, make that a neighbor with a kid, he grumbled as he stacked a load of logs into a canvas carrier. When he'd built his house, he'd bought the most remote piece of land he could find around Sweetwater. Granted, he'd had old Edna just down the road for three years, but she'd pretty much kept to herself, and he'd done the same. He'd chopped wood for her, picked up her stuff at the grocery store when he did his own shopping and made a few repairs around her place when she needed them, but that hadn't made them friends. He hadn't been looking for any intrusions into his life, and neither had she.

Maybe her ex-granddaughter-in-law had that in common with her. A man could hope.

Jayne Miller. A plain name for a far-from-plain woman. Tall, with long legs, long brown hair and a husky voice… If he was a weaker man, he might be in trouble. But he'd had a lifetime of experience at keeping people at a distance. He excelled at it.

Not that he didn't have his weaknesses. He hated every one of them.

Grimacing, he finished filling a second canvas bag, then picked up one in each hand and trudged around his house and across the snow to Edna's house. *She* came out as he dumped his load on the porch. He didn't speak when he passed her on his way back, and neither did she as she heaved a carton from the cargo area of the truck.

By the time he'd delivered and stacked a good supply of wood, she was finished with her unloading. He took the last load inside, got the fire going, then piled the rest of the logs nearby. When he turned, she was watching him. Her smile was tentative as she huddled in her coat for warmth. He could relate. He'd lost contact with his feet a long time ago.

"Thank you."

He shrugged it off, then glanced at the little girl asleep on the sofa, bundled in so many blankets that only part of her face was visible—pale skin, pale brown hair. His sister teased that he wasn't a kid-friendly person, and he didn't argue the point. He didn't think he'd ever been a kid himself, and helping raise his brothers and sister had been enough exposure to small people to last a lifetime.

Still, he nodded toward her. "What's her name?"

"Lucy. She's five."

There were worse names for a five-year-old—Edna. Bess. Tiffany. If he had a preference, it would be for nice, common names like Sarah, Beth or Kate.

Or Jayne.

Still hugging herself, she eased a few steps closer to the fireplace. He thought he should say something before leaving but didn't have a clue what. He settled for gesturing toward the fire. "Try not to let it go out." The moment he heard the words, he grimaced. His sister would unload on him if he said something so patronizing to her.

But Jayne just smiled tightly. "I won't. Thanks again for your help. I really appreciate it."

He nodded, walked outside and pulled the door shut behind him. Stopping on the porch, he tugged on his gloves, adjusted the collar of his coat, then stepped out into the snow. Inside he would have said the house was no warmer than outside, but even those few moments of heat had made a difference that he could feel to his bones.

His own house, though, really was as cold as outside, and much darker. The dogs met him at the door, sparing a few seconds for a sniff and a lick, then darting outside before he could close the door. Out of habit, he flipped the light switch, but nothing happened. He found the matches in the gloom, lit the oil lamps that sat on tables around the room, then crouched in front of the woodstove. It didn't take long to get a fire burning, though it would be a while before the room warmed to the comfort zone. He removed his coat and hat anyway, hanging them near the door, where the snowmelt could drip on the tile, then kicked off his boots. After fixing a cup of instant cocoa with hot water from the tap, he wrapped up in a quilt and settled on the sofa.

The ring of the phone seemed out of place in the still, dark room. It seemed only fair that if he lost power and heat, the phone should go out, too, but he knew better than most that life wasn't fair.

"Enjoy your walk home?" his sister, Rebecca, asked in place of a greeting.

"You bet. Sliding uphill in the middle of a snowstorm has always been my idea of a fun time," he retorted, then asked, "How'd you know I wound up walking?"

"Because you always think you'll get home before the road gets too bad and you always wind up walking." Her tone turned sly. "Anything new to report?"

"Like what?" he asked, though he knew exactly what she meant. Sweetwater, with a population not worth counting, had the most effective gossip network around. Jayne Miller had probably stopped in town for supplies or directions, which meant that everyone within a ten-mile radius knew Edna's long-absent heir had put in an appearance before she'd even reached Sassie Whitlaw's four-foot-tall metal chicken. Everyone but him.

"Come on. Jayne Miller. From Chicago. Writer of some sort. Has a five-year-old daughter named Lucy. Divorced from Edna's grandson and got the house in the divorce. What do you think of her?"

"What makes you think I met her?"

She made a *pffft* sound. "Tell me you didn't haul firewood for her."

Tyler shifted uncomfortably. Rebecca knew him too well—all his secrets, all his shortcomings. "Just enough for a couple days."

"So? Tell me about her."

"Hell, you already know more than I do." She hadn't said anything to him about being a writer, though she had spilled out everything about how she'd come to own her ex's grandmother's house. Being a city girl, she probably wouldn't have much appreciation for country living. Maybe he could persuade her to do what Edna had always refused—sell the property to him. He'd bought the rest of Edna's land before she'd died. If he could have that small section, his privacy would be complete.

The slyness returned to Rebecca's voice. "Is she pretty?"

"I didn't notice." Just as he tried to not notice the heat in his cheeks that always appeared when he lied. It was better than any lie detector, his mother used to tease.

When she'd recovered enough to learn how to tease again.

There was a moment of silence, then Rebecca heaved a sigh. "You know, what happened with Angela was an aberration. It doesn't mean you're like…" The silence that followed was heavy. Final.

When had they agreed that they would never mention their father again? They hadn't actually discussed it or anything. One day not long after his death they had just stopped talking about him, and the younger kids had followed their lead. Delbert Lewis had stopped existing for them.

Except in their dreams. Their nightmares.

Angela was another subject they didn't discuss. His old girl-friend was long gone—but never forgotten. Some of the best times in his life had been with her. So had some of the worst.

"What are the streets like in town?" he asked as if Rebecca hadn't trespassed into memories best left alone.

There was another silence, broken by another sigh. "Probably worse than the roads are out there. At least you were the only fool on the road out there."

"Gee, thanks for the compliment. Listen, I've got to change into dry clothes. I'll talk to you later." He moved the phone away from his ear, but not quickly enough to miss her quiet words.

"Yeah. Later."

Shadows danced on Jayne's eyelids, applying pressure to her eyes, then easing. She tried to pull the covers over her face, but they wouldn't budge. Tried to brush the shadows away but found something solid instead. Blindly she groped and realized it was Lucy's hand, her pudgy little fingers probing. Wrapping her hand around her daughter's, Jayne moved it away, then opened one eye enough to see a blurry face peering at her.

"I knew you was awake inside there." Tugging her hand free, Lucy jumped to the floor. "Come look outside, Mama. It snowed and snowed and snowed. It's pretty."

Jayne lifted her head from the pillow to watch Lucy dance to the windows, glanced around, then sank down again, resisting the urge to pull the covers over her head. Snow. The house. No power, no heat. The fire. Lewis. That was why she'd spent the night on a less-than-comfortable sofa, why she'd awakened every few hours to stoke the fire, why she wanted to hide her face and go back to sleep.

Of course, that wasn't an option, so she sat up and pushed

back the covers. Though Lucy had no qualms about twirling across the dusty floor in her bare feet, Jayne searched for the house shoes she'd kicked off after her last fire-stoking. Judging by the prints of her little bare feet, Lucy had explored the entire house before waking her mother. Now she was kneeling on a table in front of one window, the curtains held back in one hand, not even noticing the dust motes drifting down on her in a lazy shower.

"Look, Mom. Isn't it beautiful?"

Jayne detoured to add another log to the fire, then removed the curtains from Lucy's hand and pushed them back. "Beautiful," she agreed, then realized that it really was. Everything was covered with pristine snow. Tree branches hung heavy with it, and mundane things like trucks were turned into graceful lumps of white. All signs of her trips between house and SUV had been obliterated in the night, as well as Lewis's bigger footprints.

It was beautiful, peaceful and exactly what she needed. Just looking made her breathe a little deeper, a little slower, and eased the tightness in her chest. Maybe she hadn't made a mistake after all. Maybe this really was the change she'd needed.

"Can we go out and play?"

The idea of voluntarily going out into such wet and cold made Jayne cringe. She'd hated going out in the snow every winter of her adult life…but she'd loved it when she was a kid. Cleaning, unpacking, firewood and breakfast could wait.

"Okay. Let's get dressed."

Within fifteen minutes they were ready to go. Lucy was bundled in her favorite pink snowsuit. Lacking a snowsuit of her own, Jayne settled on jeans under sweatpants, a long-sleeved T-shirt, a sweatshirt, coat, hat and gloves. Neither of them was particularly mobile.

Lucy didn't seem to notice that moving through the snow was more hassle than fun. Even when she slipped into drifts that were deeper than she was tall, she came up coated in white and laughing. More of the tension inside Jayne eased. As long as Lucy could laugh, life was good.

Lucy was trying to start a snowman when the sound of a door closing echoed across the clearing. She popped to her feet, gazed at their neighbor's house as if noticing it for the first time, then broke into a broad grin. "Puppies!"

The dogs who'd just been freed from their house saw her at the same time and immediately detoured toward them, bounding across the snow as if it was no more than a minor nuisance. Easy to do when they were both the size of small ponies.

As Lucy moved to meet them, Jayne followed, struggling to catch up. Neither she nor Lucy had ever had any pet more rambunctious than a hamster, not even a blip on the landscape next to these creatures. The dogs were moving quickly, clearing the board fence that circled their yard in one leap, and they were so big that they could trample her little girl into the snow without even noticing it.

Ten feet out, the dogs leaped. Jayne shrieked Lucy's name, certain the next sound she would hear was her daughter's screams. Instead it was a sharp whistle that split the air. The dogs landed a few feet away and stood stock-still except for the excited quivering of their tails.

"Diaz, Cameron," Lewis called, but Jayne couldn't take her gaze from the animals to look in his direction. "Sit. Stay."

Both animals obeyed, though the smaller didn't actually touch the ground. It hovered there, butt a few inches above the snow, as if it might leap for Lucy's throat any minute now, Jayne thought hysterically…or as if it knew that snow was too cold to be sitting on, common sense forced her to admit.

"Are they your dogs?" Lucy asked as Lewis approached.

"More or less." He shifted his gaze, no friendlier than last night, to Jayne. "They're just excited to see someone smaller than them. They won't hurt her."

Maybe not on purpose, Jayne thought doubtfully.

"Cameron Diaz is Princess Fiona in *Shrek*," Lucy pointed out. "Are they named after her?"

Looking as if he had no clue what *Shrek* was, Lewis shrugged. "Maybe. I didn't name them."

"Are they boy dogs or girl dogs?"

"Boys."

Lucy splayed one mittened hand on her hip. "But Cameron Diaz is a girl, or she couldn't be Princess Fiona. You can't name boy dogs after a girl."

He shrugged again. "Like I said, I didn't name them."

"Can I pet 'em?"

"Yeah," he replied at the same time Jayne said, "I don't think—" She clamped her mouth shut at Lucy's chastising look. Greg had often accused her of being overly protective, a judgment she'd had difficulty accepting from a man who was the very personification of reckless. There was nothing overprotective about not letting her delicate little girl within snapping distance of animals who could take her whole head in their mouths.

Well-behaved animals. Whose owner was standing between them. Who hadn't yet disobeyed his command to stay despite the obvious temptation to do so.

Gritting her teeth to keep in her objections, Jayne shrugged and Lucy bounded forward. Lewis crouched, pulled off his glove and curled his fingers under. "Hold your hand like this and let them sniff you first."

Lucy yanked off her mitten and did as he directed. Both dogs eagerly sniffed her hand from all angles, then worked their way up her arm, over her body and to her face, making her giggle. "Their noses is cold! You're good puppies, aren't you?"

Jayne reluctantly agreed that they did seem to be good. Despite their excitement, they both remained seated—though the smaller one did scoot forward a few inches—and they didn't lick, show their teeth or make any threatening gestures. Though being twice Lucy's size was threatening enough, in her opinion.

"I'm Lucy," her daughter announced, gently scratching each

animal behind its ear. "And that's my mom. Mom, come meet Cameron and Diaz."

"I can see them just fine from here."

"She's afraid of dogs," Lucy confided in a confidential tone. "She doesn't like pets. She didn't even like my hamster just 'cause it got scared and bit her finger. A little blood, and she squealed."

Jayne's cheeks heated as Lewis looked at her. "It was more than a little blood," she said defensively. "And I didn't squeal. I shrieked."

"An important distinction." Was that sarcasm or amusement in his voice? It was hard to tell, so finely veiled was the tone, and his expression was totally blank.

After scratching both dogs for a moment, Lucy looked up at their owner. "My name's Lucy," she announced again. Of course, her first introduction had been made to the dogs. "I live here now. What's yours?"

"Tyler Lewis."

Tyler fitted him every bit as much as Lewis hadn't, Jayne thought. A Tyler would be handsome, brooding and rugged—a loner…until he found the right woman to share his solitude. A Tyler was hero material—strong, with an equally strong code of honor. Champion of the downtrodden, protector of the weak, guardian of—

Jayne gave herself a mental shake. This wasn't some character she was creating for her next book but a real, live individual with strengths and weaknesses, failings and flaws. Rule one—no romanticizing him. It would just lead to disappointment, and Greg had given her enough of that for a lifetime.

He eased to his feet, his six-foot-plus frame towering over Lucy. A sharp crease ran the length of his jeans legs, and his shirt, visible through the open parka, was pressed, as well. When was the last time she'd seen a man in a pair of starched, creased jeans? Probably never. Whose wife had the time to do that for him?

"Is there a Mrs. Lewis?" she asked without thinking.

His dark eyes turned a shade darker. "No."

She waited for more—*I've never married* or *There used to be*—but that was all. *No* with a scowl. "Any kids?"

"God, no." That was said with another scowl that made her want to draw Lucy safely behind her, out of his sight. A neighbor who didn't like kids—wonderful.

"Can me and the puppies play?" Lucy asked.

Jayne was about to answer when she realized that the question was directed to Tyler instead. He might not like kids, but Lucy hadn't noticed yet.

He touched the bigger of the dogs and said, "Go on." Both animals immediately sprang to their feet, and they ran after Lucy, leaving Jayne alone with Tyler.

Unable to think of a thing to say, she turned for her first good look at the house. The snow did much to soften its dilapidated facade, even lending it an air of old-fashioned charm, but that wouldn't last long. Already she could see the drips of melt coming off the eaves. By the next day the snow would be gone, and so would the charm, but the dilapidation would remain.

"A great old house," she murmured disgustedly, still able to see the pleasure of fond memories in Greg's face as he'd talked about his grandmother's home. Great old *lies* was more like it.

"Not quite what you were expecting?"

She glanced hastily at Tyler. She hadn't meant for him to hear the words, hadn't even really meant to say them out loud. She shrugged. "Not quite. Was there ever an orchard around here?"

He gestured across the road, to the neat rows of trees on the far side of his fence. "Apple trees. Edna used to own the whole mountaintop. I bought everything except the house and the acre it sits on."

Score one for Greg. And the house *did* have hardwood floors—scarred, neglected, in dire need of refinishing, but wood all the same. Presumably there had been a garden twenty-five years ago, as well. So he hadn't made it *all* up.

Tyler shifted uncomfortably, packing down the snow under

size-twelve boots. "I made an offer on the rest of it before she died, but she turned me down. She wanted some part of the family land to leave to the family." His features quirked into a grimace that made clear what he thought of such sentimental nonsense. "I'll make you the same offer."

Jayne looked back at the house. It was old, plain and needed money and a large dose of sweat equity. It made their house back in Chicago look luxurious in comparison. It was too cramped even for just the two of them, with no room for her office. Whatever money he offered could be a down payment on a more suitable place.

Unfortunately for Tyler—and maybe for herself—she *was* a sucker for sentimental nonsense and she liked a challenge. Why else would she have stayed married to Greg for so long? Why else would she be trying to support herself and Lucy on a solidly midlist author's income? She wasn't a Miller by blood, but Lucy was, and if her great-grandmother had wanted the house to pass to someone in the family, it should. God knew, Greg hadn't given her anything else…besides those big brown eyes, that charming smile and that fearless approach to life.

But, sentimentality aside, Jayne was also practical. It was one of the things Greg had liked the least about her. "Right now I have no plans to sell the place, but if I change my mind—" she looked again at the dangling shutters, the crooked porch, the paint flakes barely clinging to the wood "—you'll be the first to know."

Her answer seemed to satisfy him, judging from the silent nod he gave. He probably thought she was naive and inexperienced—a city girl who didn't know what she'd gotten herself into, who wouldn't last into summer and most certainly not through winter. And he might be right. She *had* been naive. Even knowing Greg's penchant for exaggeration, she'd believed everything he'd told her about the house. But the place had potential, and she was a big believer in potential.

"Well…" She stamped her feet to get her blood circulating.

"I'm freezing here and I need to see about breakfast. Lucy, let's go in and warm up."

"Aw, Mom—" Lucy broke off when her stomach gave a growl that would have done either of the dogs proud, then grinned. "Wanna have breakfast with us, Tyler?"

Say no, say no, say no, Jayne silently chanted, and she swallowed a sigh of relief when he did.

"No, thanks. I've got things to do."

Lucy grinned again. "Can Cameron Diaz have breakfast with us?"

"They've already eaten."

"Yeah, but they look like they could eat again."

"They look like they could eat *you.*" Jayne swung her up into her arms, then brushed away some of the snow that covered her from hood to boots. In unison with her daughter she said, "Oh, Mom…" As Lucy rolled her eyes, Jayne took a few backward steps toward the house. "Thanks again for the firewood. We really appreciated it."

As he'd done the night before, he simply nodded, then walked away. She watched him for a moment before turning and trudging toward the house.

Her house. Her daughter's ancestral home.

Their future.

Chapter 2

By noon the snow was dripping so heavily that at times it sounded like rain, plopping off the roof and puddling on the ground underneath. Tyler stood at the front window, eating lunch—a sandwich in one hand, a Coke in the other—and gazing across the yard. Supposedly he was watching the dogs run. Instead, he was seeing another snowy scene, this one a hundred and fifty miles and eighteen years away.

An unexpected snowstorm had crippled Nashville, blanketing everything in white and closing the schools early. The buses had been waiting at lunchtime, and the kids who walked to school had been lined up at the office to call for rides. Since they'd had neither a home phone nor a car for Carrie to come and get him, Tyler had hidden in the boys' room and waited until the school was quiet—the buses gone, the luckier kids picked up by a parent. Then he'd sneaked out of the building and had run all the way home, his jacket too thin and his shoes too worn to provide any protection from the snow.

Despite the frigid temperatures, he'd removed his shoes and socks outside—Del didn't like the kids tracking in dirt or snow—then let himself into the house. His first clue that something was wrong was his mother. She'd sat at the kitchen table, Aaron in her lap and Rebecca clinging to her side. Carrie hadn't laughed at his hair, frozen in spikes, or offered him a towel or fussed over him at all. She hadn't done anything but give him a sorrowful look.

Then Del had walked into the room.

"Stupid little bastard, sneaking off from school," he'd muttered as he'd advanced. "You think they don't keep track of kids down at that school? You think they don't notice when some whiny-ass little bastard sneaks out like a damn thief? You're gonna be sorry, boy, damn sor—"

Pain in Tyler's hand jerked his attention back to the present. He stared blankly at the pop can he held, crumpled almost flat, and the blood welling where a sharp corner had pierced his palm. Coke dripped from his fingers and puddled on the floor, each plop a reminder of the punishment such a spill had always brought.

An instant of panic spurted through him—*Got to get a rag, got to clean it and dry it so no one will notice.* He pushed it back with a deep breath and forced his fingers to relax around the battered aluminum. He'd taken only a few steps from the window when the doorbell echoed through the house, accompanied by Diaz's excited barks and Cameron's howl from the porch.

He would like to think the dogs were smart enough to ring the bell themselves, but a soft little-girl giggle told him he couldn't be so lucky. Grimly setting his jaw, he opened the door. The dogs shot in around him, racing through the living room and circling the kitchen island before leaping onto the couch and battling for space. Lucy would have followed them if her mother hadn't grabbed the hood to rein her in.

Her cheeks pink, Jayne smiled uncertainly. "Hi. I'm sorry

to bother you, but I saw your electricity was on, and it reminded me to call and see about getting mine turned on, too." She gestured toward the porch light that he always left on when he knew he would be home after dark. With no power, he'd forgotten to turn it off this morning, and now it glowed dimly in the bright day.

More than anything he wanted to send her away. He didn't need her in his house, looking at his things, disturbing his day. But instead he flipped the switch to off, then stepped back to allow her entrance. "The phone's on the desk," he said gruffly. "The book's under it."

Still holding on to Lucy's hood, Jayne came inside, steering her daughter toward the desk against one living room wall. She gave the wrestling dogs a wary look, and he spoke sharply. "Diaz. Cameron. Stop."

Immediately the dogs separated, each taking one end of the couch and watching the three humans curiously.

"Could you teach me how to do that with Lucy?" Jayne asked, wearing that uneasy smile again.

Lucy seemed well enough behaved to him. Though her expression said she was itching to go exploring, she didn't try to slip out of her mother's hold. Instead she was satisfied to look at everything, her brown eyes wide with curiosity. When she looked at *him*, a broad grin spread across her face and she raised one hand and wiggled her index finger in greeting.

With a brusque nod, he went to the kitchen, tossed the can in the trash, then held his hand under cold water, washing away the pop and fresh blood. The puncture wasn't deep, so instead of a bandage, he balled a napkin in his fist, then went to stare out the back windows. Immediately Diaz joined him, rubbing against his legs for attention. A moment later Lucy came over, as well. Glancing back, Tyler saw her coat hanging by its hood from her mother's hand.

"I like your house," she announced.

He grunted. It wasn't fancy—maybe fourteen hundred

square feet, one big living room/dining room/kitchen, two bedrooms and one and a half baths, with a wide front porch and a deck across the back. He'd built it himself, with help from his brothers and sister and his boss, and he'd done everything exactly the way he wanted it. It was his and his alone.

Lucy touched her reflection in the window, then giggled. "Look. I'm having a bad hair day. That's 'cause I've been helping Mom clean. See?" Her fine hair stood on end, and what looked like the remains of a cobweb spread across the wild strands. It was a good look with the smudges of dirt that marked one cheek and her chin before spreading down the front of her shirt.

He couldn't think of anything to say to her comment, but she didn't seem to notice.

"You have any kids?" When he shook his head, she frowned, then wistfully asked, "Are there any kids around here?"

He knew everyone who lived along the road by sight, if not personally. He rarely had anything to do with them. He rarely had anything to do with anyone. He saw the Ryans—his boss Daniel, Sarah and their kids—every workday. He saw his own family on Sunday afternoons, and Zachary and Beth Adams and their kids maybe twice a month.

He wasn't a real sociable person.

"The Trumbulls have some kids, but I don't know how old they are," he said at last. "They live about halfway back to town. And Sassie Whitlaw's grandkids live with her part of the time. There's a girl about your size."

The wistfulness disappeared as she giggled again. "What kind of name is Sassie?"

Not much different from Lucy. It was an old name for a young girl.

A strand of hair fell forward to rest on her cheek, and she brushed it back with delicate fingers. "Do you have any animals besides puppies? Like maybe horses?"

"No." There were cats in the barn, but they were no more

sociable than he was. He kept their water dish full and supplemented their field-mouse diet with dry food, but that was the extent of their interaction.

"My dad said I could have a horse when we moved here. He said we'd have a barn and everything. He said we'd have trees filled with apples to give 'em for treats, and I could ride my horse to the store and to school." Suspicion settled over her features, making her look years beyond five. "There's no barn at our house. Daddy was little when he came here to see his grandma. I think he didn't remember very well."

Was there ever an orchard around here? her mother had asked that morning with the same sort of look, and just before that she'd all but snorted, *A great old house.* Clearly the Miller home had fallen far short of her expectations. Because her ex had a faulty memory—or a problem with the truth?

Lucy edged closer to the glass. "You have a barn," she announced. "What's in it?"

"The tractor. Some tools. A workshop."

She tilted her head to look at him. "What kind of workshop?"

"You're awfully nosy today." Jayne came up to stand on the other side of the kid, combed the spiderwebs from her hair, then tried without success to remove them from her fingers. Her cheeks turned pink as she surreptitiously scrubbed them off on her sweatshirt.

"I'm bein' neighborly," Lucy disagreed. "That's what Grandpa says people do in the country. Isn't it, Tyler?"

Not me, he almost blurted out, but he just shrugged instead.

"They said we should have power by five," Jayne said. With her gaze locked on something outside, it was hard to tell whether she was addressing the words to her daughter or him. "Do you think the roads are clear enough to go into town and pick up a few things?"

The snow had been melting steadily all day, leaving great patches of ground showing everywhere that wasn't in the shade, and the temperature was warm enough for a light-weight jacket. How could the city girl not realize the roads would be clear? "Sure."

"We'd be happy to give you a ride to your truck on the way."

He'd be happy to say no. It wasn't much of a walk, and he could use the exercise to clear his head. He couldn't begin to guess at what made him say, "I'd appreciate it." Maybe because then they would be even. She wouldn't feel as if she was in his debt for the firewood and there wouldn't be any reason for further contact between them.

Her smile was uneasy but relieved, too. "Okay. Let's go."

Tyler Lewis had less to say than any man Jayne had ever known.

Maybe she was just accustomed to talkative sorts. Her father could chat up anyone about anything, and Greg had never let a little thing like having nothing to stop him from saying it. Tyler, it seemed, was just the opposite. While taking care of the electric, water and gas accounts, she'd listened to his conversation with Lucy with half an ear. Surely he had more than those brief little answers to offer.

But he wasn't offering them to her. Without a word, she and Lucy had waited while he'd locked up, then the three of them had walked back to Edna's house, where he and Lucy, still silent, waited while she locked up—laughable when practically every stick of furniture sat on the front porch—before loading into the Tahoe. Peripherally she watched him fasten his seat belt, then rub his long fingers over the leather armrest as if testing its texture. They stilled as his attention turned to the outside mirrors, automatically adjusting and lowering when she shifted into reverse, then returning to their preset position when she shifted into drive.

His mouth quirked slightly. Remembering that she'd told him Greg had taken everything of value? This truck was worth two, maybe three times the sorry little house and its one-acre setting. Knowing divorce was on the horizon, she'd had the sense to put it in her name only when she'd bought it.

Unable to bear the silence one moment longer, she asked, "Do you work in town?"

"No."

She'd forgotten one of the rules she'd learned early in her career—no *yes* or *no* questions when conducting an interview. "Where do you work?"

He pressed the button that turned on the heater in the seat, then turned it off again before offering a halfhearted gesture to the west. "A few miles over that way."

"Are you a farmer? A rancher? A housekeeper? A nanny?"

His mouth quirked again. With impatience? "A carpenter."

"Do you frame houses, make cabinets, build decks?"

Finally he glanced at her and said in the softest of voices, "I see where your daughter gets her nosiness."

Her face warming, Jayne slowed to a stop. They were at the bottom of the first hill, where a pickup old enough that its faded color could be one of any number was parked sideways across the road.

"Here you go."

"Thanks." He opened the door, ignored the running board and slid to the ground. Then he looked back. "Furniture. Tables, chairs, entertainment centers, desks…if it's wood, I build it."

Not a carpenter but a craftsman—and a modest one at that. She didn't meet many modest people in her business. Authors had to believe their work was good or they would never open themselves up to crushing rejection by trying to sell it.

With a nod that passed for goodbye, he closed the door, crossed to his truck with long strides and climbed inside. It might be ten years older than her Tahoe, but the engine started on the first try and revved powerfully, and it had no problem with the mud as he straightened it out, then drove past.

"I like him," Lucy remarked from the backseat. "He doesn't treat me like a kid."

Jayne wasn't sure he knew how to treat kids. As far as that went, she wasn't sure he knew how to treat adults either. But maybe it wasn't all people he had a problem with—just those who invaded his privacy.

Lucy amused herself with a movie on her portable DVD player for the drive into town, while Jayne amused herself with comparing Greg's stories with reality. Virtually everything about the house was a lie, and based on what she was seeing today, so was everything about the town. A quaint little town, like Mayberry from *The Andy Griffith Show?* Ha!

Sweetwater was a few blocks of shabby little buildings surrounded by a few more blocks of old houses and, on the outskirts of town, even shabbier businesses. There was a town square, and the downtown buildings were mostly old, mostly built of stone, but that was the extent of the quaintness. The welcome-to-town sign didn't include a population, probably because people were leaving a lot quicker than they were coming. It looked sleepy and dreary and depressing.

How had she let herself believe that, for once, Greg wasn't exaggerating?

Because she'd needed to believe. She'd needed a change, and after he'd cleaned out their joint bank accounts, this had seemed the best choice left her.

"Mom, I'm hungry," Lucy piped up from the back.

So was she, and it appeared they had a grand total of two places to choose from—a diner near the courthouse and a convenience store on the edge of town that sold gas, hunting licenses, hot dogs and sandwiches. She opted for the diner.

Deprived of her DVD player for the walk from their parking space to the diner, Lucy looked around wide-eyed but didn't comment on the town. Neither did Jayne. She might find it disappointing, but she certainly didn't want to pass that on to her daughter.

The diner was warm and filled with good smells. Jayne helped Lucy out of her jacket, then slipped off her own before sliding into a booth that fronted the plate-glass window. A twenty-something waitress brought menus and offered a cheery greeting and coffee before leaving again.

"I like Sweetwater," Lucy announced. "It's pretty."

Pretty? Jayne's gaze darted to the view outside the window. Pretty old. Pretty shabby. It was the sort of place where one of her heroines would end up when everything else in her life had gone to hell and she found herself at rock bottom.

But *her* life hadn't gone to hell. It wasn't as if she had no place else to go. She could have stayed in Chicago. She could have settled anywhere.

But Sweetwater had one advantage over those options—Edna's house. With no rent or mortgage payments, she'd figured that the savings she'd secreted away would last about eighteen months, barring emergencies, in southeastern Tennessee. That meant no outside job, no trying to work full-time *and* be a mother full-time *and* write full-time. She was a fast writer when Greg wasn't scaring her muse into hiding. In eighteen months she could finish her current book and write two, maybe even three books on a new contract. In eighteen months she could be on her way to getting her career back on track.

That same money wouldn't carry her through the end of the year in Chicago.

Just that thought gave the town a little brighter gleam.

They ordered hamburgers, and Jayne was all but drooling over the crispy thick-cut fries that came with them when the bell over the door dinged with a new arrival. She looked up to see another young woman, in her early to midtwenties, wearing jeans, a turtleneck under a heavy flannel shirt and boots with thick ridged soles. Despite the lumberjack clothes, there was something amazingly feminine about her, and it had nothing to do with the stylish blond hair or the three pairs of hoops that graced her earlobes.

Sorting through the stack of mail she carried, she called, "I'm back, Carla."

The waitress appeared in the pass-through window. "How's your mom?"

"She's fine."

"How's Tyler?"

"Not answering his phone, as usual."

One of Jayne's heroines might jump to the conclusion that this lovely woman and Tyler were involved. Truth was, Jayne didn't care beyond the fact that it would answer her question whether Tyler was antisocial with everyone or just her. Curiosity—that was all it was.

"His new neighbor's here," the waitress said with a gesture, and the woman turned to give them a speculative look. After a moment, she started their way.

Jayne dropped her gaze back to her burger. Her sweatshirt was dusty and cobwebby, and she hadn't bothered with makeup this morning, not when she was still wearing the remnants of yesterday's application. The last thing she needed was to meet someone who would make her feel dowdy even all dressed up—especially someone who might or might not be romantically involved with her neighbor.

But the woman didn't detour away. She didn't stumble and fall flat on her face or disappear into thin air but glided to a stop at the end of their table. "You must be Jayne."

Jayne smiled politely. "Yes, I am. This is my daughter, Lucy."

"Hi, Lucy. I'm Rebecca Lewis. I understand you've met my brother Tyler."

That made Jayne feel marginally better. Sisters were less intimidating than girlfriends—no matter that she had *zero* interest in the man in question.

"What do you think of Sweetwater?"

Jayne glanced out the window, then back at Rebecca. "It's… different."

Rebecca showed no offense. "It's small but boring, which is not always a bad thing. We grew up in Nashville—at least, until Tyler was fourteen and I was nine, when we came here to live with my grandparents. I liked the change." She pulled a chair from the nearest table and sat down. "I take it you're…" With a glance at Lucy, she hesitated. "Do you use the *D* word?"

Lucy seemed preoccupied with driving the ketchup bottle around the table with one hand while eating fries with the other, but she was never really tuned out. She often repeated something overheard during her most oblivious act. For that reason, Jayne had been as honest with her as a five-year-old deserved.

"Yeah. Lucy's dad and I are divorced."

"Too bad," Rebecca said, then shrugged. "Or maybe not. I've got a few ex-boyfriends that I was more than happy to see the last of. The rumor mill says you're a writer."

"Historical romances." Jayne was never sure what response that news would bring. There were the inevitable snickers and insults about trashy sex books and bodice rippers—not that one of her characters had ripped a bodice ever in his life—along with polite disinterest. Some people wondered why she didn't write *real* books, and some, bless their hearts, were fans of the genre who were tickled to meet a real-life author.

"Really. That's cool. How many books have you sold?"

"Eight." Four in the eighteen months before she'd married Greg, and only four more in the following six years. There was a depressing statistic.

"Do you write under your own name?"

"No, I write as…Rochelle Starr." Jayne hated admitting to her pseudonym. It was so overblown, so fake.

But Rebecca didn't even blink. Instead she teasingly asked, "So, after selling eight romance novels, do you have any special insight into men?"

She laughed. "Yeah. They're alien life-forms."

"Isn't that truth? So you already know everything you need to get along just fine with my brother."

Jayne didn't *want* to get along with Tyler, other than in a neighborly fashion—and she meant big-city neighborly, where you smiled and waved when you passed, helped each other out in an emergency but otherwise lived separate lives. She wasn't looking for a man to share her life. She wrote fantasy love stories, and fantasy was one thing she already knew a lot about. She didn't need living, breathing inspiration.

"Speaking of Tyler, could you save me a trip and give him something for me when you go home?" Rebecca asked.

Jayne's smile was fixed in place as she gave the only answer she could. "Sure."

"I'll get it now." Rebecca left her seat and disappeared through the swinging door into the kitchen.

By the time she returned, Jayne and Lucy were finished with their meals and Jayne had pulled out a twenty to pay the check Carla had delivered. Rebecca brushed it away. "It's on the house. Consider it our welcome to Sweetwater."

"Thank you."

Rebecca set a large brown bag on the table. The top was folded over, and an envelope with Tyler's name on it was binder-clipped to the fold. A chill emanated from it, suggesting its contents were frozen. Food? Did Rebecca make it her duty to make sure her big brother had a good meal from time to time?

"Thanks for delivering this and, like I said, welcome to Sweetwater. I hope I see a lot of you."

"I'm sure you will," Jayne said as she left a tip for the waitress, then helped Lucy into her coat.

After all, the diner's only competition in town was a hot dog at the gas station.

Country music played on the stereo, nothing but a distant hum until Tyler shut off the sander. While running his hand over the surface, he hummed a few bars, but humming was as far as it went. The last time he had sung a song, his mother had remarked that he sounded just like his father, then burst into tears. That had been the end of singing for him.

This piece was the final door to the entertainment armoire he'd been working on for the past few weeks. It was his own design, built of walnut and carved with a rising-sun pattern on the upper two doors. It had turned out better than he'd expected—good enough to offer to the same pricey shops that sold Daniel's work. But it was going into his living room, where few people besides him would ever see it.

He'd begun working with Daniel when he was fifteen. Life had been tough then—his mother away, adjusting to Sweetwater after Nashville, trying to fit in when kids talked about his family both behind his back and to his face. All the adults had agreed that he needed something constructive to occupy his time. Since Zachary couldn't train him in the legal trade, his good friend Daniel had offered to teach him carpentry. They'd meant to keep him busy and out of fights, but instead he'd found a career.

He might never get rich at it, but his house was paid for, he had money in the bank, and he liked going to work every day. That counted for a lot.

A shadow fell across the open door, catching his attention an instant before Lucy Miller stepped into sight. She was carrying a grocery bag, clutching it to her body with both arms, and her eyes were wide as she looked all around. Disappointment curved the corners of her mouth. "You can't even tell it's s'posed to be a barn. Where's the hay? Where do the horses go? Where do the cows go?"

His muscles tightened as he picked up a tack cloth and began wiping down the door, removing the bits of dust that inevitably escaped the sander's vacuum bag. He didn't like interruptions, especially from a talkative neighbor whose mother was pretty and needful. "Where's your—"

Before he could finish, Jayne appeared behind her daughter, her cheeks flushed. "Lucy, I told you—wow." Stepping around

Lucy, she came farther into the room, to the table where the finished door was lying. She reached out, almost touched the carving, then drew back. "Did you do this?"

"Yeah."

"Wow," she murmured again, then turned to look around. He didn't have to look to know what she saw—neatness that bordered on compulsion. A place for everything and everything in its place. He'd learned at an early age that there was hell to pay for disorder—and usually someone else paid it. Now that he lived alone, there was no one to care whether he put something in the wrong place, but it was a hard habit to break.

Jayne walked around the room. A stranger in his workshop was even more disruptive than in his house. He wanted her to leave—even if some small part of him appreciated the way she trailed her hand along the counter. The way she sniffed the fresh lumber stacked against one wall. The pleasure she took in studying the few finished pieces.

"This is gorgeous," she said, ending up back at the armoire door. "Are you going to sell it?"

He shook his head.

"But you could."

The comment made his cheeks warm and made him feel... flattered. But hell, hadn't he just acknowledged that to himself before Lucy had come in? And he had the expertise to make that determination. So what did it matter that she agreed with him?

It didn't.

"How long have you been doing this?" she asked, stopping on the opposite side of the table where he worked.

"Thirteen years."

"Since you were a kid." She sounded impressed.

He didn't argue that thirteen years ago he'd lived through more than most people did in their entire lives but merely shrugged.

"Mom, this is cold," Lucy complained, shuffling forward

as if the weight of the paper bag was almost more than she could bear.

"I told you to let me carry it." Jayne took it from her, then set it on the table next to the newly sanded door. "We met your sister while we were in town. She asked us to bring you this."

Tyler gave the bag a suspicious look. It wasn't the contents that made him wary—Rebecca gave him food from the diner once or twice a week, as if he would starve if left on his own—but the fact that she had already managed to meet Jayne and roped her into playing errand girl. He would have seen Rebecca the next day or definitely the day after that. The handout could have waited until then, except that she hadn't wanted to wait. She'd wanted to send Jayne Miller knocking on his door.

She wanted him to have a life.

"There's a letter on it," Lucy pointed out, stretching onto her toes to see over the top of the workbench. "Don't'cha wanna read it?"

Not particularly, and not with an audience. If her mother had asked, he could have pointed out that letters were private. But she wasn't her mother. She was a nosy little kid.

He unclipped the envelope, tore one end and slid out the paper inside. It was taken from a notepad advertising the annual fall Harvest Festival in Sweetwater from the previous year, and Rebecca's loopy writing covered the sheet. *She's pretty, she's smart and she has a nice laugh. Invite them to dinner. I've packed plenty to share.*

Great. His sister was trying to fix him up. Just what he needed.

"Well? What does it say?" Lucy prompted, and Jayne hushed her. "But, Mom—"

Jayne began backing toward the door, pulling Lucy with her by the collar. "Sorry to have interrupted you. And sorry she's so nosy. As you know, she comes by it naturally. Guess we'd better get back home and cleaning again. Thanks again for the firewood and the phone and—and everything."

Tyler watched them go, then looked down at the note again. *She has a nice laugh.* Only Rebecca would find that a reason to try to hook someone up with her brother. But she was one up on him. *He* hadn't heard Jayne laugh yet. Those few minutes when she'd been looking around the shop were the most relaxed he'd seen her. The rest of the time she seemed nervous and talked too much or not at all.

He tossed the note aside, then looked inside the bag. Usually she sent him servings for one or two, but not this time. There was a large pan of lasagna, ready for the oven, along with a frozen pie made with apples from his own trees, a container of vanilla ice cream and a loaf of Italian bread, no doubt already sliced and spread with garlic butter. She'd definitely packed plenty to share, and had even sent him someone to share it with.

As if it was that easy.

He took a break to carry the bag to the house. After putting away the food, he filled a glass with water from the tap, then stood near the kitchen island and listened. Except for the heavy breathing from the dogs asleep on the sofa, the house was quiet. Always quiet. He told himself he liked the peace. Fourteen years of screaming, angry shouts and sobs had given him a fine appreciation for silence.

But it was a little less fine lately than it used to be.

Invite them to dinner. It might not be the friendliest invitation, but he could do it. And then what? They would expect conversation—at least Jayne would. Lucy would be happy to talk all by herself. He wasn't very good at making conversation and never had been. Maybe it was just his nature or maybe it came from all those warnings he'd been given as a kid. From his mother, usually whispered while smiling through tears: *Promise you won't tell anybody, Tyler. He didn't mean nothin'. He never means nothin'.* And from his father: *You say one word to anyone, boy, and I'll shut your mouth for good.*

Tyler had believed him and kept his mouth shut. Until his father lay dead and his mother was taken away in handcuffs.

Old habits were hard to break, and keeping to himself was his oldest habit of all.

Chapter 3

On Friday morning Jayne went outside, strolling to the edge of the road before turning back to face the house. It was barely seven o'clock, but she'd been up more than an hour and she'd finally done all she could to improve the inside of the house. Today, with its promise of sunshine and warm weather, she would work on the outside.

The grass in front needed mowing—*after* she'd dragged off those nasty rugs she'd tossed out the day before. Of course, she didn't have a lawn mower, but she could buy one. She'd noticed some bulbs poking up their heads in what had once been flower beds, so she intended to weed around them to give them a better chance. And she hadn't needed more than a look out the back windows to see that there was a small jungle there. She wanted to clear it before she lost Lucy in there.

Behind her a sharp whistle sounded. She watched as Cameron and Diaz came flying from the woods, leaped the fence and disappeared inside. She didn't get even a glimpse of their master.

She returned her attention to the house, thinking about paint and shutters and repairs, and only vaguely noticed the closing of a door, the revving of an engine. As the old pickup drew nearer, though, she couldn't help but wish she'd done more than drag her fingers through her hair. A little makeup would have been nice, along with a T-shirt that hadn't seen better days long before Greg had tossed it her way. Not that she was looking to impress anyone.

Listening to the truck, she calculated when to turn and give a neighborly wave. Tyler didn't return it. But fifty feet past, the truck lurched to a stop, and he backed up until he was beside her. Leaning across, he rolled down the window. "I can take those rugs to the county dump in the morning." His tone was brusque, and his expression matched.

"Thanks. I was wondering what I'd do about them." Not true. In her thoughts about the rugs, she'd gotten only so far as getting rid of them—not how.

The truck rolled forward a foot or so before stopping again. Tension rolled off him in waves, from his scowl to his clenched jaw to his fingers on a death grip around the steering wheel. "I can fix that bottom porch step, too."

She wanted to tell him, thanks, but no thanks. She could hire someone to do that for her or get how-to instructions from the Internet and fix it herself. But fixing it herself was liable to lead to more extensive repairs, and anything she didn't have to hire out was money that would last just a little bit longer. Without a steady income, that mattered.

"Thanks. I'd really appreciate that." As long as he was being accommodating—more or less—she went on. "Is there a place in town where I can buy a lawn mower and a weed trimmer?"

For a long moment he was still, then with a rueful shake of his head he removed a key from the ring in the ignition and offered it to her. "This goes to the door around the corner from the workshop. Everything you need's in there."

She backed away a step. "I can't— What if I break something?"

"You know how to use a lawn mower and a weed trimmer?"

"Yes, but—"

Impatiently he held the key a few inches closer.

With reluctance Jayne held out her hand, and he dropped the key in it. "Thanks." She seemed to be saying that a lot. She wasn't comfortable with being so beholden to someone, especially someone who was begrudging about his generosity.

"I'll get the stuff for the step today."

She nodded, and so did he, then shifted into gear and drove away.

In her line of work, heroes often had tortured pasts. What would Tyler's be? An unhappy upbringing? If so, it didn't seem to have had the same effect on his sister. A broken marriage and broken heart? When she'd asked if there was a Mrs. Lewis, his answer had been blunt, to the point, but all his answers were blunt and to the point. Some tragedy that had happened between his teen years and the time he'd isolated himself up here?

She rolled her eyes. If she wanted to fixate on a hero with a tortured past, there was one inside the house on her computer, just waiting for her to resolve the big conflict that was keeping him apart from his heroine. Tyler wasn't a character and he wasn't a hero—at least, not hers.

After finishing her coffee, she went inside to check on Lucy, still asleep in the smaller of the two bedrooms. Her daughter gave a soft sigh, then snuggled deeper into her covers as Jayne backed out of the room. She would probably sleep another hour, maybe two. She wouldn't even know that Jayne had left her to go down the road to Tyler's.

She found the door the key fit on the north side of the barn. It was wide and opened into a large, clean storage room. The lawn mower was pushed into a space apparently built for it, with a shelf above for the gas can and a few quarts of oil. The trimmer occupied a shelf nearby, with another gas can, more oil, extra line and the owner's manual. Other shelves and nooks held a chain saw, an edger and a lightweight utility cart, and

Peg-Board on the walls was filled with hand tools, work gloves and safety glasses. There was even one small shelf that held bug repellent.

Tyler Lewis was one seriously organized man.

She loaded a variety of tools into the cart, pushed it outside, then locked up again. With the key deep in her jeans pocket, she headed back to her own house. There, she checked on Lucy once more, then pushed the cart around to the edge of the overgrown backyard.

Clearing it was a daunting prospect. Where to begin?

The author in her answered: begin at the beginning. She revved up the trimmer and began clearing the tall weeds in an ever-widening arc, uncovering rocks, logs and a fifty-gallon drum Edna had apparently used for burning trash.

Despite the early-morning chill, sweat coated her skin, along with grass clippings clinging to every exposed surface, when she cut the engine.

"Well, she doesn't look like a city girl today, does she?"

Jayne spun around to find Lucy, looking like a sleepy doll in her nightgown, and Rebecca standing next to the cart. "Good morning," she said, shoving damp hair from her forehead, then brushing at the grass flecks that clung to her hand.

"You're working bright and early," Rebecca remarked. "I thought I'd bring you a treat from the diner. Our cook makes the best sticky buns in three counties and has the blue ribbons to prove it. Don't tell me you've already eaten."

Jayne's stomach answered with a loud growl as she pulled off the safety glasses. "I've only had coffee. Sticky buns sound wonderful."

"What're you doing, Mom?" Lucy asked. "You woke me up with all that noise."

"I'm cleaning up this mess."

Lucy gave the slightly improved yard a doubtful look. "You're gonna need help."

"And you *are* help. Isn't that lucky?"

"The three of us can have it clean in no time," Rebecca said as she led the way back around the house.

Jayne was startled. They were talking about a lot of hard, dirty work. "I appreciate the offer, but you have your own work."

Rebecca waved away her response as she sat on the top porch step, where a large bag waited. "I'm the boss. I can take off whenever I want. Besides, I've done this sort of thing before. I helped Tyler clear the land for his barn. When is he coming over to fix that step?"

Slowly taking a seat one step down, Jayne asked, "What makes you think he is?"

"Because I know my brother. He'll tell you he's not neighborly, but the only one he's kidding is himself. If not for him, Edna never could have stayed out here until she died. He took care of everything she needed."

She opened the bag and started setting out food. She added napkins, plastic forks and salt and pepper shakers, then smiled brightly. "Dig in."

Jayne ate half a biscuit-egg-and-ham sandwich before finally murmuring, "Tomorrow morning."

Mouth full, Rebecca raised her brows.

"Your brother's coming over tomorrow morning to fix the step. And to haul those rugs to the county dump."

The information didn't seem to surprise Rebecca in the least.

Jayne watched Lucy sneak the egg from her sandwich, wrap it in a napkin, then slide it behind her on the step. When she looked back at Rebecca, she saw that she was watching, too, and smiling. "Are you married?"

Rebecca's smile didn't waver. "No. But I came close. I've been engaged four times. It's just that when it comes time to say 'I do,' I don't."

What made a woman so skittish of marriage? Jayne wasn't going to pry as to why. Maybe when she knew Rebecca better. When she was sure she wouldn't also pry for information about Tyler.

They ate until the only thing Jayne wanted was a nap, but when Rebecca got to her feet, ready to work, Jayne pulled herself up, too. "You get dressed and brush your teeth," she told Lucy. "Put on old clothes, okay? Then come on around back."

They chose a place to start a burn pile, then began cutting the clumps of shrubs Jayne had trimmed around. For a time Rebecca offered advice—how to keep the shrubs under control; who to call for a new trash barrel; where to buy a window air conditioner.

Finally, though, when the pile of cut branches was as tall as they were, Rebecca's conversation turned personal. "How long have you been divorced?"

Jayne stopped in the act of pulling at a branch from one of the fallen trees. Getting used to thinking of herself as divorced had been tough. But for so much of her marriage she hadn't felt very married, either. She and Greg had become more like roommates—and not particularly friendly ones. They'd lived as if they were single long before it had become fact.

"Sore subject?" Rebecca asked softly.

Shaken from her thoughts, Jayne smiled. "No, not at all. we were married six years. We've been divorced five months."

"Did he break your heart?"

Jayne glanced at Lucy, who'd given up on dragging smaller pieces of debris to the burn pile and was now crouched in the grass, watching ants march along an unseen trail. "No, no heartbreak. Just a lot of disappointment, in him and myself. I married a charming, irresponsible man and expected him to transform into husband- and father-of-the-year material. I knew better. I knew he was just six months of fun and fond memories. But—" she looked at Lucy again and smiled "—I got pregnant. I was old-fashioned enough to want to be married before the baby was born, and he swore he was ready to settle down. Unfortunately, he was just a kid himself."

He was all about fun, games and living for the moment. What had appealed to her before Lucy was born had become frustrating after. She called him unreliable. He said she was rigid. He couldn't act his age. She didn't know how to have fun. He was careless. She was a bore.

Six years. Was that a testament to their commitment or their foolishness?

In a casual voice Rebecca said, "It's funny, isn't it? Your Greg is a kid in an adult's body, and Tyler's been grown up since he was about three. He's the most responsible man you'll come across."

Responsible? Jayne wouldn't argue that. Unfriendly, distant, aloof—those were true, too. But she kept that to herself when she answered just as casually, "How lucky for the women in his life."

Rebecca snorted. "Right now that's you, Lucy, my mom and me."

Bending, Jayne took the clippers to the suckers growing around the trunk of one of the fallen trees. "Too bad I'm not looking for a relationship."

Rebecca was undaunted. "Hey, sometimes you find the best things when you're not looking. Like this." She pulled back a layer of vines she'd cut to reveal a small statue. Cast of concrete, it was two feet tall—a small girl in pigtails carrying a bucket with a puppy sticking its head out.

Jayne admired it, then returned to work. *Sometimes you find the best things when you're not looking.* That sounded like something her heroine Arabella's sister would tell her. In fact, she was pretty sure one of her heroines' friends had said exactly that.

The thing was, it was true in a romance novel. But life wasn't a romance novel. Her years with Greg had proven that. She was the only one in control of her happily ever after. And she knew one thing for sure.

It wasn't going to rely on a man.

Rather than haul his saw over to the Miller house, Tyler walked over early Saturday morning, took the necessary measurements and was on his way back to the shop when a small voice called, "Hey! Wait up!"

He grimaced, then wiped the expression off his face before turning to face Lucy, leaping from the steps to land flat-footed in the recently mowed grass. She wore red boots with a white-and-purple nightgown that left her arms bare, and her hair was standing up in all directions. She ran to meet him, flashing a grin. "What're you doin'?"

Regretting this offer. "I'm going to fix that step."

"Can I help?"

He glanced back at the house. The front door was open, but there was no sign of Jayne. "Where's your mother?"

"Asleep. She was pooped last night."

He'd seen the pile of branches when he'd come home the night before and been impressed. She'd made good use of his lawn mower, trimmer and chain saw and had a nice stack of firewood against the north side of the house. He wouldn't have figured she'd even know how to start the chain saw.

"You'd better wait for her to get up."

"Aw, that could be a while." Her face fell, then she grinned again. If her pale hair was curly instead of straight, she'd look like a greeting-card angel…at least, until it came to the red boots. "I won't get into nothin', I promise."

She didn't have much experience with being denied what she wanted—no more than he had in doing the denying. Besides, he would be in the shop only a few minutes, and as long as she stayed away from the tools…

"Okay." He started walking again, realized she was running to keep up and slowed his steps.

"Where're Cameron and Diaz?"

"Out running in the woods."

"Where do they go?"

"I don't know."

He would have sworn she'd gotten in another fifteen questions in the few minutes it took them to reach the shop. Once inside, she started again. "What's that?"

A table saw. A router. A belt sander. A palm sander.

"Why do you have two sanders?"

"Because they do different types of sanding." He picked up the lumber he'd gotten in town the day before, marked the measurements and took it to the saw. He was about to flip the power switch when her face popped up on the opposite side of the table.

"What're you doing?"

"Come here."

She ran around the table, her boots clomping on the cement, and he swung her up onto the workbench behind him. She didn't weigh as much as an armload of good oak boards. "Sit here."

"But I wanna help." Her bottom lip poked out as she pointed to the saw. "I want to do that."

"Maybe some other time." When she was twice as old and half as curious. If she and her mother stayed around that long.

He cut the board to size, measured it again, rounded off the sharp edges, then started toward the door. He was almost outside when Lucy spoke again. "Hey. You forgot me."

She was sitting there, boots swinging way above the floor, arms outstretched. He switched the board to his other arm, caught her around the waist and swung her to the floor. It had been a lot of years since he'd held a kid, but for just a moment the sensation was so familiar. How many times had he picked up Rebecca, Aaron, Josh or Alex? Dozens. Hundreds. When they'd been scared, when they'd been tired, when they'd needed to feel safe… He'd been their safe place, according to the court-ordered psychologist they'd seen.

And this mountaintop was his safe place. Alone.

"Look, there's a squirrel. If you had a horse, I'd take care of him for you. I'm gonna be a cowboy when I grow up. Our TV doesn't work up here. Does yours? What's in those woods? Mama doesn't have any sisters. Or brothers. Rebecca brought us breakfast yesterday and helped us clean the yard. Is she really your sister?"

That caught his attention. He laid the board next to the tools he'd left earlier and picked up his hammer. Delivering breakfast seven miles from town sounded like Rebecca. So did pitching in on hard work. She would have done it for anyone who needed the help…though he was pretty sure he knew her motive for doing it for Jayne.

"Yeah," he said at last. "She's my sister. Don't you think we look alike?"

Lucy crouched beside him and screwed up her face as she studied him. "No. She's real pretty. And her hair's blond and yours is brown, and her eyes are blue and yours are brown."

He didn't share even the faintest resemblance with Rebecca and their brothers. They took after their mother's side of the family, while everyone agreed that *he* was the spittin' image of his father.

He'd rather look like dirt.

Using the hammer, he tapped the cracked board loose, then handed it to Lucy. "Why don't you put that on the rubbish heap around back? Watch out for those nails."

Holding it with exaggerated care, she headed around back.

The new board was a perfect fit. He made sure the wood underneath was in good shape, then positioned it and had just driven in the first nail when the screen door swung open.

"Lucy, what in heaven's name—"

Squatting put him at eye level with Jayne's feet, which were bare, the nails painted pale pink. His gaze naturally moved up over her ankles, calves, knees and thighs before reaching the hem of her T-shirt. It was red, barely long enough to be modest, and across the chest were white letters proclaiming *Smart women read romance* ♥♥♥ *I write it.*

One foot moved to rest on top of the other, and a slender hand tugged at the shirt, pulling it from the curves it naturally wanted to cling to. "Oh. I thought… I didn't realize…excuse me." Quickly she backed up and disappeared inside the house.

And his gaze had never made it higher than the words emblazoned across her breasts.

Shaking his head to clear it, he positioned another nail and gave it a sharp rap, missing his thumb by a hair. By the time he refocused and hammered in the next few nails, she was back, this time wearing jeans, unlaced running shoes and another T-shirt. Her hair was pulled back in a ponytail, and her brown eyes were uncommonly alert, as if she'd received a rude awakening.

"I'm sorry. I forgot you were coming by this morning. I overslept."

"So Lucy said." Accustomed to solitude, he worked when he wanted without worrying about disturbing anyone. He hadn't given any thought to the fact that a little hammering on her front porch might wake her. "I can come back later."

"No, of course not. I'm up. I should have been up hours ago. When I had another job, I always got up around five so I could get a few hours' writing in before I had to take Lucy to day care, then go to work myself. It's just that then I worked in an office and never did anything more physical than housework and running after Lucy in the evening. After working in the backyard yesterday, I was…" Apparently running out of air, she drew an audible breath.

"Pooped?"

With a smile that was more grimace, she eased herself onto the top step, carefully rested her ankle on the opposite knee and tied her shoe. "Lucy again, huh?"

He nodded and went back to hammering.

Moving as if it pained her, she lowered that foot, raised the other and tied that lace, then stretched her arms over her head, though not too high. "Your sister was a huge help yesterday."

She could be. She could be a huge pain, too. She was so determined to fix Tyler's life—meaning find him a woman—while she kept guys around only long enough to break their hearts. She wasn't interested in marriage, she told him. He did her the courtesy of believing her, but she refused to return it. All he needed, in her opinion, was a woman—and not of the one-night variety.

When all he really needed was to be left alone to live his life the way he thought best.

"I can't believe how warm it turned after that snow."

He glanced at her and saw that her face was tilted to the morning sun, eyes closed, a smile on her lips. Her skin was clear, tinged with the faintest of gold, and her upper lip curved into a cupid's bow. With her hair pulled back, she seemed youthful, while he felt every one of his twenty-eight years and then some.

She looked as if she didn't have a care in the world...but no one knew better than he that looks could be deceiving. Her husband had run out on her and taken just about everything. He'd lied to her about the house and left her with a daughter to be both mother and father to. Those were cares. Even the mere mention of divorce had been enough to send his mother into a state of panic. She couldn't have handled being a single mother without a lot of help. Even then, he'd been the real parent figure.

Jayne opened her eyes, looked around, then frowned. "Where is Lucy?"

"She went to throw the old step away."

She stood cautiously and walked to the end of the porch, leaning over the rail. It shifted beneath her weight. "Lucy!"

A solid thudding signaled the kid's approach a moment before she came into sight. "Hey, Mom. I was watching the ants. They're cool."

"Well, leave them outside where they belong. What are you wearing?"

With a grin, Lucy stuck her foot out. "The boots Grandma gave me last Christmas."

"Those are snow boots, stinker. And I was referring to your nightgown. We don't go running around outside in our night-clothes."

Yes, you do, Tyler thought, and at the same time her cheeks flushed pink.

"Go in and get dressed. And brush your teeth. And comb your hair. And put on shoes."

"Oh, Mom." Resting one hand on Tyler's shoulder, Lucy hopped over the bottom step, then stomped to the top. "You are *not* fun." An instant later the screen door slammed behind her, then the stomps faded into the distance.

"Of course, her father is *always* fun," Jayne muttered, turning to lean back against the rail, arms folded across her middle.

"I wouldn't do—"

The screech of nails pulling from wood interrupted Tyler's warning. Her eyes widened and her arms flapped as she tried to regain her balance, but it was a losing battle. The entire section of railing fell to the ground, and an instant later she landed on top of it.

Dropping the hammer, Tyler bolted to the end of the porch. The color was drained from her face, making her eyes appear darker in contrast, and her mouth was moving, but no words were coming out—just short, gasping breaths. He knelt beside her but didn't touch her. The back of her head had connected with the ground, and the railing had broken her fall across the middle of her back. At best, she was going to have some nasty bruises. At worst...

She took a breath, long and quavering, and tears gathered in her eyes. If she started crying, he was outta there. He would go home, call Rebecca, then disappear into the woods with Diaz and Cameron. He'd comforted all the weepy females any man should have to face by the time he was ten; he was out of the business. He didn't even remember how. Hell, he'd never even known how to comfort a stranger.

"Are you all right?" he asked, his tone more curt than he'd intended.

She took a steadier breath and slowly sat up. It was awkward lying half on the ground, half on the railing. Touching her was even more awkward, but he did it, lifting her to her feet, holding her until she was steady enough to stand on her own. The instant he let go, she sank down on the porch and scooted back with a wince. There was color in her face again, bright red to match the shirt she'd worn earlier.

"I was thinking I'd rather park at the side of the house than out front," she remarked in a shaky voice. "Now all I need is some steps here, and I can do that. Easiest bit of demolition I've ever done."

"Yeah. Well, next time, ask and I'll show you a less painful way to do it."

She smiled thinly as she moved experimentally, then quickly became still again. "That's a good idea. But let's pretend there won't be a next time. Hell, let's pretend there wasn't a *this* time. Okay?"

Pretend that she hadn't fallen. That he hadn't helped her up. Hadn't held her hand in his.

"Okay," he agreed.

Yeah. Sure. Like he was going to forget it.

Jayne hurt—from the bump on her head all the way down to her little toes. Small-town living wasn't supposed to be hazardous to her health. She was going to be black-and-blue tomorrow, to go along with all the muscle aches from yesterday. She'd be lucky if she could sit at the computer long enough to do anything besides check her e-mail.

She shifted position, and a tiny moan escaped her, enough to make Tyler, finishing up with the step, look her way. His expression was mixed—some concern but mostly discomfort. "Do you need to see a doctor?" he asked after hammering in the last nail.

"No, I'm fine. Just a little sore."

"You hit your head."

She raised her hand to the lump there and winced. "Yeah, but I didn't lose consciousness. I'm fine." It was true, too, except for the headache that was starting to throb. And the tender place right across her middle in back where the rail cap had broken her fall. She was convinced she could feel it swelling and purpling even as she sat there.

"There's one of those twenty-four-hour clinics about thirty miles from here."

She smiled and stood up. "Really, I'm all right." It was nothing a few aspirin tablets and a hot bath wouldn't cure.

He was watching her, gaze narrowed, as if he didn't quite believe her. Of course, distrust went with the tortured past of a dark, brooding hero. Fortunately, before he could pursue the subject further, Lucy came bursting out of the house.

Stopping at the top of the steps, she planted her hands on her hips. "You finished without me! I was gonna hold the nails for you!"

Jayne took a few cautious steps away from the porch. When she didn't trip, sway or feel even the slightest dizziness, she bent to pick up the railing section. Long nails protruded from one end, top and bottom, curving outward in an oddly graceful way. Only one nail remained at the other end, rusted and bent only near the tip, while the wood where the top nail should have been was gone.

"Do you really want steps here?"

She looked up to find Tyler standing a few feet away. Her daughter stood behind him, feet planted as his were, hand on her hip, other hand resting on the porch floor, as his were, even though the porch floor was level with her nose. Jayne smiled faintly at the sight. Lucy liked role models. For two years she'd pounded away on a toy computer while Jayne wrote, and whenever she visited her grandparents, she wore an apron around the house and said things like "Mercy me" and "Goodness gracious." The one person she'd never mimicked was Greg. But then, she'd always copied adults.

"Well?" Tyler prompted.

With a blink, Jayne refocused on the section of railing in her hands. "Can I just stick this railing back up there?" she asked.

He shook his head. "This is rotted and it's split here and here. You'd have to replace both these pieces. You can buy a premade section and put that up or…" He gazed away, his jaw tight, before finishing. "Or we can do new steps if it's what you really want. It's not a big job."

She hesitantly said, "I can pay you for your time."

Something crossed his face, then disappeared. "No, you can't," he said shortly. "Do you want the steps or not?"

"Yes, please." Her voice was small. She took a breath to strengthen it. "I can help you."

A muscle twitched in his jaw an instant before he said, "Lucy will help. Won't you, Lucy?"

Her daughter's head bobbed.

Tyler glanced at his watch. "I'll get my truck and load those rugs, drop them off, then stop by the feed store—they sell lumber, too. They should be finished by this evening."

Jayne nodded, but he was already walking back to the front steps to gather his tools. Lucy matched him stride for stride, then stood on the new step and watched as he left. As Jayne climbed the steps, she caught her daughter's hand and pulled her, backward, into the house with her. "Did you do everything I asked you to?"

"I got dressed. And I put on shoes." Lucy stuck one foot into the air to show a pink sneaker with elastic laces. "And I brushed my hair." Grabbing handfuls of it, she lifted it into the air, then let go. Some of it stayed up.

"And did you brush your teeth?"

Clamping her lips together, Lucy garbled an answer.

"Go brush your teeth." Jayne gave her a push toward the bathroom, then went into the kitchen to take some aspirin. The muscle aches were getting better the more she moved. She hoped the headache would improve, as well. Otherwise, she was in for a fun day with Tyler hammering and Lucy helping. Not that she would complain even if her head exploded.

Tyler was the most responsible man she would come across,

according to Rebecca. That was proving to be true, and it was such a novelty that Jayne wasn't quite sure what to think. Greg had broken plenty of stuff, but he'd never fixed a thing. He'd never offered his time or his help without the expectation of something substantial in return. He'd never put in a full day at work, which explained why he'd been fired from as many jobs as he'd quit. He'd never accepted responsibility for anything.

A responsible man in her life other than her father…quite a novelty indeed.

By the time Tyler returned in his truck, Jayne had pulled on a pair of work gloves and walked out to meet him. He glanced at her as he slid his hands into his own pair of well-worn gloves. "I can handle this."

"I can help."

Instead of arguing, he shrugged and picked up one end of the nearest rug. She bent, too, with a quiet intake of breath as the movement pulled the bruised skin on her back, and gathered the other end in her hands. Immediately moisture soaked through her cotton gloves. "Eww, it's wet."

The snowmelt had turned the dirt that permeated the fibers into mud, as well as given life to a smell words couldn't do justice to. It was enough to make her shudder all over.

They heaved the rug into the bed of the truck, then picked up the others. As soon as the last rug left her hands, Jayne stripped off the gloves. She was tempted to toss them into the truck bed, too, but why waste them? They could go into the laundry with all the filthy towels and cloths she'd used in cleaning.

Tyler held his gloves in one hand. "I'll be back in a few hours—"

"Could we go with you?"

The question surprised her as much as him. There was still plenty for her to do here. Laundry, last night's dinner dishes, a little research for the next scene she would be writing.

"I'd like to see where the dump is," she went on when he

didn't speak. "My furniture's arriving next week, and I'll be getting rid of some of Edna's stuff. That way I'll know where to take it."

He still didn't say anything.

"I can pay for the stuff for the steps, too. And I'd like to get some paint samples. I really want to paint the house, both inside and out. I'm guessing they sell paint there, too. I mean, what's the use of lumber without paint to put on it? Well, that's a dumb question. We're living in a pile of lumber with very little paint. But anyway—"

He raised one hand, and she gratefully stopped talking. "Okay." That was all he said, then he walked around the truck and climbed behind the wheel.

Jayne stood there a moment, surprised by his easy concession, before turning and hurrying into the house. Lucy was still in the bathroom, the water running in the sink, so she washed her hands at the kitchen sink, then went into her bedroom. "Luce! Hurry up in there! We're going into town with Tyler!"

There was nothing she could do with her hair, but she did a quick makeup job—foundation, eye shadow, eyeliner and lipstick. She met Lucy in the hall outside the bathroom, her hair damp where she'd combed it down. Lucy puckered up for a kiss, and Jayne bent, but instead her daughter blew minty-fresh breath full-force in her face. "Better?"

"Much. Let's go."

Lucy raced across the yard while Jayne locked up. By the time she'd reached the truck, Lucy was already buckled into the center section of the bench seat and swinging her feet, chattering about her very first ever pickup ride.

Compulsively neat, responsible and endlessly patient. Jayne was learning more about her neighbor every day.

And appreciating it.

Chapter 4

Every soul Tyler knew in the county was in Sweetwater that day. Saturday was a time for running errands. What had possessed him to let Jayne and Lucy come along? He could blame Jayne and her nervous rambling. It had seemed easier to say okay than to listen to her.

And blaming her was better than admitting that some part of him might have *wanted* them to come. For five years he'd worked hard at not wanting, and in just a few days…

No. Better to blame her.

She stayed quiet on her side of the seat. Though the sun wasn't overly bright, she'd pulled a pair of dark glasses from her purse as soon as they'd cleared the trees that shaded their road and had kept them on. Occasionally he caught her rubbing her temple as if trying to ease an ache there. Maybe he should have insisted that she go to the doctor…. But she was an adult. Surely she knew better than he if she needed medical care.

Though he was too damn familiar with people who refused to seek care when they needed it. How many times had he watched his mother cope with injuries because a hospital visit raised questions she couldn't answer? How many times had he nursed his own aches in silence?

Too many.

If not for Lucy, the trip would have been uncomfortably quiet, but she kept up a running commentary. She was the most curious child he'd known. It never occurred to her that he might not be interested in what she had to say. Must be nice to have that kind of confidence in yourself.

The dump was located two and a half miles south of town. He paid the couple bucks' fee, unloaded the rugs with the help of the attendant, then turned the truck back toward town.

When they reached the edge of town, Lucy spoke. "Hey, Tyler?"

"Yeah."

"I'm hungry."

He grimaced. It was barely ten o'clock, and the last place he wanted to go with them was his sister's diner. Rebecca would take it as a sign that her efforts to fix him up were working and she would never give him any peace.

Jayne roused from her silence. "Sweetie, we'll be home before too long and we can eat then, okay?"

"But I'm hungry *now,* Mama. Doesn't a sticky bun sound good?"

Jayne paled as if just the idea might empty her stomach.

"Have you eaten anything at all?" Tyler asked. When she shook her head, he said, "Maybe you should. Oatmeal or crackers or something."

She considered it a moment, then nodded, and he wondered why the hell he'd opened his mouth. Because old habits were hard to break. He'd been taking care of too many people for too many years. But those people—except for Edna—were family. Jayne wasn't.

He didn't even want to think *Jayne* and *family* in the same sentence.

Frowning, he turned right on Main and found a parking space near the diner. Lucy skipped ahead, and Jayne matched his pace, which slowed the nearer they got.

They both reached for the door handle at the same time, their hands about an inch apart on the worn metal. Hers was so much smaller than his, delicate, well suited to typing, soothing a little girl…or arousing a man.

She made a choking sound that was probably meant to be a laugh and withdrew her hand. "Sorry," she murmured and stepped back so he could open the door.

Mouthwatering aromas drifted from the diner. Just inside, Jayne stopped and took a tentative breath. Testing to see if the smells would aggravate what already ailed her? Then she smiled faintly. "Smells good. Where do you want to sit?"

"Doesn't matter." He could already feel the speculative gazes on them. A quick glance around the room showed that practically every soul he knew was there, and they were all curious.

Lucy charged toward the nearest empty booth. As they followed, Rebecca, her arms filled with dirty dishes, detoured to meet them. "Hey, Lucy, Jayne." Bumping her shoulder against him, she winked. "Bubba."

He scowled at her back as she continued to the kitchen.

Lucy climbed onto one bench and slid across to make room for Jayne. Tyler claimed the other bench, his feet bumping hers as he settled in. He muttered, "Excuse me," then her foot nudged his and she repeated the words.

How long had it been since casual contact with a woman had seemed so significant? Since the woman had been Angela. Look how badly *that* had turned out.

He slid his feet as far back as he could.

Balancing three glasses of juice with a coffeepot, Rebecca returned. After filling their mugs, she asked, "Is it okay if I steal Lucy for a minute? I'd like to introduce her to Jordan Ryan."

Great. Next Lucy would want to eat with Jordan, which would leave him and Jayne together. Alone. In front of everyone.

"Sure," Jayne said with a smile. Before she could get up, Lucy scrambled over her, jumped to the floor, slid her hand into Rebecca's and headed for the counter, where Jordan sat with her sister, her brother and the Adams twins.

Tyler rested his hands on the tabletop, absently scraping one fingernail across a scar on the other hand. He was uncomfortably aware of his grandparents and two of his brothers seated at a far table and of Daniel and Sarah Ryan sharing a nearer table with the Adamses. He knew what they must be thinking—the same thing Rebecca did. That he needed to give up his isolation. That it was time for him to settle down and start a family. That he needed a woman.

That Jayne Miller could be a very easy woman to need.

His jaw tightened. He doubted that last thought was in anybody's mind but his, and he couldn't afford it. He couldn't let himself want what he couldn't have.

Across the table she shifted. When he raised his gaze, she smiled a little. She was pretty when she smiled. But, hell, she was pretty when she didn't smile. "Looks like Lucy's found a new friend. Do you know Jordan?"

"She's my boss's daughter." *Scrape, scrape* went the nail over the scar. The mark was old, white, barely raised. An old injury at work or a souvenir from Del? He couldn't remember.

"Which one is your boss?"

With a breath, he locked his fingers together, then tilted his head to the right. "The big guy over there is Daniel. Sarah, his wife, is on his left. The others are Zachary and Beth Adams. They're lawyers." They'd saved his mother's life and made a huge difference in his. He owed them—and the Ryans—a lot.

"Is Jordan Daniel and Sarah's only child?"

"No." He pointed out D.J. and Kate, who, according to her mother, had a crush on him. He hoped she was wrong. He was almost twice Kate's age. He'd changed her diapers when she was little. She should be interested in someone a whole lot younger…who'd seen a whole lot less.

"The twins are Brendan and Colton Adams," he finished.

"The two young men over there—" she gestured toward the wall "—seem very interested in you. Who are they?"

"My brothers, and it's you they're interested in."

"I guess strangers must be something of a curiosity."

Tyler looked to see if she was kidding. She didn't appear to be. A thousand strangers could march through the door, but unless they were young, female and pretty, Alex and Josh wouldn't spare them a glance.

Jayne met all three of their requirements.

"So you've got two brothers and a sister. Nice."

"Three brothers. Aaron must be working this morning."

"Wow. I'm an only child. Greg has a brother, but he never stays anyplace long enough for the dust to settle. Their parents are divorced and living in California and Texas, so all Lucy's got is my parents and me, and they're three states away. They live outside Chicago, in the same house I grew up in. It's really—"

Abruptly she caught her breath. Her cheeks flushed pale pink, making her look younger, more vulnerable. He'd always had a weakness for young and vulnerable—Rebecca, the boys when they were little, Angela. For as long as he could remember it had been his responsibility to take care of them, to help them out, to protect them.

But Jayne could take care of herself, and the only threat he was responsible for protecting her from was *him*.

That knowledge made his gut tighten. He reached for his coffee, his hand unsteady, then drew back, hiding both hands beneath the table, staring hard outside. It wasn't fair. The first half of his life had been tough enough to live through. Did it have to affect the rest of his damn life? He wasn't to blame for those years. His father was. The justice system was and, to some extent, his mother was. He'd been the victim, not the villain, but he was still paying. It was his future shot to hell, his life in some sort of purgatory.

It wasn't fair, damn it!

Through the buzzing in his ears he became aware of a distant voice—Rebecca's. He forced his breathing to steady, forced the anger and the hopelessness away and shifted his gaze to her. She stood next to the table, order pad in hand, smile in place. She wasn't angry, wasn't bitter, didn't have control issues. For a moment he resented her like hell for it. But just for a moment. If anyone in the family had to keep paying for Del's sins, he was the best choice. He was the strongest, the most capable. He could do what had to be done.

He could resist temptation.

Even if he didn't want to.

"…wants a sticky bun and a hamburger," Rebecca was saying. "Is that okay?" She waited for Jayne's nod, then turned to him. "What about you, Bubba? Breakfast or lunch?"

It took forever to relax the muscles in his jaw, to unclench his teeth. "Breakfast."

"Two eggs over easy, ham and hash browns, plus one order of my special oatmeal, coming right up."

After she left, the silence dragged out. He tried to think of something to say but couldn't. Maybe the less he knew, the less he would want to know. The less he would want, period.

But when Jayne raised one slender hand to massage her temple, he asked, "How's your headache?"

Smiling, she guiltily lowered her hand. "It's going away."

And he knew where it was going—straight into the bull's-eye between his own eyes. And it was going to be an ache aspirin couldn't cure.

Only time. Strength. And solitude.

Rebecca's special oatmeal—rich with butter, brown sugar and pecans—had been exactly what Jayne needed to settle her stomach and help the aspirin get her headache under control. She still had plenty of aches by midafternoon, but they were all below the neck—thankfully, or the pounding of hammers and the whine of the saw outside would have sent her crying into the woods.

She'd offered her help once again with the steps, and Tyler had turned her down once again, saying that Lucy would provide all the help he needed. If she were a more sensitive person, her feelings might be hurt that he so obviously didn't want her around. Instead she was grateful for the attention— and lack of annoyance—he showed her daughter. Greg's time for Lucy had been limited, and he'd always grown bored quickly. He'd visited her only twice after he'd moved out, and in the five months since the divorce she hadn't seen or talked to him at all. She needed someone like Tyler—a man who acted like a man—to balance what she'd seen in her father.

As long as she didn't get too attached...

Pushing away from the computer she'd set up on the dining table, Jayne stood with a grunt. All she'd done was sign on to download her e-mail—a few from friends, a lot from the author loops she was on—and check the ranking of her last book on Amazon, and her traitorous body had already stiffened up on her. Maybe she would get in better shape once they were settled in. Hiking through the woods and up and down the mountains should help with that. Granted, she couldn't do much hiking on her one acre, but surely Tyler wouldn't mind if they explored his property. Especially if it kept them out of his way.

She opened the windows in every room to let the fresh air in, then breathed deeply of pine, springtime and fresh-sawed wood. Outside, Lucy was asking probably her thousandth *Why...?* question. Tyler's answer came in a quiet, patient murmur.

Smiling, Jayne picked up the paint chips she'd gotten at the feed store and held them, one at a time, at arm's length in front of a bare section of wall. White, or anything tame like it, was out of the question. And so was brown, when so much of the house was already brown. Mint-green was okay. Yellow was nice and sunny. And cranberry—

"That would look good with white trim," Tyler said from the doorway.

Surprised, she glanced at him. A man who knew colors. Must be the craftsman in him. "That's what I was thinking. And yellow in the kitchen, peach for my room, light green in the bathroom and lavender for Lucy's room."

"Aww, Mom…" Lucy pressed her face to the window screen from outside. "I don't want purple again. That's a baby color."

"Lucy, you *loved* your lavender bedroom at home."

"I was little then, and *this* is home. I want…" She ducked out of sight, slipped through the small space in the doorway that Tyler wasn't filling and studied the chips in Jayne's hand for all of three seconds before pointing. "That one."

The chip she chose was orange. Not the delicately hued peach at the far end of the strip that Jayne had selected for her own walls but traffic-cone orange.

"How about this one?" Jayne pointed to a much paler shade, but Lucy shook her head and tapped the pumpkin color again.

"Maybe this one?" It was a medium tint—still too orange for her tastes but not nearly as bold as the other.

But again Lucy shook her head. "And a black floor and ceiling," she added decisively.

The queasiness returned to Jayne's stomach. "As small as that room is…it'll look like some kind of Halloween cave."

"You could just say no," Tyler said.

She could, Jayne thought as Lucy raced off to her room with the paint sample in hand. But why bother? With luck, Lucy would enjoy her room for a while, then grow tired of it and want something more suitable. "It's only paint," she said with a thin smile. "And I can always keep her door shut."

It was impossible to tell from Tyler's shrug whether he approved of her decision.

"How are the steps coming?" she asked as she sorted out the paint chips she'd chosen.

He blinked as if remembering why he'd come inside. "They're done."

"Wonderful." She went outside and walked to the edge of the new steps. They were straight and solid, with sturdy rails on either side, and pristine except for the Lucy-size footprints where she'd tested them. "These are great. How can I repay you?"

He moved around her, then took the steps two at a time to the ground. "Don't fall down them."

"I'll do my best," she said drily.

He'd already cleaned up his work space and loaded his tools in the back of his truck. Other than the sawdust littering the ground, there was nothing else to show he'd worked there—no discarded nails or cast-off bits of lumber. He was amazingly neat.

"Seriously, thank you very much. This was way beyond being neighborly."

He looked up at her, his gaze narrowed. "I'm not neighborly."

He'll tell you he's not neighborly, Rebecca had said, *but the only one he's kidding is himself.*

"Right," Jayne agreed. "It was way beyond being unneighborly."

With a curt nod, he went to his truck, climbed in and drove off. Instead of parking in the driveway, he went around back, no doubt to put everything away in its place in the shop. She almost felt sorry for him—he'd offered an hour or two of his time on his day off and had wound up working most of the day, as well as finding himself the unwanted center of attention.

But it was hard to feel sorry for him when the day had turned out so well for her. Okay, so she'd broken the porch railing and banged up herself in the process. She'd also gotten rid of those stinky old rugs and gotten a new set of steps.

Besides, maybe Rebecca was right and Tyler did need a life. Not with Jayne, of course—not in the way Rebecca was thinking. Jayne had only three priorities in her life at the moment—her daughter, her career and her house. But it seemed to her that Tyler had spent way too much time alone. If she and Lucy could help bring him out of his shell, that was A Good Thing….

Wasn't it?

Tyler left work Monday with a smashed thumb—the result of thinking about the wrong thing with a hammer in his hand—and an invitation to return for dinner. With Jayne and Lucy.

An invitation? He snorted. *Command* was more like it. He'd tried to get out of it, but Sarah wasn't taking no for an answer. So here he was, wasting time that would have been better spent in his workshop, taking the neighbors he didn't want to a dinner he didn't want. As the crow flew, it was less than four miles to the Ryans' house. As the truck drove, it clocked in at just under ten. It promised to be a long drive and a longer night.

"How long have you worked for Daniel?"

He glanced sideways to see that Jayne had finally lost interest in the acres of forest they were passing and was focused on him instead. She wore her hair down tonight, a sleek length of light brown that fell past her shoulders. Instead of her usual jeans and T-shirts, she wore khaki pants that fitted snugly and a white top that hugged every curve. Tall, slim but with the aforementioned curves, she looked less like old Edna than any neighbor should.

His throat was suddenly tight, and he used clearing it as an excuse while he recalled her question. Oh, yeah. Work. Daniel. "Since I was a kid."

"You say that as if you're so old now." She paused, and when he didn't say anything, she asked, "How old are you?"

"Twenty-eight."

She snorted. "You're still a kid."

"How old are you?"

"Thirty."

He wouldn't have guessed she was older than him, but then, he'd always felt older. It had something to do with his earliest memory—quieting Rebecca's fearful wails while their father's rage and their mother's sobs echoed through the house. Or his second earliest memory—learning to change Rebecca's diaper because their mother was hurt too badly to do it herself.

Carrie had always blamed herself, and sometimes Tyler had, too. Sometimes he'd known the beatings were *his* fault—he'd put something away in the wrong place, he hadn't kept the younger kids quiet enough, he hadn't done his own chores quickly enough to help out with his mother's. It had taken a long time to put the blame where it belonged—on Del Lewis himself. No excuses, no reasons that mattered, no scapegoats. Just Del.

And he'd paid for it eventually. Punishment had come years too late, but it had come.

"Tyler, are you—"

A hand touched his arm, and he yanked away, jerking the steering wheel and sending the truck careening toward the opposite shoulder. The wheels spun, then fishtailed in loose gravel, and he eased up on the gas pedal as he steered back onto the right side.

Lucy and Jayne were watching him, curiosity on Lucy's face, concern on her mother's. Sweat had collected on his brow, and his fingers were knotted so tightly around the steering wheel that the tips had gone numb. He'd gotten lost in a past that he wished he could forget. But how could he? He was the one most like his father. He had Del's hair, his eyes, his looks, his voice, his temper. He couldn't afford to forget.

Jayne's hand was still in midair, where she'd jerked back after touching his arm. He'd zoned out, and she'd tried to get his attention—that was all. And he'd overreacted.

His face grew hotter. He turned the nearest air-conditioning vent so it blew directly on him, then forced his muscles to relax enough to allow an awkward shrug. "Sorry. I—I was…"

"Are you okay?" Jayne asked conversationally, as if he hadn't practically run them off the road. That was for Lucy's sake, of course. She didn't want to scare the kid. Neither did he.

"I'm—yeah." He waited, half expecting her to ask to return home. She could drive herself to the Ryans' or she could decide that anyone who would invite him to dinner wasn't someone she wanted to spend time with.

But she didn't say anything. She simply lowered her hand to her lap, clasped both hands and gazed straight ahead.

After a moment, Lucy closed the book she'd brought with her and came to the rescue. "Jordan has a tree house with a ladder and two rooms and a porch. She's gonna show it to me, and I'm gonna climb up in it."

"Maybe you shouldn't—" Jayne began.

"It's a great tree house," Tyler said at the same time. He felt her look his way but kept his gaze on the road. "Daniel and I built it when Kate wasn't much bigger than you. Sometimes in the summer the kids sleep in it."

"Wow." Lucy's tone was a reverent whisper. "That beats sleeping in a real bed anytime."

"Sleeping in a *tree?*" Jayne scoffed. "Remember when you fell out of the bunk bed at Grandma's? That's nothing compared to falling out of a tree."

Lucy looked at her, then turned to Tyler. "Has Jordan ever fallen out?"

"No. No one has. There are railings all around the deck, and when they sleep up there, they sleep inside."

Jayne shot him another look, this one sharper than before. "And just think of all the bugs and the mice and the snakes. All sorts of creepy-crawlies come out at night."

"I bet your idea of roughing it is sleeping in a fancy RV," Tyler murmured.

"You'd be wrong," she answered haughtily. "My idea of roughing it is—" she ruined the snobbish effect with a smothered giggle "—staying in a cheap motel."

"Didn't your father ever take you camping?"

"No. *His* idea of roughing it is staying in a hotel without room service. Did your father take you?"

He should have expected her to turn it back on him. "No," he said shortly. He lied. They'd gone camping a few times. On the last trip, Del had threatened to leave Tyler alone in the mountains if he didn't stop whining. It hadn't mattered that he'd fallen ten feet—with a little help from his father—and broken an arm, split his lip and blacked one eye. Del had just wanted him to suffer in silence, the way his mother did.

Grateful to have returned home from that trip with the same number of kids they'd left with, Carrie had managed to dissuade Del from any more campouts.

And to this day Tyler didn't wander far from home.

"My parents are supposed to be here Thursday morning with our furniture," she remarked.

How was he supposed to respond to that? Was she merely stating facts or did she expect an offer of help from him? He wasn't obligated to her. Her folks would manage to get the truck loaded; the three of them would get it unloaded. They wouldn't need his help.

"They're going to stay a few days, then they're going on a cruise to celebrate their thirty-fifth anniversary."

"And they wouldn't let me go," Lucy piped up, her tone incredulous.

"Can you imagine not wanting your granddaughter along on your anniversary cruise?" Jayne laughed softly as she rumpled Lucy's hair. Rebecca was right. It *was* a nice laugh.

"I'm telling you, they'll get bored on that big old boat without me," Lucy insisted. "Don't'cha think, Tyler?"

Him, Jayne, a tropical cruise, no Lucy. He *couldn't* think.

He followed the highway for less than a mile before turning

west onto another winding road. The pavement disappeared after
a mile or so, and the gravel petered out not long after that. The
dirt was hard-packed and rutted as it curved back and forth, up
and down, to the top of the mountain. The woods grew right up
to the edge of the road in places, far enough back in others to
pasture a few head of cattle. Houses were few and far between,
trailers mostly, with an occasional wood-framed house dropped
in.

"That looks like a great place for a Halloween spook house,"
Jayne said as they passed the last house before the Ryans'.

Lucy stretched up as far as her seat belt allowed for a look.
"Oh, Mom, it's just an old house. There's nothing spooky about
that."

"Use your imagination, Lucy. Candles in the windows, spiderwebs in the corners, creaking doors, dead bodies in the bedroom…"

The house was where Sarah had lived before she and Daniel
got married. Tyler didn't know much about their lives before
he'd come along, but he did know they'd been married fourteen
years and Kate was fifteen. They had apparently dealt with
whatever had kept them apart, though, because he'd never seen
two people happier together…unless it was Zachary and Beth.

That was how a marriage should be, Carrie repeatedly
reminded him and Rebecca. Not like hers. Things could be different.

Different for other people. Maybe even for Rebecca. But for
him?

Before he had to answer that question, the road ended in a
clearing in front of the Ryan house. He parked next to Zachary's SUV and cut the engine. Jayne was out of the truck and
lifting Lucy to the ground before he managed to unbuckle his
seat belt. The people inside were like family to him, but he'd
still rather be home alone than walking into the house with
Jayne and Lucy.

Kate answered the door, politely greeting Jayne and Lucy

and giving him one of her shy smiles. Before they'd gone more than five feet in, Sarah joined them, wrapping her arm around Tyler's waist. He was prepared for the contact this time.

"I half expected you to weasel out," she murmured before turning a welcoming smile on her guests. "Jayne, Lucy, I'm Sarah Ryan. We're glad you came and glad you gave us an excuse to get *him* over here."

"I work over here," Tyler reminded her. "I'm here five days a week."

"But that's work. This is play. You do remember play, don't you?" She gazed at him a moment, clearly not expecting an answer, then let go to take Jayne's arm and Lucy's hand. "Let me introduce you to everyone."

Relieved, Tyler headed across the room to where Daniel and Zachary were standing near the fireplace.

"I talked to Masterson today," Daniel said after exchanging greetings. "I told him about that armoire you're building."

Jeff Masterson owned a chain of shops across the northeast that sold handcrafted furniture for amazing prices. The first time Tyler had heard how much the dining table he was working on would sell for, he had practically cut one leg a foot shorter than the others. He'd had no trouble believing that Daniel's work was worth that kind of money, but his? No way. Not even with Daniel's label on it.

"He said he'd like to see it when it's done. Said it sounds like something one of his regular customers is looking for."

He was talking about selling it. For a whole lot more than Tyler had put into it. Of course, there was more than the materials. He'd spent a lot of hours on the piece...but that was just time. He had plenty of it.

"I don't know," he said at last. "I'll think about it."

"What's to think about?" Zachary asked. "You make furniture for a living. He sells furniture for a living. Why not let him sell yours?"

"He sells stuff like Daniel's."

"You make half the stuff with my name on it," Daniel pointed out.

It wasn't the same, but Tyler didn't know how to explain it. Instead of trying, he shrugged and repeated, "I'll think about it." To signal the end of the discussion, he turned to look around the room. Lucy had disappeared with Jordan. The boys were playing video games in one corner. Kate was sitting in a chair, reading with a cat on her lap, and Jayne was seated on the sofa, talking and laughing with Sarah and Beth. She looked comfortable, as if she'd known them forever.

"You're being watched," Zachary warned.

Tyler looked at the other two women, taking turns watching him watch Jayne. His face warming, he turned his back to them.

"Aw, there's no crime in looking at a pretty woman," Daniel said. "What's it like having a neighbor again?"

"I liked it better before they moved in." It was hard to achieve isolation when people lived just fifty feet down the road. He was always aware of them. Even when they stayed inside, out of sight, there was her SUV, the lights behind curtained windows, the toys scattered on her porch to remind him.

It was even harder when he saw them.

"Every man needs a distraction from time to time," Zachary said with a grin. "And, son, there are worse distractions than a pretty woman. Who knows? Maybe you'll settle down with this one, and everyone can fuss over someone else for a while."

Suddenly chilled, Tyler moved a few steps closer to the fireplace, though no fire burned there. He was as settled as he was ever going to get. Del and Angela had made sure of that. He'd accepted that fact and lived with it for five long years.

Why was it so damned hard to accept *now?*

Chapter 5

All in all, Monday night's dinner was about equal parts success and failure, Jayne reflected a few days later. Tyler couldn't have been more uncomfortable if he'd had the sentiment tattooed on his forehead, but she'd really liked Sarah Ryan and Beth Adams. The food had been great, the company enjoyable. Jordan was Lucy's newest best friend, and Kate was an aspiring author. Lucy had an invitation to ride Jordan's pony the following weekend, and Jayne had an invitation for lunch with Sarah and Beth the next week.

But Tyler hadn't spoken one word on the way home.

They hadn't seen him since beyond glimpses as he drove past on his way to work and again when he came home in the evening. But he'd taken to parking his truck around back and, apparently, using the back door. Not that she was spying on him. She just happened to be able to see his front door when she sat at her computer. The fact that she'd had to move the dining table from the kitchen to the living room to accomplish that was inconsequential. The fact that she'd *wanted* to accomplish that was a little disconcerting.

He was on her mind way too often. A person would think she'd never seen a handsome man before or been baffled by his behavior. Not true. Greg was very handsome, boyishly so, and she'd been at a loss to understand him throughout their entire marriage and divorce.

How could he take everything? How could he have zero concern for the quality of his young daughter's future? How could he cut Lucy out of his life without the slightest of regrets? If he'd never wanted to see Jayne again, that would have been fine—though his feelings for her had never been strong enough to include a *never* or *always*. But to not care if he ever saw his daughter again…his sweet, funny, adorable daughter who'd loved him better than he deserved…

No matter how often she considered it, the idea still stunned her.

"Are they here yet?" Lucy asked impatiently, tugging on Jayne's arm.

With a sigh, Jayne refocused on the present. It was Thursday afternoon and they'd been waiting forever for her parents to arrive—or so it seemed. Bill and Clarice had gotten a late start out of Chicago the day before, then had stopped along the way to visit with old friends. Instead of the midmorning arrival he had predicted, it would be closer to five when they pulled up.

"There they are—right in front of us. Can't you see them?" Jayne lifted Lucy to sit on the porch rail but kept her arms securely around her middle. Her mother had called a few minutes earlier to say they were close by. Neither she nor Lucy could sit still long enough to wait inside.

"Oh, Mom, you're silly."

"*I'm* silly? *I* didn't ask if they were here when I could see they weren't."

Lucy sagged back against her, a warm, solid weight. "I've missed Grandma and Grandpa."

"I have, too, babe." Not once in the months Greg had been gone had Lucy said the same about him. How sad—more for him than her.

"I miss Tyler, too."

Jayne swallowed hard. She didn't want Lucy to get too attached to anyone who wouldn't be a regular part of her life. She was way too young to have her heart broken. "There's no reason to miss him. He's still over there every night. You've seen his lights."

"Yeah, but I haven't seen *him.*"

"Just because he's our neighbor doesn't mean we have to see him all the time. He came over when we needed help, and if he ever needs our help—" *fat chance* "—we'll go over there. That's what neighbors do."

Lucy's bottom lip was pouty. "I haven't even seen Cameron Diaz in forever. I miss them, too."

Jayne hid her smile in baby-fine hair. If Lucy merely missed Tyler the way she missed the dogs, there was nothing to worry about. Now that they had a place without traffic, close neighbors or city ordinances, maybe they could have a dog of their own—something cute and cuddly that could sleep on the floor beside Lucy's bed and keep Jayne company once Lucy started school. A shih tzu or a dachshund.

The rumble started so low that Jayne paid it no mind until Lucy started bouncing on the rail. "Here they come, here they come!"

Sure enough, an orange-and-white moving van slowly lumbered into sight down the road. Lucy leaped to the ground and raced to the edge of the yard, and Jayne followed. She would have jumped up and down, too, if it hadn't seemed undignified.

The van shuddered to a stop and her father swung to the ground, scooping Lucy into an exuberant embrace. Jayne went to the passenger side to help her mother climb down and was immediately pulled into her hug.

After a moment, Clarice pushed her back to study her intently. "Oh, we've missed you so much! How are you?"

"I'm fine, Mom."

Arm in arm, they walked around the truck, then Clarice stopped short. "Oh, mercy…this is a joke, right? The real house is around back or—or—" She looked around for an explanation. Finding none, she looked back at Jayne. "Greg strikes again."

They traded off so Jayne could greet her father and Clarice could hold Lucy. When that was done, Jayne said, "It's not so bad, Mom. The side steps are very sturdy."

"They look brand-new," her father said.

"Of course they're brand-new," Clarice said, her mouth pinched. "The old ones probably collapsed."

"Actually," Jayne confessed, "there was a railing there. I leaned against it and it broke. So we replaced it with steps."

"It broke…and you fell."

Jayne waved her hand negligibly. "Just a few bruises, that's all, and they're gone." *Liar,* the fading mark across her back taunted with a twinge. "It's really not bad. Just wait until I paint it. I've already done most of the inside. Come and see." She pulled her mother across the yard to the steps, and Lucy and Bill followed. Inside she stopped in the center of the cranberry-hued living room with its fresh white trim and opened her arms wide. "See?"

Her father took one quick look. "I didn't know you could paint."

She grinned. "I didn't know I could either. But the man at the feed store told me everything I needed to know."

It took Clarice a moment longer to give in. "It's pretty. It'll be nice once we get your furniture in here, though it's a shame we can't do something about these floors first. Once they've been stripped, sanded and refinished, they'll be beautiful." Still talking to herself, she turned the corner into the newly yellow kitchen with Lucy on her heels, reappeared a moment later, then disappeared down the hall.

Bill slid his arm around Jayne's shoulders and held her near. "Are you disappointed?"

She leaned against him, taking comfort in his embrace. "At first I was, more in myself than Greg. I knew better than to believe anything he said. But…" She broke off and looked around. With their things scattered around, the place was feeling more like home every day. She'd put a lot of work into it. She was proud of what she'd accomplished and was looking forward to what she would accomplish in the future. "It's not fancy, but I don't need fancy."

"You met anybody yet?"

"Our neighbor, his sister, a couple of families. Lucy's got an invitation to go horseback riding this weekend. The town is small and it's nothing like Greg described, but…" She shrugged.

"What is?" Bill asked drily. Jayne knew he'd been disappointed that she'd gotten pregnant first, had never been convinced Greg was worthy of his only daughter, had adored the very air Lucy breathed from the moment of her birth and had tried, always tried, to accept Greg fully and without reservation into their family. He'd never quite succeeded. "Tell me about your neighbor."

Jayne's gaze automatically went to the front window. Tyler should be home soon—and, she suspected, he would come over for the first time since Monday. That caretaker gene he resented probably wouldn't let him stay inside his house or workshop while she and her father unloaded the moving van. Maybe she would tell him they didn't need his help. They could manage.

"Is he old, stooped, deaf and so boring you can't think of anything to say?"

She blinked, then focused on her father's grin. "No. He's young, handsome and unsociable. He wants to be a hermit, but he just can't stop himself from helping out when someone needs it."

"You might want to keep that first part from your mother. She'll worry less about an unsociable neighbor than she will a young and handsome one."

Jayne laughed. "She's got no reason to worry, believe me. Besides, she'll probably see for herself while you're here." She rolled the sleeves of her T-shirt up a few turns, dusted her hands together and asked, "Shall we get started unloading?"

"First we need to get this furniture out of here or we're going to run out of room real fast. Do you want to save any of it?"

She looked around. The sofa and chairs were older than she was, the springs broken down, the fabric worn through in places. The same description applied to virtually everything— old, broken and worn. Not even someone down on his luck would find much use for it. "I think I'd like to keep that table—" she gestured toward the long narrow table pushed against one wall "—but the rest of it can go."

"Then grab an end."

Between them they maneuvered the sofa out the door and down the steps, then left it in the front yard. One chair followed, then another. They worked steadily—Jayne and her father carrying stuff out while Lucy and Clarice moved their personal items into the bathroom and out of the way. They were in the larger bedroom, trying to take the bed apart, when a distant bark sounded outside and Lucy's ears perked. "Cameron Diaz!" she shouted and raced from the room.

"Cameron Diaz lives next door and barks?" Clarice asked, her brows arched.

"Our neighbor's dogs—Cameron and Diaz," Jayne explained. She was holding the foot of the mattress several feet in the air while her father tried to rip the fabric free from the metal springs that had snagged it. She hadn't known that beds had once come with bare metal springs.

"Do you have a sharp knife or a pair of scissors?" her father asked, his voice muffled by the mattress looming over his head.

Her shoulders were starting to ache from holding the mattress neck-high. "The kitchen knives aren't very sharp, but there's a pair of manicure scissors in the bathroom, Mom—"

"Here." Tyler's voice came from behind her, but by the time she'd turned her head, he'd moved to stand between her and her father. He offered Bill an open pocketknife, handle first, then took the weight of the mattress from Jayne.

Go ahead, a devilish voice goaded. *Tell him you don't want his help.*

Maybe she would once the throb in her shoulders went away. Once that smelly mattress and the rusty, sharp-edged springs were out in the yard with the rest of the junk. Once she'd finished taking a long, appreciative look at him. He looked just as he should for having come straight from work—sawdust on his jeans, smears of stain across his shirt—and he smelled of wood and sweat and pure sexy male.

She stepped back to allow him to take her place—the better to observe him—and her mother came forward to meet her. *Who is* that? Clarice mouthed.

My neighbor, Jayne mouthed back.

Clarice's brows reached for her hairline.

"You keep doing that, Mom, and I'm getting you BOTOX for Mother's Day," Jayne said aloud. "Mom, Dad, this is Tyler Lewis, our neighbor. Tyler, my parents, Bill and Clarice Jones."

Everyone murmured something appropriate, then Tyler looked at her over his shoulder. "Your maiden name was Jayne Jones?"

She offered a phony smile. "Yes, it was." Plain, common, everyday-average. She'd heard comments about it all her life.

Finally Bill finished cutting the fabric around all the sprung springs and Tyler hauled the mattress to the floor, standing it on its side. It was so broken down that it wobbled, then collapsed in on itself.

Bill returned the knife, then extended his hand. "Pleased to meet you."

Jayne had tried to shake hands with Tyler the day they'd met—only a week ago—but he'd refused. After sliding the knife back into his jeans pocket, he gave Bill a strong shake, then took hold of the mattress again. "You want this on that pile outside?"

"Yeah. That's the stuff we're getting rid of."

The two men left the room, balancing the mattress between them. Clarice followed them to the bedroom door, watched until they turned the corner into the living room, then fanned herself with one hand. "I see why you didn't mention him."

Jayne took hold of the springs and managed to lift the end an inch or two before something caught. Letting them fall back to the frame, she faced her mother. "What was to mention? He lives down the road. He builds beautiful furniture. He has two dogs and he keeps to himself."

"Is he married? Gay?"

Jayne blinked. The closest Clarice ever came to swearing was *Mercy me,* a phrase she'd learned from her grandmother, but she could still surprise her daughter with the words that came out of her mouth. "No, and I don't think so."

"Homicidal? A drunk? A pervert?"

"Mom!"

"If my only daughter and granddaughter are living down the road from him, I have a right to know more about him."

"You know everything I know." Except that his family and friends thought a great deal of him. That he was a nicer guy than he wanted to admit. That he'd practically run them into a ditch when she'd touched him in the truck Monday night.

She'd thought about that the past few days—more than she should have. He hadn't shrunk away from Sarah's embrace or her father's handshake. Was it only her touch he'd found offensive? Or had he confused her with someone in his past? His features had paled and taken on a distant look, sweat had popped out across his forehead and he'd clenched the steering wheel so tightly that she wouldn't have been surprised if it had turned to dust under the force.

What had he been thinking? Who had he been remembering?

She gave a start when Clarice touched her shoulder, though far more subdued than Tyler's had been that night. "What?" she asked, finding her mother watching her with concern.

"It's too soon, honey."

"For what?"

Heavy footsteps sounded in the living room, and Clarice nodded in that direction. "It's only been five months, Jaynie. You need time to get over that, to put it in the past." She glanced at the men in the hallway and hastily repeated, "It's too soon."

As she turned away to remove empty drawers from the warped dresser, Jayne didn't know which surprised her more— that Clarice assumed she was romantically interested in Tyler or that she needed time to get over Greg. She'd been over Greg for years. She had cared deeply for him, but she had never loved him, and he hadn't loved her. If anything about the marriage still affected her, it was sadness that she'd married a man she didn't love. Marriage was too important, too…well, sacred, and she hadn't entered it with the respect it deserved.

And she wasn't interested in trying again just yet.

Though, she admitted, stealing a look at Tyler's back in the dresser mirror, he was certainly handsome enough to tempt a less susceptible woman. In a white T-shirt that stretched across broad shoulders and faded denim that clung to narrow hips and long legs, with nicely bronzed skin and brown hair a shade too long, he could make any living woman look twice—even her mother.

Even her.

Her arms full of drawers, Jayne left the room ahead of the men, grateful her mother stayed behind. She dumped the drawers on the growing rubbish heap, saw that the hallway was blocked while her father and Tyler worked to get the bed-springs through and waited on the porch, watching Lucy throw sticks for Cameron and Diaz to retrieve.

She *would* marry again. She was only thirty. She wanted

more children. She believed in love and marriage and happily ever after. But she was in no hurry. With modern medicine, she had ten or more childbearing years ahead of her. Her biological clock hadn't even wound up yet. And though she wondered what it was like to be loved the way her father loved her mother—or her heroes loved her heroines—she wasn't desperate to find out. When the time was right, it would happen. In a year or two or five.

And when it did, just like her father and mother, just like her heroes and heroines, she would know. Her parents had denied it for a time—and so did her characters—but deep inside, they'd always known. She would look at the man and just *know*.

She didn't even know what to think when she looked at Tyler.

Except that he was handsome. Kinder than he wanted to be. Looked better in faded jeans and a T-shirt than any man should.

But that was the professional in her. Noticing handsome men was part of her job—how lucky was that? But to the woman in her, he was a neighbor—a handsome one, to be sure, but still just a neighbor.

Unlike her parents and her characters, she wasn't in denial. She was simply stating the facts.

It took an hour to clear the furniture from the house. Tyler's footsteps echoed as he walked through the rooms, now empty except for the sofa table that held Jayne's computer and papers and the personal stuff piled up in the bathroom. Mrs. Jones was vacuuming before they started bringing in the new stuff, and Mr. Jones was outside with Lucy, getting acquainted with Diaz and Cameron.

Jayne, he saw when he stepped outside, was on the porch, watching them. She glanced at him, then turned back. Her hair was pulled up in a ponytail that she'd braided and secured with a green band. Her T-shirt today read, *Warning: What you do may appear in my next book!* and her jeans fitted like a second skin.

He had once asked Rebecca how she could breathe in such tight jeans, and she'd laughed before explaining the miracle of stretch fibers.

"You don't have to help unload," she remarked when he stopped a few feet away.

He'd told himself that when he'd seen the truck out front on his way home. He'd parked around back, entered the house through the rear door and let the dogs out for a run, turned on the television and drunk a bottle of water, all the while telling himself that. They were three able-bodied adults, and Lucy could do her share. They hadn't asked for help, and he didn't owe it to them. If Jayne wanted to live on her own, then she needed to learn to *live on her own*. She shouldn't expect anything of him.

But the expectations were within himself. He couldn't say his mother had raised him to be the friendly sort—in fact, they'd been taught to not even speak to the neighbors for fear of what they might say. The old lady who'd lived next door to them in Nashville could have collapsed on the sidewalk in front of them, and Carrie would have rushed them inside and locked the door.

But while Carrie had discouraged him from all outside social interaction, taking care of the kids, protecting them, keeping them safe—that had been his job from the day Rebecca was born. Hiding them, comforting them, shielding them, taking their punishment…

He felt Jayne glance his way and he met her gaze. Her eyes were brown, like his, but so much more. Flecked with gold. Filled with warmth. Friendly. He missed warmth and friendliness. Missed softness. Missed wanting and needing and having.

But they came at too great a price. He'd barely survived the first time. He wouldn't survive a second time. But damn if he wasn't tempted….

"I guess I should be thinking about dinner. They were supposed to be here hours ago, and we would have been done by now and could go out to eat. But they decided to visit some friends in Kentucky and time got away from them. So here we are and I don't have anything planned to cook, to say nothing of the fact that in a little while my kitchen's going to be filled with boxes."

He waited for her to take a breath, then said, "I have stuff in the freezer—that bag you delivered for Rebecca last week. Lasagna, bread, an apple pie and a half gallon of ice cream." It had seemed pointless to cook the entire meal for himself. The pie he could have finished off, but he would have been stuck eating lasagna the rest of the week.

"You wouldn't mind sharing?"

Actually, he'd been offering to give it to her, but Rebecca *had* wanted him to share the meal. And better to eat her cook's good food than a sandwich standing at the island while his neighbors enjoyed it. "We can eat at my house when it's ready."

She pushed away from the rail. "Thank you," she said, and he thought for a moment that she was going to lay her hand on his arm before she walked away. His muscles tensed as she considered it, then with a taut smile, she lowered her hand and went inside.

He told himself that was relief spreading through him.

Even if it did feel like disappointment.

Leaving the porch, he went to his house to leave the bread and the pie on the counter to thaw and to put the lasagna in the oven. He set the alarm on his watch, then stepped out the front door to find Lucy and the dogs on the porch swing. She jumped to her feet and fell into step with him. "Hey, Tyler."

"Hey, Lucky girl."

She giggled. "That's not my name."

"Are you lucky?

She thought about it a moment, then grinned. "Yep."

"Are you a girl?"

"Yep."

"Well?"

She resorted to skipping to keep up, so he shortened his stride. "I'm gonna sleep in my own bed tonight," she said. "And I'm gonna have all my clothes and books and toys, and Mom'll have all her clothes and books. Have you ever read one of my mom's books?"

"No."

"My grandma read one and said, '*Jaynie!* Where did you learn such things?' I asked what things and she wouldn't tell me. I think there's lots of kissin' and other yucky stuff in 'em."

"When you get older, kissing won't seem so yucky."

"Do *you* like kissing?"

Tyler stumbled over a nonexistent bump in the road. It had been so long since he'd kissed a woman that he hardly remembered what it was like.

Liar. He remembered. More every day.

To distract her, he crouched, bringing himself to her level, and studied her face intently. She stood still for a moment, then shifted. "What're you doing?"

"Trying to figure out how that little tiny nose of yours can belong to someone as nosy as you are. By rights your nose should be about this long." He measured a foot with his hands, and she stretched out her arms to try to reach them.

"Then my nose would run into doors before I could open 'em and it would go into rooms before me, and when I sneeze, it'd get snot all over the place."

"And people would see you and say, 'Look at that nosy little girl.'"

"You're silly, Tyler," she said with a laugh before she raced across the yard, calling, "Mom, you know what Tyler said?"

He slowly straightened. No one had ever called him silly in his life. Of course, no one had ever seen him the way Lucy did. Everyone in Sweetwater knew his background. They knew he'd testified at his mother's trial, that he and the other kids had been under a psychologist's care for years, that his one attempt at a serious relationship had ended badly.

They thought they knew everything…but they didn't know the worst of it.

Lucy didn't know his history and didn't care. He didn't treat her like a kid, he had dogs and he didn't mind her questions. That was all that mattered to her.

Too bad the rest of the world wasn't so easy.

Too bad *he* wasn't so easy.

With everyone out of the way, Mr. Jones backed the moving van into the yard and Tyler pulled out the ramp, resting it on the top porch step. He swung himself up onto the ramp and raised the truck door just as Jayne joined him. He looked at the contents, then her. "Just how big did your ex tell you this house was?"

"Two stories. Huge. Too big for the three of us."

"Did you know he had a gift for telling stories?"

Finally she pulled her gaze from the furniture and boxes to give him a dry look. "I was married to him for six years. I knew. I just…"

"Wanted to believe?" His father had been a master liar, and for too many years, even after he was dead, his mother had wanted to believe. He'd destroyed their family, but he had never managed to beat the naiveté and the hope out of her. "And look what believing got you."

If the sarcasm in his voice bothered her, it didn't show in the shrug that made her ponytail sway side to side. "It got me a house that will keep us warm and cool and dry—if a little bit crowded—in a beautiful location with a neighbor who tells my daughter her nose should be this long to show how nosy she is." She opened her arms as wide as they would go, stretching the T-shirt across her breasts. "I have the peace to get a lot done. The people I've met so far are very nice. The neighbor, it turns out, is very handy and he makes my daughter laugh. That's A Good Thing."

So he was handy and he made Lucy laugh. He'd received better descriptions—though he usually hadn't trusted them—and others that were much worse. This one had some merit and some basis in truth.

With a sigh, she moved forward and picked up a box marked *Toys*. Mrs. Jones and Lucy helped her with the boxes while Tyler and Mr. Jones carried in the furniture. They had to take the doors off the refrigerator to get it inside, and the only place it fit was in the dining area. There were more boxes of kitchen things than the kitchen would hold, and Lucy's toys and clothes were stacked to the ceiling in her room.

When Tyler, Rebecca and their brothers moved from Nashville to Sweetwater to live with their grandparents fourteen years ago, everything they'd owned had fit in four paper grocery bags.

They were about three quarters through when his alarm sounded. Lucy led the way to his house, where everyone washed up and gathered at the dining table while he served the lasagna, took the bread from the oven and put in the pie.

"Did you make this?" Jayne asked, rubbing her fingers back and forth over the inlay pattern that formed a rectangle within the rectangle of the table itself. "It's beautiful."

It was a casual compliment that brought a more-than-casual heat to his gut. He shrugged as he laid a stack of napkins in the middle of the table. "It didn't turn out the way I wanted."

She nodded as if she understood. "Sometimes I spend a lot of time writing a passage that just doesn't feel right when it's done. Even though I don't know exactly what's wrong with it, I have to throw it out and start again."

She did understand. The table didn't have any obvious flaw he could point to and say, *That's the problem.* It was more subjective than that—maybe the legs should have been rounder or squarer or the inlay simpler, the stain a shade lighter or a shade darker.

"You *made* this table?" Mrs. Jones looked at it from one end to the other, then bent to check the legs. When she sat up again, she looked surprised. "You actually made it? Bought chunks of raw wood and cut it and stained it and inlaid it and put it all together?"

"Mom, I told you he built beautiful furniture," Jayne said.

"Well, yes, but seeing it makes it mean more. You're very talented, Tyler."

"Thanks," he murmured.

With nothing left to do in the kitchen, he finally sat down. Lucy sat at the head of the table, her mother and grandmother at right angles to her. That left Tyler the empty seat across from Mr. Jones.

And next to Jayne.

Everyone else talked so much that he didn't have to. Instead he ate and tried to remember a Lewis family meal that had been filled with easy conversation and laughter. There had always been the fear that something would set Del off—he wouldn't like Carrie's choice of dishes, one of the kids would spill something, Carrie would cower too much or not enough. Del had liked her scared but not *too* scared. Tyler supposed that might have pricked at the bastard's conscience—if he had one.

"So, Tyler…" Mrs. Jones's voice broke into his thoughts. "We know you have a sister. What other family do you have here?"

He blinked. "My grandparents. My mother. Three brothers. A few aunts and uncles and some cousins."

"What about your father?"

His hand cramped, and he looked down to see that he had a death grip on his fork. He forced his fingers to unclench and laid it on his plate, then lowered his hands to his lap. "He died a long time ago."

"I'm sorry. He must have been fairly young. An accident?"

"Yeah," he lied.

"I'm sorry," she repeated. "That must have been tough on you and your brothers and sister."

"Yeah," he lied again.

What would they think—this nice, normal, average family—if he told them his father's death had been the best thing to happen to his family? If he told them that his mother had killed his father after a particularly brutal beating? That she'd waited until he'd fallen asleep and then she'd stabbed him twice in the chest with a butcher knife?

They would be shocked. Everyone was.

And they would wonder whether he had the same violent tendencies. Everyone did.

Everyone around him had become experts on domestic abuse, had spouted the statistics regarding the sons of abusive fathers who grew up to become abusive themselves and the daughters who entered into their own abusive relationships. They'd talked about the unbroken cycle and they'd watched him, because he was, after all, most like his father. He was the angry one, the hot-tempered one, the one in trouble in school. They'd pegged him for the one most likely to follow in his father's footsteps.

And though they didn't know it, he hadn't disappointed them.

Revulsion shuddered through him, masking the *beep-beep* of the timer. He shook his head to clear it, jerkily scraped his chair legs across the wood floor and went to take the pie from the oven and the ice cream from the freezer. When he turned, he almost bumped into Jayne carrying a handful of dishes to the sink. "I can do that."

"I know you can. And I can help."

She stood there, refusing to back off, close enough that he could feel the warmth radiating from her, could smell the flowers and spice of her perfume. That scent had lingered in the house after her brief visit last Saturday and in the truck when they'd returned from Daniel's on Monday. After he'd dropped them off, he'd pulled around back and just sat there, breathing deeply, wishing…just wishing.

The next day, despite the morning chill, he'd driven to work with both windows down, letting the wind chase away the last whiff of the fragrance.

If she was challenging him to see who was more stubborn, she would lose. But who said it was a challenge? He hated being in debt to anyone. If he was going to take, then he damn well wanted to give, too. Wasn't it possible she felt the same way?

With a shrug, he stepped aside. While he dished up the pie and ice cream, she cleared the rest of the dishes from the table and left the leftover lasagna on the stove. She carried Lucy's dessert to the table, then came back to pick up two more plates while he reached for the last two.

"See?" she murmured in a voice meant for him alone. "That wasn't so hard, was it?"

If she only knew.

Chapter 6

The first thought in Jayne's mind Saturday morning was, *Please, God, another hour's sleep.* But she knew it wasn't going to happen. The rental truck's engine was rumbling out front, nearly blocking out Tyler's and her father's voices, Cameron and Diaz were barking and her mother was in the kitchen making too much noise.

A moment later the smell of freshly brewed coffee filtered through the sheet that covered Jayne's nose. Eyes squeezed tightly shut, she pulled the cover down and peeked to find Clarice holding a mug over her, fanning the steam her way.

"Life's tough when you have to make your bed on the living room sofa, isn't it?" Clarice asked, sitting on the coffee table.

Jayne sipped the coffee and sighed. She loved real coffee, but almost always resorted to instant. As if the extra few minutes the brewed stuff would take was too much to spare? "Mmm. Give me enough of this, and I can get some real work done. I haven't written a word since we got here."

"You've had other things that needed doing. Once you're all unpacked and settled in, you'll write."

Jayne knew she was right. She was already feeling the pull. As she'd set up her desk in the corner of the living room the day before, she'd wanted to sit down, boot up the computer and dive right into the current manuscript. She always felt that need whenever she was away from it for too long.

"Your father and Tyler are going to take all that junk to the dump," Clarice said. "Lucy has reminded me no fewer than seven times that we're supposed to drop her off at the Ryan house for her first horseback-riding lesson. Are you sure that's a good idea?"

"What's the worst that could happen?"

"She could get thrown or stepped on."

"I'm sure Sarah and Daniel Ryan wouldn't let their six-year-old or her five-year-old friend ride a horse that's prone to throwing or stepping on its riders." Truth was, Jayne wasn't wild about the idea of Lucy on an animal that outweighed her so tremendously, but she was trying not to be overprotective. She'd accepted Cameron and Diaz; she was thinking about getting Lucy a dog of her own; she'd even let her climb up into the Ryan kids' tree house—though she was drawing the line at letting her sleep there.

"Well, come on," Clarice said as she stood. "It's time to rise and shine."

Jayne groaned and sank deeper against the sofa cushions.

"Here come your dad and Tyler."

Gulping the coffee she'd just taken in her mouth, Jayne held out the mug to her mother, threw back the covers and made a hasty retreat to the bedroom her parents were using. Her mother's laugh followed her, because she'd fibbed. There was no squeak of the screen door, no creaking floorboards, no deep voices. When Jayne returned to the living room, both men were still outside, still heaving Edna's discards into the back of the rental truck.

"He's a nice boy," Clarice said when Jayne joined her at the open door after retrieving her coffee. "Troubled, though."

Nice, yes. Boy, absolutely not…and thank heavens for that. Jayne would feel way too guilty if she was this preoccupied with a boy.

The troubled part was also accurate. Troubled pasts were much easier to deal with in a book than in real life. On paper, she could always strip traumatic events of their lasting effects. She could provide the love, acceptance and healing that a character needed to find his or her happily ever after. She could guarantee them that.

Real life held no such guarantees.

"I imagine it goes back to his father," Clarice continued. "Losing your dad at a young age can be so hard for a boy."

"Depends on what kind of father he was." When Clarice looked at her, Jayne shrugged. "You taught school for thirty-five years, Mom. You had plenty of students whose lives would have been better without their fathers in them. His father could have been abusive. Neglectful. Indifferent. He just might not have given a—"

"Damn," Clarice finished when she didn't. "I've heard the word before."

"Not from me, you haven't."

"I've read it in your books—along with a whole lot of other things. I don't even want to know where you learned all that."

"Oh, come on. I've never written anything that you and Dad haven't done." Yes, there were love scenes in her books, described as "explicit" in the mail-order book club guidelines but deemed "warm" by the review Web sites that rated such things.

"You're right," Clarice said as she pushed open the screen. She stepped outside, closed the door, then gave a wicked grin. "But you didn't hear about it from *me*."

Shaking her head, Jayne finished her coffee, then went to fold the sheets on the couch. She was holding one above her head, trying to line up the edges, when the screen door bumped

quietly. "Hey, Mom, why don't we have breakfast in town…."
Lowering the sheet, she saw Tyler. He wore his usual outfit—
snug-fitting T-shirt, faded jeans, work boots and a lack of expression—and he was much better than a cup of steaming
caffeine for getting her heart pumping. "Oh. You're not Mom."

"Nice of you to notice," he said drily. His gaze dropped to
read her shirt—*Everyone has a book inside them. I just fed mine
a box of chocolate.* "How many of those do you have?"

"T-shirts with sayings? I never counted." She shrugged. "A
lot of writers' groups sell them to raise money."

His gaze slid down again, this time going past her white
denim shorts to her sandals before coming back up. Suddenly
the morning felt about ten degrees warmer than it had. "As soon
as we get Edna's refrigerator, we'll be ready to go."

She nodded, then picked up the sheets and her pillow, clutching them to her. "What are the odds of all your family and
friends being at Rebecca's again this morning?"

"I don't know. The odds of me being in town two Saturdays
in a row are pretty slim."

"Do you want to chance it and have breakfast? Or should I
wait until you and Dad are gone to suggest it?"

He thought about it a moment, then shrugged.

"Is that a yes-I-want-to or no-I-don't?"

"It'd be okay."

"So enthusiastic," she teased, but inside she was delighted
that he'd said yes without looking as if every minute would be
torture. "Why don't we meet you there? Then when we're done,
you guys can go to the dump and we'll take Lucy to Jordan's."

He shrugged again before heading into the kitchen. Rolling
her gaze heavenward, Jayne took her bedding into the bedroom.
The hallway that had seemed more than spacious when she'd
painted it a few days earlier was now cramped with floor-to-
ceiling bookcases lining one side. Another bookcase took up
most of one living room wall, and another left precious little
space to maneuver around the bed in her bedroom. She could

have put one or two of them in storage, but then where would her books go? She wouldn't know how to live without them around her.

Their stuff had certainly made the house...cozy, she decided—sounded so much better than cluttered or crowded—but she didn't mind. It was now officially home. That made up for a lot.

As Bill came in, Jayne went outside. She stood next to her mother and Lucy while Tyler and Bill wrestled the old refrigerator out the door and onto the truck. For its compact size, it weighed a lot, and she couldn't help admiring the muscles flexing and bunching in Tyler's arms and across his back as he worked.

With a start, she realized her mother was enjoying the same view of her father.

She *would* have that someday, she promised herself. Mutual love, admiration, respect...and lust. Not temporarily, not for a few months or a few years, but lasting a lifetime. She would still get as tingly looking at him in thirty years as she did the first time she laid eyes on him. The bonds between them wouldn't grow old and dull but would strengthen with time. They would love each other forever.

Starting someday.

"You want to drive?" Mr. Jones asked, holding out the keys to the truck.

Tyler had started driving when he was fourteen—his granddad's tractor or the old farm truck. He'd never driven anything as big as the moving van—or as lumbering, he discovered in the first few minutes. It was like a turtle on wheels and kicked up enough dust that Jayne, in the Tahoe, went around them after less than a quarter mile.

"I appreciate you being so much help to my daughter—and to me," Mr. Jones said. "I forget I'm not as young as I used to be. This whole process would have been quite a job without you."

"It's not a problem," Tyler murmured.

"Clarice worried about them moving here. Jayne's lived in Chicago all her life. Her mother just couldn't understand why she'd suddenly pack up and move south—and to a place where she doesn't know anyone. I told her, maybe she just needed a change of scene—someplace that didn't remind her so much of Greg."

Then moving into his grandmother's house didn't seem the best choice. But Tyler didn't think Greg had anything to do with Jayne's decision to move. She didn't act at all regretful, bitter or even disappointed over the end of her marriage.

Or was that just what he wanted to think?

His jaw tightened. He didn't care if Jayne was broken-hearted. If she'd loved Greg Miller with every fiber of her being. If she'd been devastated by the divorce. She was his neighbor—not his friend, not a potential girlfriend, not a potential anything. She was no different than Edna.

Right. And when was the last time he'd admired the way Edna's jeans fit? Found himself looking at her legs? Noticed how she smelled? Remembered how she smelled days later?

After a time, Mr. Jones asked, "Have you always lived in Sweetwater?"

Tyler slowed to a stop at the highway, looked both ways, then pulled out. "No. We lived in Nashville until I was fourteen."

"Tough age to move. Have to adjust to a new school, new kids, a small town after a big city."

Had to adjust to the fact that his mother was on trial and, later, in prison for killing his father. Had to know that he and his brothers and Rebecca were a burden his grandparents couldn't afford. Had to listen to the teasing of the other kids and endure the curious stares and whispers everywhere he went. Had to bear the watching—by his grandparents, his shrink, his teachers, the school counselor, hell, everyone—as if he were a bomb about to go off.

"It wasn't so bad," he said at last, and it wasn't even a total lie. He and the kids had been a burden in Nashville, too—God knows, Del had told them so often enough. There had been teasing, curious stares and whispers there, too. Though most kids in their schools had been poor, the Lewises had been the poorest. Del hadn't made a lot of money, and every penny he'd spent on them was one less he could spend on booze.

The simple fact was life had never been easy. His grandmother said some people were just meant to have more than their share of trials and tribulations. It seemed the whole damn Morris/Lewis family was included in that group.

"Would you leave Sweetwater if the chance arose?" Mr. Jones asked.

Ten years ago, that had been Tyler's dearest dream—graduate from high school and leave Tennessee forever. Go someplace where no one had ever heard of his parents, where he could make up any kind of background he wanted.

But taking care of his family was a habit he couldn't walk away from, and if he'd left the few friends he had, who knew if he ever would have made more. At least here he wasn't totally alone, as he would almost certainly be anywhere else.

He shrugged as the outskirts of Sweetwater came into sight ahead. A little shabby, a little down on its luck, but... "It's home."

And he knew better than most that "home" could be good or bad. Sweetwater, for the most part, had been pretty good.

By the time they reached downtown, Jayne, her mother and Lucy were window-shopping along Main Street. "Clarice's favorite pastime," Mr. Jones remarked. "She's a world-class shopper."

"A person's got to have a hobby," Tyler remarked as he turned into the empty parking lot that backed the bank, where he could take as many parking spaces as he needed.

They locked up the truck and walked back to Main. Jayne, Lucy and Mrs. Jones were waiting on the corner near the diner.

As soon as she saw them, Lucy charged inside, no doubt, Tyler thought drily, to claim a booth that would put him in too close proximity to her mother.

But he was wrong, he saw when he followed the others inside. Lucy was sitting on a stool at the counter, swiveling from side to side and talking animatedly—as if she had any other way—to Rebecca. She broke off and patted first the stool on her right, then the one on her left. "Sit here, Grandpa. Grandma, you sit here."

The Joneses exchanged looks. Clearly sitting on a bar stool wasn't their idea of comfort, but they wouldn't refuse her. What was a little discomfort when you got an ear-to-ear grin in return?

Jayne sat next to her mother, which left Tyler with the stool on the end. Sitting at the counter had the added benefit of keeping his back to the rest of the diners. They could talk or look if they wanted, but he didn't have to know it.

"So you're Lucy's grandma and grandpa," Rebecca said as she passed out menus. "She was telling me how much fun she's had since you got here. I'm Rebecca Lewis."

"Oh, Tyler's sister," Mrs. Jones said, leaning forward to look at him. "You don't look a thing alike."

"No," Rebecca agreed, giving him a wink on the side. "But we're so much alike inside that it's scary. Can I start you off with coffee?"

"Do you see yourself as a lot like Rebecca?" Jayne asked quietly while the others debated decaf and the real stuff.

He knew she disliked his shrugs—he'd seen the eye-roll— but he gave one anyway. He and Rebecca had both suffered at their father's hand. They both had scars inside where no one could see them. Where he avoided relationships altogether, she went through men like water through a sieve. He was antisocial while she was very social—but even her friendships were only surface-deep. He kept to himself physically as well as emotionally, while she kept herself hidden, even from him. "We probably have more in common than not."

She nodded as if that answer had told her something she wanted to know. Her next words gave no hint of it, though. "My parents are leaving tomorrow. Lucy will be so sad."

"Then maybe you should move back to Chicago, where she doesn't have to be sad."

She gave him a sidelong look. "You'd like that, wouldn't you?"

The question didn't require an answer. That was what he'd wanted from the beginning and still did. He wanted his privacy back. Wanted to believe that he was in control. Wanted his life the way it was before she'd intruded.

Didn't he?

Maybe not, a sly voice whispered in his head.

"Sorry to disappoint you, but we're here for at least eighteen months or so. Depending on the cost of living and how long my savings lasts. After that, if I get my career back on track, we stay forever. If I don't…" Some of the pleasure left her expression. "We move to a place where I can find a full-time job and write on the side."

Eighteen months, and they could be gone. He could buy Edna's house and that last acre, and his isolation would be complete. But after eighteen months of neighbors, of seeing them and talking to them and answering Lucy's ten thousand questions, how lonely was his isolation going to be? Today was only the tenth day since they'd moved in and already they had made things different. After five hundred and forty days…

Deliberately he led the conversation back to the original topic—Lucy having to tell her grandparents goodbye. "Or you could persuade your folks to move down here. They're retired. You're here. Lucy's here. What's keeping them in Chicago?"

She stared at him—just stared, mouth open—until Rebecca came to stand in front of them, order pad in one hand, coffeepot in the other. She reached across and closed Jayne's mouth with one finger. "Good way to catch flies—not that there are any flies in *my* restaurant. What will you two have?"

"The usual," Tyler said, and Rebecca smirked. "Already got it down. Jayne?"

Still looking at him, she murmured, "Pecan waffle. Hash browns. Diet Coke."

"Jeez, Bubba, what did you say to her?" Rebecca asked but didn't wait for an answer.

"Does the diet pop balance out the sugar, starch, oil, butter and syrup?" he asked as he emptied a packet of sugar into his coffee.

"Of course it does. Everyone knows that." Jayne shook her head, setting her hair swaying, and the faint tropical scents of her shampoo drifted on the air. "If my parents moved down here to be close to us and I had to move again to find a full-time job, they would never forgive me."

"How hard is it to earn a living at writing?"

"It depends on a lot—sales, expenses, how fast you can write. Fifteen percent of my income goes to my agent. I'm self-employed, so another big chunk goes to taxes. At my current advances and with the money I've saved, Lucy and I can get by on two books a year until the savings run out. Then either I need bigger advances or I'll have to do three books a year."

"I thought Greg took everything of value."

Her smile was faint but satisfied. "Everything he knew about. For the last few years we were married I put all my writing income in an account he knew nothing about."

Divorce must have been inevitable if she'd begun planning for it that long ago. Maybe that had made the actual end of the marriage easier to bear. It wasn't as if he'd surprised her with, "Hey, I don't love you anymore. I want out." On the other hand, living in a dying marriage couldn't have been fun.

Because he didn't want to know—how she'd felt, whether she'd loved Greg, whether she'd been hurt—he stuck to the subject. "How do you get bigger advances?"

"Get my name out there, get published more often, hope that my publisher will support me. Truthfully, other than writing the best books I can as fast as I can, there's not much I can do. In the beginning, my books came out every four or five months and sales increased with each new one. Then I got married, and they started coming out every twelve to fifteen months. My sales just sort of stagnated. I'm hoping to change that by getting back to a two- or three-times-a-year schedule."

He didn't ask why marriage had changed her schedule so drastically. He was pretty sure she hadn't been just so damn happy and that Lucy hadn't been the cause of the slowdown either.

So she'd come to Sweetwater because she owned the house, it was cheap and she would have nothing but Lucy to distract her from her work. In an ideal world, that knowledge would help him keep his distance.

But considering the last ten days…he doubted it.

A week and a half ago, Jayne had said goodbye to her parents, loaded Lucy in the truck and left Bill and Clarice standing in their driveway all blue and weepy. She'd been a little blue herself, but her excitement had far outweighed it. She and Lucy were going on an adventure!

Now it was her parents' turn to drive away and leave *them* standing in the road. Doing the leaving was a whole lot easier than being the one left.

"But I don't want you to go!" Lucy wailed, her arms twined around Clarice's neck.

"We'll be back, honey," Clarice assured her, holding her tightly with one arm, patting her gently with her free hand. "It's not that far. You can come and visit us, and we'll come and visit you."

"But I don't want you to go *now!*"

Bill slid his arm around Jayne's shoulder. He'd already had his go-round with Lucy, and he looked as if he'd barely survived. "We *will* be back," he murmured. "Not often enough to interfere with your writing but so often you'll be sick of us."

"I couldn't get sick of you." Jayne thought about Tyler's suggestion the day before. With a trembling smile, she mentioned it now to her father. "You know, if you ever get tired of those Chicago winters, you could move here."

Bill's gaze shifted off to the woods that covered the hills around them. "On the way back from the landfill yesterday, Tyler showed me a couple of pieces of land that are for sale. Pretty little places just begging for a log cabin."

She gazed down the road at Tyler's house. Had he maneuvered the conversation around to available land? Taken advantage of a For Sale sign they'd passed? Probably not. He had likely been blunt and to the point, as usual. *It would mean a lot to your daughter and granddaughter if you relocated down here.*

She was holding her breath, she realized, and slowly she let it out. As if it was the most inconsequential thing in the world, she asked, "Are you considering it?"

Bill looked around again—at the wildflowers peeking up through the grass, the apple trees in full blossom, the mountains rising above them—and a solemn look came to his face. "You know, I think I am. Of course, I'd have to talk to your mother about it. After we're at sea."

Jayne nodded. "When you've just finished an outstanding meal."

"With a few glasses of wine under her belt."

"And a plate of gourmet chocolates at the ready."

He drew her into his embrace, and for a moment she closed her eyes, savoring the feel, the warmth, the smell of him. No matter how grown up she was, he would always be her daddy and she would always be his little girl. She would always feel safe from the world in his arms.

Finally he released her and, in a falsely cheerful voice, said, "It's time to get this show on the road. Lucy…" He freed her from Clarice's embrace and handed her to Jayne, then kissed her soundly. "I love you, pumpkin." He followed that with a kiss for Jayne. "Love you, too, big pumpkin."

Abruptly his face brightened. Jayne didn't need to look behind her to know that Tyler was approaching.

"I thought you might drop by to say goodbye." Bill offered his hand, and Tyler stepped up to shake it. "Thanks for all your help."

"You're welcome. Have a good trip."

"I'm getting my sweetheart on a boat and going to sea, where the wind blows, the wine flows and the nights are long and private. How could it be anything but good?" Bill teased, waggling his eyebrows.

"Oh, Bill! Not in front of the kids!" Clarice dabbed at her eyes with a tissue, removing the moisture without disturbing her makeup. "Tyler, thank you."

Arms wide, she had him in a hug before he could avoid it—and he would have avoided it, Jayne thought. She'd seen his muscles tense, caught a glimpse of panic in his eyes, then tight-jawed resignation. So it wasn't just her touch he withdrew from.

She was considering that so intently that she almost missed her mother's murmur. "Take care of my girls, will you?"

Her face turning red, Jayne looked away, but not before seeing that hint of panic return to his dark eyes.

It took a few more minutes for the final goodbyes, then Bill and Clarice climbed into the rental truck. The ground seemed to rumble as they drove away.

Lucy's wails increased for a moment, her whole body shaking as if her heart was breaking. Jayne would have cried with her if Tyler hadn't been standing there. Instead she blinked her tears away, patted Lucy soothingly and murmured silly things like *It's okay* and *Go ahead and cry.* From Lucy's perspective, it *wasn't* okay and she wasn't waiting for anyone's permission to cry.

After a time, Tyler did something she'd never seen except for the time he'd helped her up when she'd fallen—he initiated contact with another person. He reached across the space that separated them and very gently tugged at a strand of Lucy's hair. "Hey, Lucky girl. You ever been to a farm?"

Lucy's tears stopped midsob, and she tilted her head to one side so she could see him, then shook her head.

"You wanna go?"

A sniffle was followed by a hiccup. "Does it have animals?"

"Cows and calves and chickens and kittens and goats."

She lifted her head. "And a tractor?"

"Yeah."

Lucy swiped her hand across her cheeks as excitement replaced the tears in her eyes. "Can I go, Mom?"

"Whose farm is this?" Jayne asked.

"My grandparents'. The whole family gets together on Sundays for dinner." Tyler paused a moment, then added, "You can come, too."

Jayne had never been to a farm, either. The closest she got to cows was the burgers and steaks on her dinner plate. "Sounds like fun."

"I'll get the truck while you lock up."

Lucy wriggled to the ground and raced to the house. Jayne started to follow her, but turned instead. "Hey, Tyler."

He faced her but didn't stop walking. "Don't say *thank you*."

"All right." She'd said it so many times that he was probably getting sick of it. Slowly she smiled and said something else that, at its simplest, was still an expression of gratitude. "You're welcome."

Chapter 7

The Morris farm was back toward town. Where they would have made a right turn to go to the Ryans' place, instead they turned left. The dirt road was narrow and hard-worn and began a steep climb almost immediately. Trees formed a heavy canopy overhead, leaving little to see besides occasional rutted lanes disappearing to one side or the other. The road would be a pleasant walk on a cool fall day, with the leaves changing to brilliant hues, but Jayne would find it downright spooky after dark.

"Zachary and Beth Adams live at the end of the road," Tyler commented. "They've got the top of Laurel Mountain to themselves. My grandparents' farm is Laurel Valley. It's been in the family for five or six generations."

"It's hard to imagine there's a space along here open enough to farm. Have they ever considered cutting down some of these trees and letting the sun in?"

"Why bother? They're not going to plant crops in the road."

After a moment, his mouth quirked and he came *this* close to smiling. "When we first moved here, Rebecca was convinced that the bogeyman lived in these woods."

"And I don't suppose her older brother had anything to do with planting that notion in her head?"

The moment's ease faded into grimness. "Not me. I knew where the real bogeyman lived."

The temptation to touch him was so strong that Jayne laced her fingers together in her lap to avoid it. "You don't have a lot of happy memories from your childhood, do you?"

He remained quiet for so long that she thought he wasn't going to answer. At last, though, he did, in a voice barely audible. "Not so you'd notice."

After that, Lucy took over the conversation. "How many cows does your farm have? How old are the kittens? Do the goats have names?" Jayne let their voices fade into the distance and gazed at the winding road instead.

She'd never lived in a small town before, but most of her characters did. She knew what they were like—intimate, familiar. Everyone knew everyone else's business, and spreading it around was the favorite pastime. She would bet her next advance that it would be easy enough to get Tyler's story out of someone in town—the older man at the feed store who'd given her painting instructions, the chatty secretary at the insurance agent's office or Sarah Ryan or Beth Adams. Maybe even Rebecca.

And what right did she have to that information? Nothing justified her snooping into Tyler's past—not neighborly curiosity, not friendship, if she could even apply the word to their awkward relationship.

He had a right to privacy. She had an obligation to respect it.

But darn if it wasn't hard.

A dinged-up sign listed drunkenly at the side of the road, its lettering so faded that it was barely legible: Road Ends, ¹/₂ Mile.

A few yards past it, a trail angled off through the trees. Tyler turned, then slowed the truck to little more than a crawl to bump over several deep holes filled with rocks. Gradually the trees thinned, letting in a ray or two of light, then they rounded a curve and the valley opened up before them.

The road broadened, with grass growing on either side. Pastures were fenced off here and there, and crops dotted the landscape like squares on a checkerboard. In the middle sat a collection of buildings and a fair number of cars.

"Are there gonna be any kids my age?" Lucy asked hopefully.

"There should be a couple close enough," Tyler replied as he parked in the first available spot alongside the road. They walked the rest of the way. The house was plain and sturdy but wore its shabbiness like a cloak. There was a concrete porch but no roof to shade it from the afternoon sun. It needed paint and, like her own house, half its shutters were missing. The window screens were rusty and showed numerous patches, and the screen door opened only halfway until Tyler lifted it on its loose hinges.

His expression was a mix of embarrassment, belligerence and defensiveness. Did he expect her to judge his grandparents' home and find it lacking? She was hardly in a position to criticize anyone's living arrangements. Besides, she didn't care. The Morrises were apparently good, hardworking people— they'd taken in their daughter and grandchildren and were farmers. Enough said.

A din of voices greeted them as they stepped directly into the living room, but the room was empty except for a teenage girl talking on the phone. She rolled her gaze and turned to shield the conversation as they walked past.

The dining room was next and held nothing but a solid oak table, but the voices were louder, mostly female with an occasional baritone thrown in. The conversation stopped suddenly when they walked through the door into the kitchen. Eight or ten women and one teenage boy stared at them as if they'd never seen such a sight. At least two of them had, though, Jayne acknowledged as she saw Rebecca and one of their brothers.

"Grandma." Tyler bent to kiss an older woman's cheek. She was plump, with white hair and care lines etched into her face. Next to her, peeling potatoes, was a much thinner version, her pale brown hair heavily mixed with gray, her brown eyes faded, her movements nervous and jerky, even surrounded, as she was, by family. Tyler kissed her next and let her envelop him in a quick hug. "Mom," he said quietly.

"I'm glad you came," she said, her voice girlishly pitched, her smile unsteady. "And you brought friends."

A blush colored his cheeks as he made one-sided introductions. "This is Jayne Miller and her daughter Lucy. Lucy is Edna Miller's great-granddaughter."

"Hi, Jayne. I'm Ruth."

"I'm Carrie," Tyler's mother said.

"I'm Alex," his brother added.

Rebecca burst out laughing. "Do we sound like the Mouseketeers?"

"Hilda and I—" one great-aunt gestured toward the other "—went to school with Edna. That boy of hers was pretty much worthless. Was his boy any better?"

"Not in front of his daughter, Bertrice," Hilda chided. "Besides, she's here and he's not. That pretty much answers the question, doesn't it?"

"Tyler, why don't you take Lucy out and introduce her to some of the kids?" Carrie suggested.

He looked happy for the chance to escape. Jayne would have been happy to escape with him, but he and Lucy made a beeline for the back door without so much as a glance in her direction. Left behind, she summoned a smile for all the curious faces and asked, "What can I do to help?"

"If you don't mind, those eggs need peeling," Ruth said.

Jayne washed up at the old-fashioned farm sink, then started peeling the small mountain of hard-boiled eggs, all the while waiting for the conversation to resume and hoping it didn't revolve around her.

She was disappointed.

"So…how *did* Edna's grandson turn out?" Bertrice asked.

"About the way you remember his father," Jayne replied. "Self-centered, irresponsible, unreliable. What was Edna like?" Greg had told her a little about his grandmother, but he hadn't remembered much and what he had remembered had so far been proved false.

"She was a good woman," Ruth said, and all the older women in the room nodded. "Her husband died when Darren was a boy, and she worked hard to support him—even sent him to college. Never did get much thanks from him for it."

"She was good to Tyler," Carrie said, sounding timid. "She needed him, and he did a lot for her."

"We hear he's been doing a lot for you," Bertrice said.

"And enjoying it a whole lot more than he did with Edna," Hilda added with a lecherous grin.

"How could he not? Edna was old enough to be his grand-mother—"

"His *great*-grandmother," Ruth interrupted huffily. "She was a good fifteen years older than me."

"And this one's young enough and pretty enough to be trouble," Bertrice went on.

"With a capital T," Hilda finished.

Jayne couldn't help but laugh. In her entire life, no one had ever called her trouble. She was nice, easygoing and certainly never trouble.

"Okay. I think this conversation's gone far enough. Aunt Weezy, you were telling us about Crystal's new boyfriend and all his tattoos." Rebecca looked at Jayne, crossed her eyes, then grinned as one of the other women immediately took over the conversation.

Jayne peeled egg after egg, listening to dating-teenage-daughter horror stories, and was glad she'd come. She still had an ache in her stomach when she thought of her parents and the months before she would see them again, but it wasn't nearly as big as it would be if she and Lucy were moping around the house. Thank heavens Tyler had listened when she'd commented that their leaving would make Lucy blue. Such an offhand remark would have gone in one ear and out the other with Greg—even important stuff did that. But Tyler had listened, and he'd done something to help.

Whether he wanted her gratitude or not, he had it.

And a whole lot more.

Tyler leaned against the barn door, watching Lucy and his cousin Charley play with the kittens they'd rounded up. They sat on bales of hay pushed together, the soles of Lucy's sneakers pressed against Charley's bare feet, making a diamond-shaped corral for the kittens. The animals could have easily escaped, but they liked the attention too much to wander away.

"You don't have to watch over them. They're not going to get into trouble here."

He glanced at Rebecca as she sauntered toward him. "I know. But her mother gets antsy."

"She needs to realize she's not in Chicago anymore."

"I think she's probably figured it out," he said drily. "You abandon her to the old women's mercy?"

"Hey, you're the one who ran out first. I've never seen you leave a kitchen so fast."

He didn't comment but gazed toward the house. An assortment of tables and chairs were spread across the backyard, about half of them occupied by the male members of the Morris family. The women cooked while the men talked and made a stab at watching the kids, the women served while the men ate and the women cleaned up while the men talked. He would call them traditional. Jayne probably saw them as sexist.

"I was surprised you brought them," Rebecca remarked.

"Her folks left today. Lucy was crying and her mother looked like she was about to start, so…" He finished with a shrug.

"Aw, come on." She poked him in the ribs with her elbow. "Admit it. You wanted to bring them."

"Lucy had never been to a farm before—"

She poked him again, harder this time. "You *wanted* to bring them. You like spending time with them. There's nothing wrong with that, Bubba. Just admit it."

He bent to pluck a piece of straw from the nearest hay bale, then ran it between his fingers. What good was admitting it when he would also have to admit that nothing could come of it? Living alone was hard enough without wanting something he couldn't have.

"What happened with Angela—"

He stiffened and turned away, striding into the barn, but Rebecca followed him. "Damn it, Tyler, it was a long time ago! It was a freak thing—and I'll bet you money it was her fault. You can't—"

"*Her* fault? How can you say that?"

She folded her arms stubbornly across her middle. "Because I knew her. She was a whiny, selfish, demanding little bitch. I can't count how many times I wanted to snatch her bald and tell her to grow up." Then her voice softened. "And because I know you. You're not like him. You're *not*."

He leaned toward her and said stiffly, "Only because I work at it. Because I stay in control. Because I keep people at a distance. *All* people. I *know* how I have to live. What I have to do. What I can and can't have."

Rebecca glowered at him. "That's bull."

"Great. Now I'm getting advice from the queen of broken hearts." He glowered right back. "Your life is as much a wreck as mine, just in a different way. You want to fix somebody, fix yourself."

They were staring heatedly at each other when a small voice broke the silence. "T-Tyler?"

He turned to find Lucy standing just inside the door, looking confused. "Th-the bell's ringing."

Filtering through the angry hum in his brain came the sound of the old school bell, mounted on a post near the back door. Years ago it had routinely been used to call the men in from the fields. These days it rang only on Sundays, to summon the children from wherever they played.

He glanced back at Rebecca, still scowling at him. He wanted to say something—*I'm sorry. Mind your own business. Leave me alone.* But he walked away without a word for her. "Come on, Lucky girl. That means dinner is ready. Are you hungry?"

She fell into step with him. "Mom says I'm always hungry. After we eat, can you show me the creek? And can I sit on the tractor? Maybe we'll catch a fish and you can have it for dinner with us. Or maybe you'll let me drive the tractor. Do you think you'd let me do that? If I say please and I'm really, really good?"

He glanced back at the barn, where Rebecca was barely visible in the doorway. She thought because they'd grown up together, because they'd gone through the trauma of life with Del, that they had come through it the same. But she wasn't the one everyone had deemed a risk. She wasn't the one they'd watched, expecting the worst.

And Jayne didn't even know what "worst" to expect. Though she would find out the sorry truth about his family before long. If Rebecca didn't tell her, someone else would. *Watch out for that neighbor of yours. Del Lewis used to beat his wife something fierce, until finally she stabbed him right in the heart. And that boy, Tyler, he's just like his daddy. Hot-tempered and angry. Never seen anyone angrier than him.*

Fourteen years ago the angry part had been true. He'd been filled with rage against his father, his mother, the police, the courts, himself. He'd gone to bed every night, praying to wake up in a different world, in a different life, but nothing had ever changed.

Until Angela.

He'd been more inexperienced than any man of twenty-one should ever be. He hadn't dated in high school. Just getting through the day had required all his energy.

Angela had come to town for a teaching job. Just out of college, she hadn't known his story at first, and when she'd heard it, she hadn't cared. Other people hadn't cared—the Adamses, the Ryans—but she had been different. He'd been dazzled by her, had fallen for her, had even found himself thinking about marrying her—

He drew up abruptly, inches from Jayne as she turned from setting a dish of deviled eggs on a table. He stared at her and she looked back, her brown gaze warm and friendly. That quickly, he couldn't call Angela's face to mind. Her hair had been blond, her eyes blue, her smile practiced, but he couldn't turn those details into an image. For years she'd haunted him…and for that moment she was gone.

"Hi," Jayne greeted before dropping her gaze to her daughter. "Hey, sweetie, did you see the kittens and the goats?"

"Yeah. One of those goats tried to eat my shirt and it chewed on my hair. See?" Lucy gathered up a handful of it. "It's got goat slobber on it."

"Eww. Why don't you run inside and get washed up?" Jayne watched her go, then turned her attention back to Tyler. "Are we supposed to segregate to eat?"

He glanced around. Most of the men were seated together, though a few of his younger male cousins were settling in with their families. "We can sit wherever."

Hilda paused on her way past. "Oh, we saved you a table. Right over there."

They both looked to see a card table set for two in the shade of an old oak, the floral sheet serving as a cloth fluttering in the light breeze. It was far enough away from the others that their conversation would be private—provided they had any.

Jayne was grinning when she looked back at him. "Your family is so subtle. They did everything but check my teeth and look to see if I had childbearing hips."

Heat rushed into his face. "We don't have to…"

"And disappoint the old ladies?"

Would *she* be disappointed if he refused to sit alone with her? He wasn't sure he wanted to know. And truth was, he wouldn't be any more uncomfortable alone with her than he would be with his family and her. As she'd pointed out, they weren't exactly subtle.

"It's okay," he said with a shrug as his grandmother called for attention from the back steps.

"Everyone bow your heads. Bertrice, you want to do the honors?"

Tyler obediently ducked his head and closed his eyes. For a moment the silence was heavy, with nothing but birdsong in the distance. Then Bertrice's strong voice broke it. "Dear Heavenly Father…"

He'd been raised to pray before every meal, every night before bed and any other time there was a need, and he'd done it for years before he'd finally realized how few of his prayers were ever answered. He had no doubt there was a God; it just seemed that He, like so many others, thought it best to keep His distance from Tyler. Now he bowed his head and remained quiet, but he didn't pray—didn't even listen to the others' prayers. There just wasn't any point to it.

Once Bertrice's *Amen* had been followed by a chorus from most of the adults, his grandfather clapped his hands. "Fill your plates and dig in!"

Tyler moved back out of the way and watched. The old men went first, followed by the children, the younger ones helped by mothers or aunts. Jayne walked along the table with Lucy, whose eyes were wide at the array of food displayed before her. Once her plate was full, she squeezed in at the picnic table scaled down to kid size with a half dozen of his cousins, looking as if she'd known them forever.

Jayne came back to stand beside him. "You have a nice family. Do they all live in Sweetwater?"

"No. My grandparents and my family are the only ones who live here, though the rest are still in the county."

"They're nice," she repeated. "And this is a nice tradition."

"Everything today is just nice, isn't it?"

She looked at him as if she didn't quite know how to respond, then settled for a subdued smile. "Including, no matter how you fight against it, *you*." Without waiting for a response, she joined Rebecca at the end of the line and picked up a foam plate, plastic utensils and napkins.

"How old is she?"

It took Tyler a moment to pull his gaze from Jayne and to look at his brother, Aaron, hands shoved in his hip pockets, definite interest in his eyes. "Too old for you."

"I don't know. I'm pretty open-minded. I figure I could go up to…oh, I don't know, ten years older. You're not even that."

"Sorry. You're not my type."

"No one is." Aaron spoke matter-of-factly, which gave his words an added punch. When his kid brother thought he was hopeless… "So how old *is* she?"

"You have to ask her."

"You don't know, huh? That's okay. I'll find out. How long has she been divorced?"

Several years longer emotionally than legally, Tyler thought. "What does it matter?"

Aaron's grin was cocky. "Well, if she's on the rebound, she won't be as picky about the guy she hooks up with."

She hadn't been picky enough in the first place or she never would have married Greg Miller. She wouldn't make that mistake again, especially with a daughter to think of.

"You going to introduce me or do I have to do it myself?"

"Do it yourself," Tyler said. "But don't bother her while she's eating." Thanks to his great-aunts' meddling, that was *his* job.

He was surprised to realize, as he moved into line behind Jayne, that he really did mean *thanks* to his great-aunts.

Jayne stretched out on a quilt in the dappled shade of a maple, her sandals kicked off, her head resting on one fist. She'd eaten her fill of wonderful home cooking, including a sampling of desserts she didn't need, and had offered her help with the cleanup, but the great-aunts had declined. Instead they'd rounded up all the teenagers, male and female alike, and were supervising their work in the kitchen. She'd been surprised by the departure from tradition.

"You look too comfortable."

She smiled up at Rebecca, carrying a sleeping baby. When she patted the quilt, the woman sat down, then settled the baby between them. "She's adorable," Jayne said, gently touching the bib of the baby's pink overalls.

"He, actually," Rebecca corrected. "Hand-me-downs. He's the only boy in a family with three girls. Fortunately by the time each girl turned about two, they started wearing pretty much unisex clothes, so he won't be scarred for life."

Jayne touched her fingertip to the baby's hand, and he instinctively wrapped his fingers around hers. His mouth worked for a moment on an imaginary bottle, then he settled into a soft, whispery snore. "This must have been a great place to grow up."

"Greater for some than others," Rebecca replied with a hint of bitterness, then she shrugged. "It was okay. A little crowded but okay."

Jayne could see the house hadn't been built for three adults and five children. It didn't look as if it could possibly have more than two bedrooms, and small ones at that. "Did you have a hard time adjusting to small-town living?"

"No. But I had a real hard time adjusting to not having my mom." Rebecca's mouth tightened and she quickly went on. "What about you? Missing Starbucks and the mall and the big-city social life?"

Where was your mother? Jayne wanted to ask. *Why didn't she move here with you?* But she knew avoidance when she saw it, so she kept the questions inside. "I like plain coffee, I'm not a big shopper and I had no social life. But I do miss some of the conveniences—the all-night grocery stores. The bookstores. The variety of restaurants. I've enjoyed every meal I've had at your place," she continued hastily. "But sometimes I get a craving for Thai or sushi or Vietnamese."

Rebecca made a wry face. "If you'd said Mexican or Italian, I could probably help you out. But I'm pretty sure Thai, sushi and Vietnamese aren't in my cook's repertoire."

"I can always make an occasional eating trip into Nashville or Atlanta."

"So a week and a half here hasn't convinced you that you made a mistake?"

"No. Exactly the opposite, in fact."

Rebecca gave her a sidelong glance. "Does my brother have anything to do with that?"

Automatically Jayne's gaze shifted to Tyler, leaning against a board fence at the edge of the yard, listening to his mother. She hadn't been watching him. He'd left the table to push Lucy on the swing, and then had taken her to the barn to climb over the tractor. She'd been tracking her daughter's movements, not his.

Though at that moment she couldn't say where Lucy was, while she'd known exactly where Tyler was.

"Wow. When it takes that long to answer a question…"

Jayne blinked before focusing on Rebecca. "What? Oh—"

"Never mind," Rebecca said. "I think I figured out the answer."

Figuring a change of subject was in order, Jayne eased her finger free of the baby's grip, then gently stroked his chubby arm. "Do you want kids?"

"Sometimes. Other times I think I'd make a great aunt or godmother. What about you? Is Lucy enough or do you want more?"

"Yes," Jayne replied with a laugh. "She's a handful. But I'd like to have a couple more. I'm an only child and I always envied people like you."

"You can have all four of my brothers," Rebecca said, then drily added, "In one way or another."

Just the thought of all the ways she could "have" Tyler raised Jayne's temperature. "I just think it's kind of lonely for an only. I had cousins that I saw all the time, but it wasn't the same. I wanted a brother or sister to be part of my family and I want Lucy to have that, too."

"What if the next man you marry—"

"The last man," Jayne interrupted. This divorce might not have left her brokenhearted, but she was *not* going to be a two-time loser.

"—doesn't want children?"

Was she hinting that Tyler didn't? As Lucy ran over to climb the fence and grin up at him, Jayne thought she'd never known a man besides her dad to whom playing a paternal role came more naturally. Sure, it had taken Tyler a little time to warm up to Lucy, but no one watching them now would suspect that he might not like or want children.

After talking with Lucy for a moment, Tyler said something to his mother, then pushed away from the fence. Carrie smiled indulgently as Lucy jumped down and strode alongside him, coming across the lawn toward them.

Abruptly Jayne turned her gaze back to Rebecca. "I guess that's something we'd have to deal with. I'm great at compromise. It was the only way my marriage to Greg lasted as long as it did."

Tyler and Lucy stopped at the edge of the quilt. "He's a fat baby," Lucy announced.

"How do you know he's a boy?" Jayne asked. "He's wearing *pink*."

"He *looks* like a boy, Mom. Sheesh." After an exaggerated shake of her head, Lucy said, "Tyler an' me are going wading in the creek. Wanna come?"

She was debating it when Rebecca gave her a sly look. "You ever been wading, city girl?"

"Of course I have. There was a fountain in the park down the street from my parents' house and—"

Rebecca snorted, and a faint look of amusement came into Tyler's gaze. "A fountain...that's not wading. That's only a step above getting into the bathtub barefoot. Wading has to be done in natural bodies of water—creeks, lakes, rivers, oceans—"

"Mud puddles," Lucy offered helpfully.

"And mud puddles," Rebecca repeated with a wink for her. "Fountains don't count. Go on. See what you've been missing."

Jayne got to her feet, stepped into the sandals she'd kicked off earlier and gave Rebecca a smug smile before following Lucy away. They walked along the fence, past the barn and a short distance along a barbed-wire fence. Stopping, Tyler lifted a wire loop from a fence post, then swung back what she'd thought was merely another section of fence. She walked through the gate, then stopped suddenly. "There are cows in this field."

"It's a pasture, and they won't hurt you."

"Are you sure? I'm wearing sandals."

Tyler gave first her leather shoes, then her an odd look. "Do you think they're going to recognize the hide of some distant relative and want revenge?"

She felt like mimicking Lucy's exaggerated head-shake. "I mean, they're not made for running."

"Why would you want to run?" He secured the gate once more before facing her. "If there was a bull in here, you'd have reason to worry. But I wouldn't take you in a pasture with a bull. As long as you don't bother the cows, they're not going to bother you."

"Just be careful not to step in cow poop, Mom," Lucy said as she set off across the pasture, her stride long and sure.

As Jayne followed her, Tyler fell into step with her. "Next time you go to a farm, wear real shoes."

"Thank you for that advice I could have used before we left the house."

"Just remember it next time."

She opened her mouth to respond but found she *had* no response. *Next time?* He intended to invite them back again? Today's invitation had been a pity invitation. He'd known she and Lucy were blue. But the next time they wouldn't be blue. It would be because he liked them.

Or he thought they needed to meet enough other people that they would leave him alone.

She *really* wanted to believe he liked them.

The creek marked the change from pasture to woods. It snaked back and forth, splashing over rocks, gliding like silk over moss. At its narrowest point, it was six feet wide and so clear that it looked only inches deep, though according to Tyler, it ranged from several feet to neck-deep on him.

"The best place to wade is on the other side and downstream."

"How do we get there?" Lucy asked.

"There's a crossing down to the left."

Jayne knew better than to expect an honest-to-God bridge—that would have been entirely too lucky. But it didn't seem out of line to hope for a sturdy plank of wood stretching from one side to the other or even a massive fallen tree.

Yep, it was way out of line, she acknowledged when they reached the crossing. It was stepping stones—and not nice flat ones, either. Rocks of different sizes and shapes, some breaking the water's surface by only an inch or two, a few big enough for both feet, more that would support only one.

"Oh, boy!" Lucy charged forward, but Tyler caught her by her shirttail.

"Your legs aren't long enough, Lucky girl. Come here and I'll give you a ride." He crouched, gripped her under the arms and lifted her onto his shoulders.

She giggled as he stood again and waved her arms wildly. "I

can see the farmhouse! Hellooo, Rebecca! Hellooo, Miss Carrie!"

Something tight and painful and sweet caught in Jayne's chest. Greg had never carried Lucy on his shoulders, never had a nickname for her, never had anything at all for her beyond a spare minute here or there. He'd been there at her birth, had known her every minute of her five-year existence and he'd never shown her a fraction of the attention or care that Tyler had.

If she'd been destined to make a mistake of her first marriage, why couldn't it have been with someone like Tyler? Someone who still would have been there for his daughter after the divorce? Someone who considered others, who didn't always put his own needs first?

But Lucy would have been a different person if she'd had a different father, and Jayne wouldn't change who she was for all the reliability in the world.

Balancing Lucy, Tyler stopped at the edge of the bank. "You might want to take those shoes off."

"Good idea." They were adorable sandals, but they weren't the most supportive footwear around. She probably stood a better chance with bare feet. Besides, she would hate to see what creek water would do to leather and beadwork.

Clutching her shoes in one hand, she gingerly took the first step. The rock was warm from the afternoon sun and remained solid beneath her weight. The second stone was only eighteen inches away. It shifted a little but was no cause for concern as she crossed to the third.

Ahead of her, Tyler was moving more quickly—of course, with ridged-sole boots and the experience of having made the crossing dozens of times—and Lucy was chattering. Jayne was dimly aware of their reaching the other bank, of him swinging Lucy to the ground and her daughter exclaiming with delight over something only she could see.

"Watch that last rock," Tyler said. "It wobbl—"

Jayne shrieked as she lost her balance. Her right foot splashed into cold water up to midcalf before he caught her flailing arm and hauled her to shore…and right up against his body.

Her breath was gone, her lungs utterly depleted of air. He was solid and strong and *warm*. His hand held hers just above his heart, the beat slow and steady. The rise and fall of his chest was shallow, as if he was hardly breathing, and the look in his eyes…hunger. Need. Desire.

Oh, yeah. She hadn't seen it directed her way in a very long time, but she'd written about it often enough to recognize it.

Slowly his fingers relaxed their grip on hers, but he didn't let go. Instead he flattened her palm against his chest, then laid his hand over it, and his free hand slowly reached out, catching hold of her shirt, clenching, pulling it taut.

A moment ago chills had been spreading from her quick dip in the creek. Now she was too hot to breathe, to think, to do anything besides lean against him, stare at him, feel him. If he let go, if he walked away, she would sink in a heap to the ground. If he didn't let go, didn't walk away, she would…

His gaze slid to her mouth, and her legs trembled. She would…

He bent, his mouth coming closer, and everything inside her dissolved. She would…

"Tyler! Come quick! Come see what I found!" Small footsteps crackled over dead leaves, then a hand tugged at his arm, giving him a shake, giving Jayne a shake. "Come on, Tyler, quick, before it runs away!" Lucy urged, pulling him harder.

He didn't say, *I'll be right there, Lucky girl*. He didn't send her back to keep an eye on whatever it was while he finished what they'd started.

No, he let go of Jayne's hand and her shirt and he took a step back, taking his support and his strength and his incredible heat with him. He took another step back, then a third one, and his gaze met hers again—dark, distant, aloof…and regretful. He hadn't *wanted* to kiss her…but he regretted that he hadn't.

Slowly, deliberately, he turned away. His voice sounded totally normal when he asked, "What did you find, Lucky girl?"

"It's a yertle—you know, like in *Yertle the Turtle.* And he's all curled up inside his little house, but sometimes he peeks his head out…." Lucy babbled on, her voice growing fainter as they disappeared over the crest of a rise.

Wow. He hadn't even kissed her, and her heart was racing, her stomach tumbling. If his mouth had actually touched hers, if they'd shared their first intimate, needy, hungry kiss, she would probably be too weak, too dazzled, to stand. Thanks to Lucy's turtle, though, that was only a guess.

She hoped the darn thing curled up inside his little house and got stuck there forever.

Chapter 8

Daniel Ryan's workshop was nothing fancy—just a large square building sitting directly beside the house and connected to it by a broad covered porch. There were windows on three sides, generally blocked by furniture in various stages of construction, stacks of lumber and shelves of stains, paints and oils, with an oversize set of double doors, similar to those on a barn, at the west end. Those were open Tuesday to allow in the afternoon light and air that smelled of Sarah's flowers.

Tuesdays were Daniel's day to do paperwork, so Tyler was alone in the shop, bent over a worktable, hand-sanding the last of three small door fronts to a china hutch. With its intricate cutouts, the piece reminded him of a filigree locket his grandmother had, elaborately patterned and looking much more fragile than it actually was. Each door measured only twelve by fourteen inches, but the three had taken almost as much time as the rest of the hutch combined. Why not do a raised-panel door front and be done with it? he'd asked Daniel the first time he'd watched him labor over such intricate fretwork, and his boss had replied, *The difference is in the details.*

That was the first but by no means the last time he'd heard it.

He blew away the dust, wiped the door with a tack cloth, then ran his fingers over it, searching for places that needed attention. When a shadow fell over the door, he looked up to find Kate standing there expectantly. She was smiling, but it wasn't the bashful smile she usually gave him. This one was filled with anticipation.

"Hey, Kate." He glanced at the clock on the wall. He hadn't realized it was time for school to be out. Nearly time to go home…and maybe see his neighbors.

"Guess what I got today?" Without waiting, she shoved her hand into the padded envelope she held and came out with a book, thrusting it toward him. "It's Rochelle Starr's first book. It's been out of print forever and it's really hard to find, but I tracked it down at a used bookstore in Oklahoma. Isn't that cool?"

After wiping his hands on his jeans, Tyler took the book. It was the first time in his life that he'd held a romance novel, much less paid attention to it. *Western Knight* was emblazoned across the top, *Rochelle Starr* across the bottom, and in the middle was a half-dressed cowboy embracing a barely half-dressed woman in front of a backdrop of stark mountains. "Rochelle Starr. Is that Jayne?"

Kate nodded. "I found this and two others at used bookstores and I ordered her newest two online. That leaves only three more to track down. Do you think she'll sign them for me?"

"I'm sure she'd be happy to." He flipped open the back cover and found a photograph of Jayne, several years out of date, smiling and looking polished. Sophisticated. Like the city girl she was. *Winner of numerous writing awards, Rochelle Starr makes her home in Chicago.* Not much of a biography, without even a mention of her husband and daughter. But maybe she hadn't had either of them yet. She looked awfully young in the picture.

"Is she working on a new book?"

Tyler handed it back to her and returned his attention to his work. "I don't know. I imagine so."

"When does her next book come out?" Kate asked.

"I don't know. You'd have to ask her."

"I checked her Web site, but she hasn't updated it in the past month. She really should, you know, to keep the readers coming back. She needs to put a new picture on there, too. She's prettier now than she is in the one that's there. Does she write every day? Because I've heard that writers *have* to write every day, but I think, jeez, get a life. Just because writing every day works for one person doesn't mean it works for everyone else...." Color turned Kate's cheeks pink. "Why are you looking at me like that?"

He was sure "that" was bemused. He hadn't heard Kate say so much at one time since she'd realized that boys were good for more than pestering and playing soccer with. "I was just wondering how Jayne got control of your mouth. She tends to run on at times."

The blush disappeared and was replaced with a smug smile. "Maybe it's a writer thing." After sliding the book back into its envelope, she thrust it out. "Will you ask her to sign it for me?"

His first impulse was to refuse. Jayne would probably enjoy being asked by Kate herself and she could certainly answer Kate's questions better than he could. But taking the book meant an excuse to go next door when he got home. It was pathetic, but he needed that excuse. Besides, Kate said she'd ordered other books. She could get those signed in person.

"Sure. Just leave it."

She beamed a smile. "I'll put it in your truck where you won't forget it." She was halfway out the door, where she ran into her mother, before she called, "Thanks, Tyler. Hey, Mom."

Sarah set a plate of oatmeal-raisin cookies—his favorite—

and a can of pop on the table, then gazed after her daughter. "She looked happy. You weren't flirting with her, were you?"

He gave her a dry look. "I barely manage civility."

"That's because you're out of practice. A handsome young man like you should be flirting with all the girls—except mine." She softened the last words with a smile. "What are your plans for this evening?"

"Don't have any." Besides taking advantage of her daughter's request to deliver the book to Jayne.

"We're going on a picnic. D.J. has decided he's interested in astronomy, so we're taking dinner up to the clearing to eat and stargaze." Unmindful of the dust, she leaned against the table. "I fixed extra."

He didn't want an invitation to dinner. He got them often enough and accepted from time to time, but not this evening.

"I've packed it into a basket. Why don't you invite your neighbors out to share it with you? Living all their lives in Chicago, they've probably never seen just how magnificent the night sky can be."

She expected him to say something noncommittal—*Maybe* or *I'll think about it*—or to turn her down outright. She was surprised when he said, "Sure. Thanks."

A smile almost as high-wattage as Kate's lit her face. She looked as if she wanted to seriously gush, but she settled for squeezing his hand. "Great. Stop by the kitchen before you leave."

He was rarely in a hurry to leave work. It wasn't as if he ever had a reason...until now. He hadn't seen Jayne since he'd dropped her and Lucy off at their house late Sunday afternoon. He'd thought about her, though, way too much, and about how Lucy had the damnedest timing. Just two or three minutes, no more than five, and he wouldn't have cared about her interruption—or she might have been interrupting a whole lot *more*.

But, no, she'd had to come right *then*. It was probably for the best that she had, but just once he hadn't wanted what was best. He'd just *wanted*. Thought he could have.

For a time.

By the time he ate the cookies, drank the pop and finished sanding all the curves and curlicues on the door, it was quitting time. He cleaned up his work space, then washed up at the sink in the corner. Outside, he brushed the sawdust from his clothes and stomped it from his boots before entering the house.

His first stop was Daniel's office, where his boss was sitting at his desk. Daniel was a big man, well over six feet and two hundred pounds of solid muscle, and looked as rough and tough as the mountains outside. There had been a time when he'd lived even more alone than Tyler. Until Sarah had come along and changed everything.

Tyler had never been intimidated by him. He'd lived fourteen years with an average-build man with average looks and charm to spare who was far more dangerous than the biggest, toughest social outcast around. No one seeing Daniel now with skinny little Jordan sitting on his lap and reading aloud from a school-book would be intimidated, either.

When Jordan took a break, Daniel swiveled them both around to face Tyler. "You heading home?"

"Yeah. I got that last door sanded. I'll start the finish tomorrow."

"Hey, Tyler, we're going on a picnic," Jordan said.

"I heard. Have fun."

"We always do," she said firmly, leaving no room for argument.

With a nod, Tyler went on down the hallway to the kitchen. He envied Jordan that kind of certainty. The Ryans always had fun. The Lewises had always been afraid. Even a simple thing like a meal provided so many opportunities for Del to explode in anger and violence.

Some of the Lewises were still afraid.

Sarah had filled a woven basket with too much food—sandwiches, chips, potato salad, pickle spears and more oatmeal-raisin cookies. "Have fun," she said when she handed it to him. "Really. Just be who you are and enjoy the evening."

With a thin smile, he thanked her, then went outside to his truck. The envelope with Kate's book was in the center of the seat. He set the basket beside it, then backed out.

Just be who you are. Bad advice. He detested who he was. He'd rather be someone else for a while. Someone people didn't worry about. Someone with no past. Someone with at least the hope of a future.

With someone like Jayne.

"Mom."

Jayne ignored the whisper and continued to type. It was her second full day at work since the move and it had been a productive one. It felt so good to write again, to experience the story practically flowing out her fingertips. It was her favorite part of the whole process—when her characters came to life with little help from her—and when it was really flowing, she hated to quit.

"Mom." The whisper came louder this time, tickling her left ear.

"Babe, you promised me an hour and the timer hasn't gone off yet."

A hand reached past her on the right to set the windup timer on the desk next to the mouse pad. Some part of her mind noticed that the timer had, indeed, gone off, while the rest focused on the long tanned fingers that held it. Her gaze moved upward, over a muscular tanned arm to a white T-shirt sleeve, and she swore her heart skipped a beat.

"You're not working," Lucy complained. "You're typing the same letter over and over."

Jerking her gaze back to the screen, Jayne deleted the two rows of *j*'s. She saved her file, then turned the chair around to face her daughter and Tyler.

Lucy blew out her breath loudly. "Are you done now?"

"I am. Thank you for being so good."

"It was pretty boring. I napped two times." She held up her fingers to emphasize the words, then climbed onto Jayne's lap, her arm looped around her neck. "Tyler and me have been talking and we decided we want to go on a picnic."

She glanced his way again. His hands were in his pockets now, pulling the denim taut, and his attention was on the awards that hung on the wall above her desk. The Holt Medallion, the More Than Magic Award, the National Readers Choice Award, *Romantic Times* Reviewer's Choice and, the big daddy of them all, finalist for the RITA, the closest thing to an Oscar the romance world had.

"You must be good," he commented.

She allowed a small but proud smile. "I like to think so."

Then he gave her a look that hinted at amusement. "Rochelle Starr, huh?"

"I didn't choose it," she said defensively. "My editor did. Besides, I don't think a man who owns two male dogs named Cameron and Diaz can tease me about my pseudonym."

"I didn't name them."

"Who did?"

He tugged at one earlobe. "My cousin got them for his kid without asking the ex-wife, who has custody of the kid. They tore up her house and yard and went over the fence so many times that they tore it up, too. She made him take them back, and he brought them to me."

"They was Charley's dogs," Lucy announced. Abruptly she whipped up a padded envelope and waved it. "Hey, Kate bought one of your books and gave it to Tyler to give to you to sign so's he can give it back to her tomorrow. Cool, huh?"

"Yeah, cool." Jayne took the well-read copy of her first book from the envelope. "Wow. I haven't seen this in a long time— well, besides the copies I have. Can Kate read this?"

Tyler shrugged, and Lucy rolled her eyes. "She's practic'ly grown, Mom. Of course she can read."

"I mean—never mind what I mean." She set the book on the desk. "Give me a little time to think about what to say. So what's this about a picnic?"

"Can we go? Please?"

"It's going to be dark before long."

Lucy cupped her hands to Jayne's cheeks. "That's the point, Mom. You can't starlook if it's not dark."

"Star*gaze,* babe," she absentmindedly corrected her. She had to admit, stargazing in the woods at night with Tyler held a certain appeal. As long as she was being honest, she might as well admit that *anything* with Tyler—especially anything that might result in a kiss—held the same appeal. "Okay. I don't know what I've got to fix—"

"Tyler's already got the food. He says all we need is us. Come on. Let's go. And wear real shoes this time."

Jayne paused long enough to save her file to a flash drive, then let Lucy pull her to her feet and across the room to the hall. She changed from sandals into running shoes, tied a light jacket around her waist, then returned to the living room. "Are we going anyplace in particular?"

"Into the woods," Lucy replied. "Where Cameron Diaz always go."

They stopped by Tyler's house to pick up the basket and quilt that waited on the porch, then Lucy led the way into the woods. A faint trail was clearly visible in the early-evening light, though Jayne worried how visible it would be when the sun started to set. "We aren't going far, are we?"

"Don't worry, city girl," Lucy called from ahead, obviously parroting words she'd heard from Tyler. "He knows these woods like the back of his hand."

"Is that true?"

He almost smiled. "Part of them. I tend to stay out of them most of the time."

"Gee, that's reassuring."

When the trail widened, Jayne slowed until Tyler came even with her. "I can't believe my own daughter's calling me 'city girl.' As if she hasn't lived her entire life in Chicago."

"You can't tell it by looking at her."

He was right. Lucy was charging ahead as if she'd been born following trails, climbing over rocks and skirting downed trees. The flutter of wings or the rustle of nearby brush didn't distract her; one would think she was accustomed to wild creatures gathering around her.

"Does she get that sense of adventure from her father?" Tyler asked, reaching over Jayne's head to pull back a low-hanging branch.

Ignoring the implication—that it certainly didn't come from *her*—she snorted. "His only legacy to his daughter—his eyes, his smile and his recklessness."

"Do you worry she'll turn out like him when she's older?"

She glanced his way, but his attention was on the trail. "No, not at all. When it comes to nature versus nurture, I vote for nurture almost every time. He may have given her an adventurous spirit, but I can balance it by teaching her to be responsible and reliable."

"But if she's genetically programmed to be irresponsible…"

"I don't believe *any* behaviors are genetically programmed. We do what we're taught or what we can get away with. Greg's parents never held him or his brother to any standards. If they misbehaved, if they talked back, if they stayed out past curfew, there were no consequences. They never had to accept responsibility for their actions and so they never have. Lucy *is* held responsible. She knows that if she does *this,* then *that* happens. She won't forget."

He remained quiet, thoughtful, until Lucy suddenly stopped. "Is this it, Tyler? Is that the rock?"

They were at the edge of a clearing where the path split in opposite directions. Straight ahead was a huge boulder, several feet high and relatively flat across the top.

"That's it, Lucky girl. Good job." Tyler set the basket on the ground, then shook out the quilt over the top of the rock. After moving the basket there, he lifted Lucy up, who was beaming with pride at her accomplishment in recognizing the spot he'd described for her.

Greg had never done a thing to make Lucy or anybody else feel good about themselves.

Tyler climbed to the top of the rock in two steps. Jayne was preparing to look for an easier way up when he extended his hand. Surprised, she grasped it and scrambled up with his help.

He was slow to let go.

She was sorry when he did.

Fingers tingling, she looked around. "Pretty place. How much land do you own?"

"Forty-two acres, more or less."

"Building furniture must pay well."

"I saved every penny I made from the time I was fifteen. I lived at home, never did anything, never had any expenses beyond what I gave my grandparents."

She smiled teasingly. "Didn't have any girlfriends?"

He didn't smile back but looked…it was a combination of pained and stony, she decided. "Just one. But it's not easy to spend a lot of money on a woman in Sweetwater."

"Then you weren't trying hard enough." She wanted to ask other questions—who was she, what happened with her, had he loved her, did he still love her. But they were in a pretty place, she was hungry, he was talking and she didn't want to bring up anything that would put a stop to that.

She sat cross-legged on the quilt and watched Lucy unpack the basket. Each sandwich was labeled *turkey* or *ham*. Lucy chose a turkey sandwich, filled her paper plate with chips, pickles and potato salad, then slid to the ground. "I'm goin' ex-plorin'," she announced as she took a huge bite of the sandwich before heading to the edge of the clearing.

"Don't go far." Jayne offered Tyler his choice of the remaining sandwiches. "How is Rebecca?"

He chose a ham sandwich and unwrapped it, then scooped potato salad onto his plate. "I imagine she's fine. I haven't seen her since you did."

"Oh. So you made all this yourself?"

His glance was sidelong and measuring. "I *can* put together sandwiches…but no, Sarah made it. They were having a picnic tonight, too, so she made extra for us."

Was that why he'd invited them? Because his boss's wife had told him to? Jayne considered that while she chewed a bite of turkey, tomato and creamy mayonnaise. Did it matter? Not really. She would prefer to think that it had been his own idea, but the bottom line was he *had* invited them. He was spending time with them. That was all that counted.

"Is Sarah looking for you to settle down, too?"

His gaze narrowed into a scowl, but it wasn't very convincing. "Every woman I know seems to think marriage is the answer to everything."

"Except Rebecca. The runaway bride of Sweetwater."

He shrugged. "She thinks marriage is the answer for me. Not her."

"And am I the only single woman in the appropriate age range in the county?"

"There are others."

"So I'm…handy?"

He gave her a wry look that wavered on the edge of becoming a smile before disappearing. "Yeah. Sure."

"That's okay," she said with a grin, and it really was. It would have been nicer if he'd said *I like you best* or *You're the prettiest* or *I keep thinking about almost kissing you.* But she could settle for that. "I've been handy before."

"Was that how Gr—" He glanced at Lucy, wandering back for chips and bites of potato salad, and broke off.

Jayne nodded. "Being married wouldn't be so bad, he decided. Instead of having to find someone to go out with, he would have me at home waiting." Actually, he'd been more blunt about it. A ready date and a ready sex partner—that was what *wife* had meant to him.

"So how do you two work it out so that you get some writing done and you—" Tyler nodded to Lucy "—don't get bored?"

"We co-op-'rate," Lucy said with a grin. "She works one hour and we play one hour. And then she works another hour and another hour and another…."

"We played at cleaning the house and we played at clearing out more of the backyard," Jayne added. "One of these nights when it's cool, we're going to have a bonfire out there, aren't we, Luce?"

"Yep. And we're gonna roast some weenies, too, and some marshmallows. We've never done that. You can come, too, Tyler. You have to, to show us how."

"Sounds like fun," he said.

And he actually seemed to mean it.

They talked little through the rest of the meal, but it was a pleasant time. Though the night was far from quiet, it was peaceful as dusk fell. Tension Jayne hadn't even been aware drained from her shoulders and her spirit felt lighter. She was as relaxed as she'd ever been—warm and satisfied and amazingly contented.

Once the last of the food was gone, Lucy packed the trash in the basket, set it on the ground, scrambled onto the rock and stretched out on her back on the quilt. "Look, Tyler, a star."

He glanced up at the sky, following her pointing finger, and said, "Actually, Lucky girl, I think that's a plane. See? It's moving."

"Stars move, don't they?"

"Yeah, but not to Nashville."

"Depends on the kind of star," Jayne murmured.

He gave her a dry look, then he turned to lie down, too, one arm bent to pillow his head. Immediately Lucy mimicked his position. "Do you know it never gets dark in Chicago?" she asked incredulously. "Even in the middlest part of the night, it's always light. Can you imagine?"

"Yeah. I used to live in Nashville."

"Was it ever dark there?"

"Not really. Not like it gets here." But there was something in his voice—just a hint—that suggested his time there had been dark enough.

He shifted his attention to Jayne. She could feel it—intensity vibrating the very air, as physical as a touch, as warming as a caress. "You're sitting there all huddled. Does it bother you being out here in the dark?"

"No." She wouldn't choose to be alone in the dark or even with Lucy anywhere, but with him there, what was there to worry about? "I'm just a little cold."

"Isn't that why that jacket's tied around your waist?"

She glanced down and warmth colored her face. "I forgot." Unknotting it, she started to pull it on, then asked, "Luce, are you warm enough?"

"Not really." To demonstrate, Lucy rubbed her bare arms vigorously. "If I can have your coat, you can have my half of the quilt."

Hmm. And Tyler occupied the other half of that quilt.

"We can go back," he suggested, but Lucy vigorously shook her head.

"I wanna see the stars! Please."

So did she, Jayne admitted privately. And she wanted to share that quilt. "Here, babe. Put this on." She held the jacket while Lucy wiggled into it, then zipped it up to her chin. The cuffs fell closer to Lucy's calves than her wrists, and when she sat down and drew up her knees, the hem slid over her legs and settled around her ankles.

Jayne lay down on the quilt, several feet separating her from Tyler. The rock still held some heat from the day's sun, and the quilt smelled of fabric softener and—she wrinkled her nose—pickle juice that had leaked from the plastic bag.

"Do you stargaze much?" she asked as she shifted into a more comfortable position.

"Occasionally. Mostly from the front porch."

"The front porch?" she echoed in mock surprise. "You mean we could be doing this from the comfort of the rockers on your porch?"

"It's not the same, Mom," Lucy patiently explained.

"I know, sweetie." There was something adventurous about lying out in the woods in the middle of the night—well, evening. Never in her life had she spent any time in the woods. Never had she listened to wild animals unseen nearby or watched the stars slowly appear in a night-dark sky—a twinkle here, a sparkle there.

Never had she done anything as innocent as stargazing with such anticipation. Who knew what might happen before the evening was over?

When she shivered again, Lucy nudged her. "Scoot, Mom." Working her hands free of the sleeves, she wrapped the edge of the quilt over Jayne, then nudged her again. "*Scoot.* I'll make you warm."

Scooting closed half the distance between her and Tyler. For a moment she actually felt the tension ratchet up in his body, as if he might move back double that distance. He didn't, though, and gradually the tension eased back to a more normal level. Lucy's plan was working—Jayne's temperature had climbed at least a few degrees—and the child wasn't even settled in against her side yet.

Resting her head on Jayne's shoulder, Lucy asked, "What's that star, Tyler?"

"I don't know. I don't know anything about them except that I like to look at them."

"Did you ever wish on 'em when you was little?"

"A time or two." He shifted, and Jayne swore that when he resettled, he was a few inches closer to her—enough that she could feel the warmth radiating from him.

"What'd you wish for?"

His expression took on a bleak air in the dim light. Hastily Jayne said, "You can't ask people what they wish for, Lucy. You know that."

"Or it won't come true," she recited. "But that's for wishes *now.* Tyler made his wishes a long time ago. Did they ever come true?"

"Yeah," he murmured. "But not the way I expected."

There were so many questions Jayne wanted to ask. What had his childhood years been like? Had he wished for escape? For security? Had he wanted to bring his father back from death? Had he wanted his family made whole again?

But she couldn't ask them and so instead she pointed low on the horizon. "I know that. It's the Big Dipper."

"Where?" Lucy asked, twisting to duplicate Jayne's point of view.

It took forever for her to locate it, but it was worth the time. She talked excitedly about learning astronomy, flying into space and, after that, maybe even becoming an astronaut.

"How does she reckon she's going to fly into space before becoming an astronaut?" Tyler asked, sounding amused, as they finally folded the quilt for the trek home.

"On a wish and a dream," Jayne answered promptly. "Imagination's a wonderful thing. You can go anywhere, do anything, be anyone."

"And what happens when she finds out it's all make-believe? That she *can't* go anywhere, do anything or be anyone besides who she is?"

Jayne undid one fold in the quilt and wrapped it, shawl-like, around her shoulders. Holding the ends together beneath her folded arms, she studied him. "Sounds like you lost your illusions at an early age."

"I never had any illusions." Crouching, he opened the basket, removed three flashlights and offered one to Lucy. "Lucky girl, watch where you're going. I don't want to have to carry you back after you fall and break something."

Lucy turned the light on and flashed it all around before holding it beneath her chin to highlight her grin. "You watch where you're going, too. I don't want to have to carry you back, neither. I'll lead the way."

"Don't get too far ahead," Jayne called.

Tyler jumped to the ground, landing lightly, then turned

back to settle his hands at her waist. He lifted her down as if she weighed nothing, set her in front of him and stood there, breathing heavily, unsteadily.

She couldn't breathe at all.

There wasn't a smidgen of chill left anywhere in her body. She wanted to throw off the quilt, but her hands were too unsteady. Wanted to take the step or two that separated them, but couldn't make her feet move. Wanted to ask him to *please* kiss her, just once, but couldn't find her voice.

And then he did it anyway.

It wasn't the hottest kiss she'd ever been given or the most erotic or the most intimate. His fingers tightened at her waist, he took that step she couldn't and he bent until his mouth was no more than a breath from hers. He brushed his lips across hers, just barely caught her upper lip, touched his tongue to it briefly, and then he was done.

It might have been the sweetest kiss she'd ever shared.

"We'd better catch up with Lucy," he murmured, turning away to pick up the basket, then gesturing toward the path.

Bemused, she flipped on her flashlight and followed the dim light ahead that was Lucy. As she walked, listening to birdsong and tree frogs, to Lucy singing "Star light, star bright" and to the solid thuds of Tyler's footsteps behind her, a smile slowly spread across her face.

She'd told Rebecca that she was convinced coming to Sweetwater had been the right thing to do. *Does my brother have anything to do with that?* Rebecca had asked.

Oh, yeah. More every day.

Chapter 9

The fresh, clean smell of rain filled the Miller house Thursday evening. While Jayne got Lucy settled into bed, Tyler closed the living room windows on the north side, where drops were blowing in, then went to the screen door to gaze out. Clouds obscured the moon and the stars, leaving his house the only other light in sight. A person might think it looked lonely over there all by itself in the dark.

Then he smiled faintly. Another person might think it looked peaceful. Like home. It was starting to *feel* more like home lately. Jayne and Lucy had come over the night before to share a pizza from Rebecca's freezer to his. With the television tuned to Lucy's favorite kids' channel—*Oh, I've* missed *this!* she'd exclaimed—her chatter and laughter as she'd played with the dogs, Jayne's help in the kitchen both before and after dinner… *So this is what a family should be like,* he'd caught himself thinking. It was so different from his own experiences that he couldn't relate the two.

Not that he, Jayne and Lucy were a family, by any means. But…they could be.

If the idea didn't scare him too damn much.

"Tell me a story," came Lucy's wheedling voice from down the hall.

He stepped outside onto the porch, closing the screen door quietly. The north end was wet, the south dry. Picking a spot in the middle of the dry area, he sat down, back against the house, knees bent, forearms resting on them.

The rain made the cool night even chillier, but he didn't return inside for his jacket. Once he put it on, it would be time to go home, and he wasn't ready for that. Not yet.

A moment later the screen door creaked as Jayne came out. He'd offered earlier to oil it, but she'd laughed and told him no thanks. An old house should creak.

Tonight she was wearing a thin tank top that fitted snugly and a long narrow skirt that reached to midcalf. With her hair down and beaded bracelets around her wrist and one ankle, she looked amazingly feminine. Amazingly pretty.

And he still couldn't call Angela's image to mind.

She'd pulled on a sweater that was too big for her. Without hesitation, she lowered herself to the floor near him, hugged the sweater tighter and sighed contentedly.

"That was a quick story."

She smiled. "Twenty-five hundred words or less—that's my limit most nights." Closing her eyes, she tilted her head back. "Listen to that."

Rain pounded on the tin roof and cascaded off to splash onto the waterlogged ground. It was a soothing sound as long as it stayed liquid. Sleet or hail, though, was a different story.

She turned to look at him. Light from the kitchen window illuminated her face—and kept his in relative darkness, he hoped. "What kind of bedtime stories did you get when you were a kid?"

"Horror stories." His father screaming out his rage, the kids screaming their fear and his mother just screaming…

She turned so her shoulder was against the wall, her knees drawn up, her hands clasped around them. "You had a tough childhood, didn't you?"

He didn't want to admit it, but there was no point in denying it, so he just shrugged.

"Do you want to talk about it?"

She asked as if it was a simple thing. After his mother's trial, he'd never talked about life in the Lewis house with anyone besides his sister and the shrinks they'd been ordered to see.

"You could find out pretty much everything in town," he replied. "Everyone knows it all."

"I don't want to hear it from someone else." Her voice softened. "How about this? I'll ask a question, and if you're not comfortable answering it, you don't."

He smiled thinly. He knew how to not answer questions.

"How old were you when your father died?"

Harmless question. "Fourteen."

"It must have been tough losing your dad at that age. Is that why you moved back here?"

"Yeah."

"Were you close to him?"

Only when he caught me off guard. When he was hitting me. When I couldn't get away quick enough. "No."

"Did you miss him?"

"No."

"What do you remember most about him?"

He'd always been so careful—when teachers had questioned him about injuries, when a school counselor had grilled him about his mother's "accidents," when a homicide detective had interrogated him about the events of that night, when Zachary and Beth had interviewed him before Carrie's trial. This time he didn't censor himself but instead gave the first answer that came to mind. "His rage."

Beside him Jayne stilled, but it wasn't surprise. He was sure of that from her expression—regret that her suspicions were proving right. Her voice little more than a whisper, she asked, "Was he abusive?"

"He didn't think so." Del's parents hadn't thought so either. That was the way of life in the Lewis household—anger, yelling, punching, beating, suffering.

He took a long breath to fill his lungs, to lighten the darkness inside him, and deliberately changed the subject. "What's it like being a writer?"

Indecision crossed her face. He knew how it went: as long as he was talking, she wanted to know more—people always did—but she didn't want to push him. After a moment, the good manners Mrs. Jones had taught her won out. She lifted her chin and spoke in a haughty tone. "Naturally it's all glamor all the time. We authors don't do such menial tasks as cooking dinner or scrubbing toilets. Our staffs take care of those things whilst we lounge about in designer peignoirs, dictating our books to secretaries and eating bonbons. And of *course* we hobnob with the rich and famous."

With a laugh, she rolled her gaze. "Really, it's a lot of hard work, often for very little reward—and often very little respect. Total strangers don't hesitate to ask how rich we are or what kind of sex lives we have. People want to know when we're going to write a *real* book. Even people we love don't think twice about insulting our books because of the sex or love scenes in them. Because we're mostly women and we mostly work at home, everyone expects us to be available at the drop of a hat to help out at school or Scouts or church. And of course virtually everyone we meet is going to write a book in their spare time someday. Yeah, and I'm going to practice neurosurgery in *my* spare time someday."

"For the record, I have no interest in writing a book," Tyler said.

"Too bad," she said with a sly grin, "because I do have an interest in operating your power tools. We could trade lessons."

He could think of things he'd much rather learn from her

than the proper way to construct a novel. While he'd been hiding away up here the past five years, she'd been married, with all the intimacies that implied. She'd probably forgotten more about sex than he'd ever known.

The thought made his voice husky and forced him to clear his throat. "What do you want to make that requires power tools?"

"Oh, nothing, really. I just want the experience of 'More power!'"

Familiar with the "Tool Time" TV character she imitated, he smiled faintly, even as he acknowledged just how much he didn't need her in his shop. No one spent time there besides him. More than anyplace else, it was his and his alone. But that didn't stop him from offering, "You can help finish the piece I'm working on."

She looked appalled. "Oh, not something real. Not *your* work. All I need is a piece of scrap lumber that I can cut and sand down to one one-hundredth its original size."

"So you don't want to construct. You want to *de*struct."

Her shrug and accompanying smile were innocent, a more mature and sultrier version of Lucy's best.

"How about I help you do both over here?" When her expression remained blank, he indicated the brightly lit window above him with a tilt of his head. "Your kitchen. You can't leave that hole there where the old refrigerator used to be."

"Why, of course I can," she teased. "But I don't want to. What are our options?"

Our. He considered that a moment. For a long time he'd been part of an *our*—his family with all its secrets, responsibilities and nightmares. The older they'd gotten, though, the less they'd needed him and the more he'd withdrawn, the less a part of them he'd felt. He'd told himself he liked the isolation—liked not having anyone to worry about but himself. Truth was, he'd had more isolation than was healthy for a man, and he'd missed being needed.

"Hellooo." Jayne nudged him with one knee. "Are you paying attention to me?" she asked with just the right amount of pout to sound like Lucy.

"Yeah. I was just thinking. We can rip out the cabinets next to that space and make room for the new refrigerator there, then frame in around it. Or we can fill that space with cabinets for a pantry."

She moved from her sideways position to sit with her back to the wall, settling in close enough that he could smell her various scents. "I'd like to get the refrigerator out of the dining area because it's so cramped, but if we get rid of those cabinets... The kitchen has so little storage anyway. I can't lose a whole set of cabinets."

"You need a smaller dining table. I've got one in the shop. If you like it, you can have it."

"If I like it, I'll buy it."

"You can *have* it," he said, giving her a stern enough look that she apparently reconsidered her next words and let the matter drop. For a moment.

After a time, though, she said, "You are a stubborn man."

"That's hardly the worst anyone's called me." *Stupid brat, a rotten mistake, worthless*—along with a few profanities, those had been Del's favorite names for him. *Troubled, disturbed, problem child*—he'd heard those at school and from other kids' parents. *Just like your father.* That was the insult he hated most.

"I can't imagine anyone calling you worse. Your family adores you. Your friends respect you. Lucy thinks you hung the moon—though not the stars. While I was checking my sales rank on Amazon today, she talked me into ordering a book on astronomy so you two can learn the constellations together."

Heat flooded his face as, perversely, he contradicted her. "Lucy's a kid with a lousy father who's just looking for some attention. The friends you've met are the only ones I've got. My father hated me, and my ex-girlfriend—"

The tension came, fast and sharp—from him and from Jayne.

She didn't say anything, didn't move, but waited, damn near breathless, for him to continue. She was looking at him—he could feel the weight of her gaze—but he refused to look back. Instead, after one endless moment, he surged to his feet. "I should go."

He didn't bother going inside to get his jacket but took the steps two at a time to the ground. The rain was cold, soaking his hair and his clothes before he'd gone fifteen feet, but he was even colder inside.

He'd reached the edge of the yard—where she someday wanted a fence with climbing roses—before she called out, "Are you still in love with her?"

He stopped where the lattice arch would go. He didn't intend to, but his feet wouldn't move. She sounded almost normal except for the faint wistfulness that kept him there. A little hurt, a little sad, a little envious, a whole lot regretful.

When he turned, she was closer than he'd expected, halfway between him and the steps. Her brown hair clung to her head, her bangs sending rivulets of water down her face. The weight of the rain tugged her sweater almost to her knees, and the thin fabric of her skirt wrapped itself around her legs.

He took a step toward her. "I can't even remember what she looked like."

"But you loved her."

Whether he'd loved Angela wasn't the point. Maybe he had. Or maybe, like Lucy looking to fill an emptiness in her life, he'd been looking for something that was missing from his and he'd convinced himself that Angela was it. Truthfully, though, if their relationship had ended any other way—and it *would* have ended; even he'd known that—he would have forgotten her soon after.

Jayne swiped her hair back from her face, then hugged her arms across her middle. "I know it's none of my business. It's just, well, writers are nosy by nature, and I just need to know…I mean, you're spending a lot of time…and Lucy and I like you…but if you're still in love with—"

He took the few steps necessary to reach her, cupped his palms to her cheeks and kissed her to silence her words. To substitute for the words he didn't have. To assure her. To assure himself.

For an instant she was startled into stillness, but when his tongue brushed her lips, she opened to him, welcomed him in a hot, hungry kiss. She didn't wrap her arms around him, though—didn't move closer or pull him closer, didn't even touch him except where *he* touched *her.* Her arms remained folded so tightly he felt them tremble against his middle.

He probed her mouth, searched, tested, until he thought he would remember the feel, the taste, the texture of her forever. Ending the kiss, he drew back just far enough to gaze at her, damp and dazed in the thin light. "I can't remember her face," he said thickly, hoarsely, "or her voice or wanting her or needing her. Since meeting you, I can't remember anything about her."

Except the most important thing, whispered a nasty little voice that sounded like his father.

He ignored it through sheer will, focusing instead on Jayne. He wanted to kiss her again, to hold her, to learn everything about her, but she was still looking stunned and still trembling—more likely from cold or surprise than from passion. She looked as if she didn't know what to say, what to think, and he couldn't begin to guess what she wanted next. Should he say good-night and walk away? Push his luck and kiss her again? Do nothing until she acted?

Before he could decide, she raised her gaze to his. "Can I touch you?" she whispered.

Of course she'd noticed that he wasn't much on physical contact. It was one of the things he'd given up after Angela— part of his punishment along with his exile. Wanting and not having was hard enough without tormenting himself with contact.

Nodding was hard. Waiting for her to act was even harder.

She untangled her hands from the sweater, lowered one arm to her side and raised the other hand until just the tips of her fingers brushed over his jaw. He swore it sizzled as cool skin touched hot skin, and he felt the sharp, raw jolt all the way through his body. After so many years alone, it actually hurt—a damn sweet hurt that he'd missed more than he'd realized.

Then she knotted her fingers in his hair, raised onto her toes and kissed him.

This was what being like his father had cost him—feeling human. Being touched. Being wanted. Being alive.

This was what he would lose again when she found out the truth about him.

Even knowing that, God help him, he couldn't stop her. Couldn't pull her hands from his hair or his chest. Couldn't let her go. Not yet. Not when he'd been alone so long. Not when he needed her so much.

Finally she stopped. She pulled away, rested her head on his shoulder and gave a soft, surprised laugh. "Oh, my gosh," she murmured. "I think I can finish that love scene now." Almost immediately she lifted her head again. "Want to come inside and get warm?"

He wasn't sure exactly what she was offering—a dry towel and a spot in front of her fireplace or *more*. Either way, if he got any warmer, his blood would boil. Somewhere he found the strength to shake his head. "I'd better go."

She didn't try to change his mind but tiptoed to kiss his jaw. "Good night."

He watched until she went inside, turned and waved, then closed the door behind her before he started toward his house. It was cold, the rain showed no sign of letting up, he was soaked to the bone and he'd kissed Jayne.

All in all, it was a damn good night.

At eleven o'clock Friday morning Jayne shut down the computer, rose from the desk and stretched. The day was bright and sunny, she'd had a very productive week and she was celebrating by taking a few hours off for lunch in town with Sarah Ryan and Beth Adams.

Listening to three women talk over lunch wasn't Lucy's idea of fun. "Are you sure Jordan isn't going to be there?" she asked for the fifth time as Jayne headed into the bedroom.

"I doubt it, sweetie. She's probably in school."

Lucy plopped down on the bed and pouted. "I wish I was in school."

"You'll be going soon enough, kiddo."

"If I was in school, I'd have lots of kids to play with and we'd swing on the swings and ride the merry-go-round and play kickball and tag and hide-and-seek."

"And sit in class all day learning arithmetic and history and geography."

Lucy brushed that off as inconsequential and sank back dramatically against the pillows. "I'm *bored,* Mom. I need to *do* something."

Jayne stripped off her nightshirt—she hadn't bothered to dress that morning since she'd known she was going out—and pulled on a red sundress that left her arms and a fair portion of her back bare. It was cool and made her feel utterly feminine. "You sound like your father." Greg had gotten bored so easily. If he wasn't going somewhere or doing something, life wasn't worth living.

Jayne went into the bathroom, and Lucy followed, closing the lid on the toilet and taking a seat. "I don't think Daddy loves me," she said of matter-of-factly.

The basket that held Jayne's makeup slid from her grasp, dumping everything into the sink. Giving her a chastising look, Lucy shook one finger in warning. "You don't play around with Bobbi Brown. It's too expensive."

Jayne looked from her to the cosmetics, then began returning them to the basket. Though she hated to defend Greg, she did so—for Lucy's sake, not his—choosing her words carefully.

"Your father loves you, babe. It's just he likes living his own way. It doesn't have anything to do with you and it doesn't mean he doesn't love you. He does. He just—"

"Loves himself more," Lucy finished for her, then gave a careless shrug. "Grandma says. But it doesn't matter. I don't think I love him, neither, so it's okay."

"Oh, Luce…" Jayne didn't know what to say. Simply providing the sperm that helped create Lucy and showing up occasionally for a bit of fun didn't entitle Greg to his daughter's love, any more than it made him a father. But it saddened Jayne, who had always dearly loved and been loved by her father, to think that Lucy was missing out on so much.

"I bet Tyler'd be a good dad," Lucy continued in that casual voice.

Oh, no. No matchmaking from the kid. No feeding the fantasies that were starting to keep Jayne awake at night.

But that wasn't on Lucy's mind. "When *he* has a little girl, he'll be way better at it than Daddy is. But, like, who isn't?"

Jayne wanted to sweep her into a hug and apologize for her lousy taste in men, but how could she apologize for the man who'd helped make Lucy the sweet, lovable child she was? So instead she started putting on her makeup, and within moments, Lucy was kneeling on the rim of the pedestal sink, watching her.

"I'm not ever wearin' makeup," Lucy announced even as she dabbed her finger in a pot of shimmery eye shadow and rubbed the color onto her cheek. "Charley says makeup is girlie."

That was twice she'd mentioned Charley in the past twenty-four hours. Presuming it must be one of the numerous kids at the Morris farm on Sunday, Jayne asked, "Which one is Charley?"

"The one with the red hair and freckles. Tyler's niece or somethin'. Her real name is something silly like Charlotte."

Jayne traded foundation for blush and a fluffy brush. "Oh, well, Charley is *so* much better for a little girl."

"Yep. She goes barefoot all the time when it's warm and it doesn't even hurt her feet. I'm gonna do that this summer. And she wears overalls. I wish I had some overalls. And she rides her pony without a saddle. I wish I had—"

Jayne headed her off by tickling the brush over her face, making her giggle. Immediately she stretched up to see her reflection in the mirror. "Oh, I look so pretty," she said in a high-pitched voice, then giggled again.

With a lump in her throat, Jayne swept her daughter into her arms and hugged her tightly. "I love you, Luce."

"I love you, too, Mom." Lucy's little hand patted Jayne's back comfortingly, then she murmured wistfully, "But I still wish I had a pony."

Lunch was lovely. Jayne and Lucy shared a corner booth with Sarah and Beth. Rebecca joined them and gave Lucy the run of the place. She helped the waitress deliver meals, clear tables and make change, delivering service with her trademark ear-to-ear grin, and when she finally joined them for dessert, she announced that she'd found her calling. She was going to be a waitress.

"And here I thought you'd want to be a famous writer like your mom," Rebecca teased.

Lucy rolled her eyes heavenward. "Sit at a computer alone with myself all day with no one to talk to? I don't think so."

Jayne tickled her. "Alone? You mean some writers get to be alone all day?"

"Being a writer is boring," Lucy announced to the other women. "You write a while and then you check e-mail and then you go to Amazon and see how your book is selling and then you look for reviews and then sometimes you get mad. Then you write some more and you check e-mail some more and you look at Amazon again because they update every hour. And you just keep doing all that all day. Booor-ring."

"I bet it's boring for you, too," Sarah said sympathetically.

In response, Lucy opened her eyes wide, then crossed them, with her tongue hanging out of her mouth to one side.

"You know, the kids get out of school in a couple hours. Why don't you go home with me and surprise them when they get there? Then you and Jordan can play together."

"Could I, Mom, could I?" Lucy asked, bouncing in her seat. "Please, I'll be real good, I always am, and you can write all afternoon. Please?"

A few hours of uninterrupted writing time was tantalizing enough. Throw in a good time for Lucy, and how could Jayne possibly turn it down? "Are you sure you don't mind?" she asked, but it was a purely rhetorical question.

"I'd love to entertain her for a few hours. And I'm very good with children," Sarah said reassuringly. "I've had four of my own."

"Four? I thought—" Abruptly Jayne broke off, but it was too late.

Sarah's smile was serene but tinged with sadness. "I had a son from my first marriage. Tony died while waiting for a liver transplant. Kate was a baby, and he was three years old."

"Oh, Sarah," Rebecca breathed. "I'm so sorry. I didn't know…."

"Most people don't. It's not a secret. It's just not something I normally bring up in casual conversation." Sarah drew a breath and smiled again, this time without the sorrow. "Why don't we plan on bringing Lucy home after dinner?"

"That would be wonderful. Thank you," Jayne said.

After a little more conversation and a tight hug and kiss, Lucy left with Sarah and Beth returned to her office on the square. Jayne was thinking about leaving, too, when Rebecca returned from cashing them out and slid onto the opposite bench. "Wow. I had no clue about Sarah's baby. How awful."

Jayne nodded. She could imagine such heartache—her career depended on it—but she didn't know if she could survive it.

"Well?" Rebecca prompted after a moment's silence.

Puzzled, Jayne shook her head in silent question.

"What's going on with you and Tyler?"

She could insist there was nothing between them, which Rebecca wouldn't believe, or she could confess to everything, which she couldn't bring herself to do just yet. She settled for the middle ground. "We've been spending some time together."

"Aha."

"With Lucy."

"Hmm."

And without. Not much. Just enough to talk a little. To kiss a little. To want a lot.

To want exactly *what,* that was the question, and Jayne wasn't yet sure of the answer. Sex was a given. Tyler's kisses weren't as smooth and practiced as Greg's had been, but they were *real—he* was real—and that counted for way more with her.

A relationship was a given, as well. Whether they used the word or not—and she suspected Tyler was of the *not* persuasion—they were *in* a relationship. Maybe not a permanent one, a happily-ever-after-forever-and-ever-true-love relationship, but it could become that. She could be very happy with that, and in the past few days she'd begun to think that he could be, too.

But what if she was wrong? What if she was setting herself up for a broken heart? She'd never had one, but she'd written about them. She knew how painful they were. And of course if he broke her heart, she couldn't continue to live within sight of his house. She couldn't be forced to see him every day, to stay there inside her little house with her heartache while he went on with life as usual.

Don't go borrowing trouble, her grandmother used to preach, and Clarice had continued the tradition. Jayne was nowhere near heartache, not yet.

But she could be on that road.

Across the table, Rebecca cleared her throat. "It seems that every time we talk about Tyler, you tend to disappear off into some other world. Are you that private about your private life or does he really require that much thought?"

Jayne toyed with her tea glass for a time before putting it away and folding her hands on the tabletop. "I realize there's a lot I don't know about Tyler." When Rebecca started to speak, Jayne shook her head and continued. "I don't want to hear it from you or someone else. I want to know that he trusts me enough to tell me himself. It's just… I don't know if that's possible for him." Trust was always an issue in her books, but her characters always came around in the end. Whatever big secrets they were hiding, the other half of the relationship accepted it. They didn't judge, didn't condemn, didn't doubt.

It wasn't as easy in real life. She couldn't control Tyler the way she did her characters—couldn't give him the trust and understanding he needed to move on into the future. He had to find those things for himself.

And if he didn't? That was too sad a possibility to consider.

"My brother's a good man," Rebecca said quietly.

"I know that."

"But sometimes he doesn't."

Jayne nodded. He'd told her he wasn't neighborly but had proven otherwise so many times. He didn't see anything special in the help he'd given her and Lucy and Edna before them, but it had been special. *He* was special. He just didn't recognize it.

"Do you think…" Jayne paused. God, it sounded so middle school to ask, *Do you think your brother* really *likes me?* "Do you think I'm…convenient…for him?"

Rebecca stared at her a moment, then burst into laughter. "You think Tyler's interested in you because you're *handy?*"

"That's the word he used." Then she frowned. "No, actually, that's the word I used. But he said, yeah, sure."

"Which *never* means yeah, sure, in that context." Rebecca

laid her hand over Jayne's and squeezed. "Trust me—if my brother didn't like you, you could be living in the same house and he would never go near you. It's got nothing to do with convenience. Personally I think it's fate."

"You believe in love at first sight?" Jayne tried to ratchet down the cynicism in her smile, but wasn't sure she succeeded.

"No. But I believe in fate. I think you were destined to move to that house. To meet Tyler. To rescue him."

"From what?" Jayne asked curiously.

Rebecca gazed into the distance for a time before bringing her gaze back to Jayne's. Her smile was thin and edged with sadness. "From his past. From himself."

She exhaled softly, bitterly. "All of us Lewises need rescuing from ourselves."

Chapter 10

"Have you made a decision about that armoire?"

Tyler turned from the sink where he'd just washed up to face his boss as he dried his hands. "I haven't really thought about it." Except that Jayne had been really impressed by it. That it would make a nice housewarming gift. That even if it wouldn't fit in her crowded house, he could keep it for her until…until…

Grimly he forced himself to finish the thought. Until she moved away, or moved into a bigger house. Like his.

"Think about it," Daniel said. "You can make good money working for yourself."

"I make good money working for you."

"You can make better money working for yourself. Enough to take care of a family."

"I don't have a family." He said the words simply, plainly. After Angela, he'd accepted that he would never have a family. It wasn't a promise or a fear but a simple fact of life. And it stung more now than it ever had before. "Is this your way of telling me I'm no longer welcome here?"

Daniel snorted. "I wasn't planning on letting you go. I need you too much here. But part-time here, part-time for yourself…"

Tyler had never thought about going into business for himself. It seemed unfair, after learning everything he knew from Daniel, to go into competition with him. Besides, the pieces he made in his spare time weren't for sale. They were to keep him busy—to keep him from dwelling on how empty his life was.

He hadn't gotten closer than fifty feet to the shop in the past four days.

"Think about it," Daniel repeated. He removed a patch of stain from the cabinet in front of him, studied the results, then began wiping the wood clean. "You and Jayne doing anything special for dinner?"

Tyler's face grew warm. "Why would we?"

"Because Lucy's having dinner here. It's not often a single mother gets an evening free. How many real dates have you two had?"

"As opposed to fake ones?" Tyler asked, leaning one hip against the worktable. "We've had dinner a couple nights this week." Three to be exact, but who was counting?

"How many without Lucy?"

He folded his arms across his chest. "How many *real* dates did you and Sarah have before you got married?"

Finally Daniel looked up from his work and grinned. "None. But we already had Katie." He examined the cabinet from all sides, then stripped off his rubber gloves. "Long story short, we met in a bar, spent the rest of the weekend together, she didn't want to see me again, a year later her lawyer—that would be Beth—showed up wanting to know if I'd take custody of our baby girl for a while. When Sarah came to get her eleven months later, we…worked things out."

Tyler didn't stare openmouthed, but he wanted to. Daniel had told him more in a minute than at any other time in all the years Tyler had worked for him. Part of it he'd already known—that the wedding had come after Kate's birth—but the rest surprised him. Sarah or Daniel hanging out in a bar? Hooking up for a one- or two-night stand? Sarah not wanting to see him again? And giving up custody of Kate, even temporarily? Sarah was the fiercest of all the mothers he'd ever known. No way she would give up one of her kids, not even to their father.

Obviously Daniel's "long story short" had left out a lot of important details.

"You don't know what to say to that, do you?" Daniel asked as he resealed the stain, then placed it with the other stains on the shelves against the wall. "Sometime I'll tell you the rest of the story. See you Monday."

With a dazed nod, Tyler walked out into the late-afternoon sunshine. The temperature had dropped a few degrees, but it was still warm. The horses were in the pasture out back. Giggles were coming from the tree house. And nearer the cat's purrs rumbled as Kate, curled in a wicker chair on the porch, scratched it. She glanced up from Jayne's book, gave him a distracted smile, then returned to reading.

On the way home he considered the prospect ahead of him—an evening alone with Jayne. They could go out on a real date, as Daniel had suggested—drive thirty miles north to Munroe for a quiet dinner that neither of them had to cook or clean up after. But a sixty-mile round-trip over mountain roads and still getting home at a reasonable time to meet Lucy meant an early dinner and spending the rest of their time driving. Not his idea of a great evening when they could do so many other things instead—kiss. Make out.

Have sex.

His grip tightened around the steering wheel. He shouldn't even think about sex with Jayne until he'd told her everything. It was only right, and he'd always—with one notable exception—done what was right. But if he told her everything, she wouldn't let him near her again, and he really needed to be near her. Even if nothing could come of it. Even if it would cost him more than he had to give.

He'd had so damn little that was good in the last five years. He was willing to pay the price for taking it now.

Lost in the bleakness of his thoughts, he was cresting the last hill before he realized it. Edna's house appeared on the left, still shabby but in a neater, less neglected way. A bright splash of color stood out on the porch—hot-rod red, blue, lime-green, yellow—a big blob of intense color set off by the silvered wood around it. The red was Jayne's dress, he saw as he got nearer, that left a lot of long, golden leg exposed, and the other colors were stripes on a hammock that, with its stand, took up nearly half the porch.

He thought about stopping, but he was grimy from the day's work. Instead he lifted one hand in response to Jayne's wave, then drove on past. After parking near the barn, he went in the back door, let the dogs out, then stripped in the laundry room, leaving his clothes in a pile on the floor to shake out before he put them in the hamper. He showered quickly, changed into clean jeans and a white button-down shirt, took two cans of pop from the refrigerator and headed across the road.

Jayne was still lying in the hammock, a book open in her lap, a glossy bookmark holding her place when the breeze ruffled the pages. With a lazy smile, she took the pop he offered, sipped it, then balanced it on the rail cap. "What do you think of my surprise? Mom had it delivered from Nashville. Did I mention she loves to shop?"

"Your dad did." He nudged the hammock with one knee and set it swaying gently. "You put that together?"

"No, but I could have." She grinned. "I came home from town to find it sitting here all assembled, with a note from Mom saying, 'Enjoy.' Want to try it?" She patted the few inches of canvas next to her.

His throat went dry. The hammock was big enough for two if they didn't mind being cozy. He wanted to get a hell of a lot more than cozy with her. He just wasn't sure how. They'd kissed only a couple of times. They'd hardly touched. He didn't know what she wanted, didn't even know for sure what *he* wanted besides *more. Her.*

"Come on," she said, her voice as soft as if coaxing a skittish animal. "I won't bite…unless you want me to." Her feet were bare, her hair mussed around her head, her smile so full and satisfied that it hit him with the effect of a punch.

With what was as close as he could come to a smile, he shook his head, then sat down on the porch floor. "What are you reading?"

She closed the book and offered it to him. It was old, the cover tattered, the pages edged with yellow. Part of the title was ripped off the cover. A flip inside revealed the rest of it: *Life in the Arizona Territory.* There were chapters on the cities, the Indians, the wildlife, the plant life. The place she'd marked detailed home remedies for common ailments.

"Interesting reading," he said drily.

"Research. When it comes to a good book, it's all in the details."

Daniel would agree with that, he thought, as he studied the bookmark. It was for one of her own books, showing another half-dressed cowboy. "I think I prefer the half-dressed woman," he remarked as he handed the book back to her.

"Yeah, well, you're not my target audience." She balanced it on the railing, then turned onto her side to face him. "Did you see Lucy at the Ryans'?"

"Yeah. She was swinging upside down from the railing around the tree house, chanting something about underpants."

Jayne's eyes widened and she'd risen a few inches off the hammock before catching herself and relaxing again. "She was not, though it sounds like something she would do. Did she tell you she's staying over there for dinner?"

"Daniel mentioned it." Tyler drew his knees up and rested his arms on them. "He thinks I should take advantage of their babysitting to take you out on a real date."

"Did he also think you should *ask* me first?"

"I don't know. I don't want to go out, so I didn't ask."

"What *do* you want to do?"

"This seems good for starters. Sitting here." *Looking at you.*

"You're way too easy to please, Tyler." She sat up, swinging her feet to the floor, tugging at her skirt. "Like Daniel, I thought we should do something since I don't have Lucy, so I bought some steaks and potatoes and mushrooms and salad mix. And Mom also sent a bottle of wine with the hammock. Do you like wine?"

"I don't drink." He shrugged. "My father was a drunk. In the beginning, that was always his excuse for hitting my mother—he was too drunk to realize what he was doing."

She nodded once, sympathy in her eyes, but didn't make a big deal of it. "Skip the wine then. I thought we could cook at your house, since you have a grill and I don't."

"Did you also think you should ask me first?"

Her smile was broad and smug. "I figured the food would be enough of a lure."

She didn't need a lure. For a few hours alone with her, he would be happy with toast and water.

She placed her feet primly together and tugged once again at the hem of her red dress. "Okay. I'm going to stand up. I haven't gotten out of this thing yet, so if I fall, don't laugh, and if I show anything I shouldn't, don't look." She scooted forward, and the hammock swayed. "On second thought, why don't you be a gentleman and help me up?"

"No one's ever accused me of being a gentleman," he said. Even so, he got to his feet and offered one hand. When she wrapped her warm fingers around his, he pulled her to her feet—and right up against him.

"See how well that worked out?" she asked. Her voice was

soft, her breath tickling his chin. Her free hand rested on his shoulder for balance, and one of her bare feet was on top of his own foot, bringing her leg between his.

Just like that, the pleasantly warm evening turned hot and the air became too thick to breathe. His heart was beating faster, his lungs constricting, his jeans growing tighter. He should let go of her, set her aside, walk away and never look back...but he couldn't. He needed this—needed the pleasure and the pain and the touching and the hope.

No matter what it cost him later.

He slid his hands to her hips, savoring the heat and the curves, imagining the warmth and softness and pale golden color of the skin covering those curves. Slowly he took a step back, then another, until the wall was at his back, and he drew her with him. Planting his feet apart, he guided her between his legs, pulled her closer until his erection pressed against her, until her hips cradled him.

Holding her there with one hand, he slid his other hand over her hip, around to her spine, up her back, over her neck, into the disheveled softness of her hair. Gently he tugged her head back, exposing her throat, and he kissed her there, right above the pulse that throbbed. His next kiss was to her jaw, then the corner of her mouth. Abruptly she twisted her head, biting at his lip, demanding a proper kiss, and he was happy to comply.

She opened to him, and he stabbed his tongue inside her mouth, stroking, thrusting. Her hips were hot against his and her breasts were nestled tight. She clung to him with both hands, urging, tormenting, pleasure and pain. Her fingers slid beneath his untucked shirt, cool against his feverish skin, and her nails scraped delicately over his nipple, making him shudder, her mouth swallowing his gasp.

Muscles taut, he pulled her hands down, settling them around his waist, but she wasn't content to leave them there. Before he could do more than release her wrists, than stroke his tongue across the silky, coarse, smooth textures of her mouth, she moved them again, this time gliding downward over his waistband, across his fly, curling around his erection in a warm, gentle, unbearable grip.

He jerked his mouth free, jerked her hands back and put her away from him. "Oh, God, don't do that. It's been so damn long…." One more touch, and he was liable to embarrass himself with his lack of control.

She didn't argue, didn't struggle against him, but smiled a lazy, womanly smile. "So, do you want to have dinner with me, Tyler? I've got the food and I'd be happy to provide the dessert."

He shouldn't. He knew damn well what *dessert* was likely to be. But he shouldn't have kissed her either. Shouldn't have spent the past four evenings with her. Shouldn't have ever spoken to her beyond a distant hello. He shouldn't have done a damn thing, and the day would come when he would regret every minute of the time he'd spent with her.

But not as much as he would regret it if he didn't.

"I'll help you carry everything over."

As Tyler unlocked his door, Jayne grimaced. "I forgot my cell phone."

"If Lucy needs to call and you're not home, Sarah will give her my number."

"Oh. Okay." She liked the idea that his boss's wife thought them enough of a couple that his house would be the second place she'd look for Jayne.

She'd liked that kiss, too. If he hadn't stopped it when he did, they would still be naked when Lucy came home—on the porch, on the sofa, in bed. She wouldn't have been particular about where.

And they were going to wind up there anyway. That fact made her stomach fluttery. She hadn't wanted sex so much in longer than she could recall. Hadn't thought that a kiss might make her combust. Hadn't felt so weak and powerful and bold and trembling and needy. Hadn't felt such *promise*. In a few hours…

She forced herself to take a calming breath as she followed Tyler into the kitchen. He set the bag of food down, then went out back to light the grill while she unpacked the groceries. The steaks were marinating in a sealed plastic bag. She'd already scrubbed and pierced the potatoes for a few minutes in the microwave, then a finish in the oven. The salad merely needed to be emptied into a bowl; she'd brought a cucumber and a tomato to add to it.

And as for dessert… She glanced down at herself. She wasn't arrogant enough to think that she could entice every man. Her breasts were on the average side, her waist could stand to be whittled an inch or two, and her hips… Jones women tended to be a tad too curvy there. But she had good legs and one distinct advantage: Tyler *wanted* her.

How cool was that?

He came back inside, the dogs on his heels, washed up and peeled the cucumber while she chopped the tomato. "Where can I find a bowl for the salad?" she asked, then followed his gesture to the cabinet to the left of the sink. She opened both doors and her brows arched toward her hairline. The bowls were nested according to size, type and color—clear glass on the left of the bottom shelf, yellow pottery in the middle, speckled blue ceramic on the right. Plastic storage bowls—also stacked by size and type—and their lids took up the second shelf. "You are seriously organized," she said, not sure whether she was impressed or intimidated.

He turned to look, and a faint sadness darkened his eyes. "My father used to beat the hell out of my mother whenever he found anything out of place. She's not orderly by nature, so I learned to help her out."

"I'm not very orderly either," she said apologetically.

"That's okay. I'm neat enough for both of us."

When he turned back to the sink and the cucumber, a small smile curved her lips. *Both of us.* She liked the sound of that.

She emptied half the salad mix into the bowl, then added the tomato before leaning against the island near him. "Did he beat you and the other kids, too?"

For a time it seemed the cucumber required all his attention. Then he shrugged. "Our mother was his favorite target. He never laid a hand on Rebecca or the boys. I would have killed him if he had." He gave her a sidelong look. "That was my bedtime prayer, my every wish—for him to die. And finally he did."

Did you ever wish on stars when you were little, Lucy had asked him, *and did they ever come true? Yeah,* he'd replied. *But not the way I expected.*

"What happened?" she asked softly.

He offered her the cucumber, ran the peelings through the garbage disposal, then faced her. His expression was stark, intense, his eyes haunted, and tension radiated through him. One hand rested on his hip, knotted into a fist. The other pressed against the countertop so hard that his fingertips were shades of red and white. "He was stabbed in the chest. By my mother."

Jayne couldn't stop the gasp as she stared at him. "Oh, my God…" Sweet, quiet, little Carrie? She was so timid, so gentle. What kind of hell had her husband put her through to drive her to such drastic action? "Tyler…"

He drew a breath so heavy that it made his broad shoulders shudder. "He had beaten her practically to death earlier that evening, and when I tried to stop him, he started on me. She just couldn't take it anymore. She told me to put the kids to bed and she waited until he passed out and she…killed him. She woke me up and told me what she'd done, and I called the police. They took the kids off to social services and they took her and me to the hospital and then they took her to jail."

"They *charged* her?"

He nodded, the look in his eyes fourteen years distant. "She was convicted of manslaughter and went to prison for eleven months. The kids and I came here to live with our grandparents, and when she got out, she came here, too." Abruptly he met her gaze. "Alex was born in prison."

"Oh, my God." She wanted to wrap her arms around him, to hold him tightly and never let go, but he looked so stiff. He wasn't in the habit of confiding in anyone, and she suspected her reaction could either encourage him to do so again or discourage him. "I'm sorry," she said at last. "He deserved a more painful death."

For a moment he stared at her, and she feared she'd made the wrong choice. But after a time, some of the strain eased from his features and one corner of his mouth quirked. "Yeah," he agreed. "If anyone deserved to suffer, it was Del." He took another deep breath—no shudders this time—then glanced outside. "Ready for the steaks to go on the grill?"

She nodded.

"How do you like yours?"

"Medium-well, please."

This time the nod was his as he picked up the steaks, a plate and tongs, then started away. She watched until the door closed behind him, then turned her back to the windows and pressed one hand to her stomach.

Dear God, his mother had killed his father! She had loved him, lived with him, borne him four children and carried the fifth—and she'd plunged a knife into his chest. The enormity of it overwhelmed Jayne.

You had a tough childhood, didn't you? she'd asked Tyler, and he'd simply shrugged. Even tonight, when she'd asked if his father had beaten him and the other kids, he hadn't exactly answered. *He never laid a hand on Rebecca and the boys.*

Which was as clear as any other answer he might have given.

A tough childhood. She hadn't guessed the half of it.

The sound of the door opening alerted her to his return. Abruptly she picked up the knife and began slicing the cucumber. Hoping her expression held some semblance of normalcy, she glanced over her shoulder as he came inside. "I didn't ask—do you like cucumbers?"

"Yeah."

"I love them, but Lucy won't touch them. When I made the mistake of telling her that's where pickles come from, she wouldn't eat pickles for months."

He came to stand at the end of the island, resting his hands on either side of the salad bowl. He looked calmer, more in control, than when he'd gone outside. "It's okay. You can be shocked. People always are."

She scraped the slices into the bowl, then laid the knife aside. "It's a terrible thing. It hurts my heart to think of you living through that. And your mother…"

"Don't you want to ask why? Why didn't she leave him? Why didn't she call the police? Why didn't she get help?"

"Serving spoon?" When he pointed to a nearby drawer, she found a spoon, then stirred the salad. "They say an abusive man is most dangerous when his victim tries to leave. As far as calling the police, who's going to protect you when they're gone? Because they do have to leave at some point, and he is going to come back. Where do you go with four children, another on the way and no job skills? What do you do when the one person who's supposed to love you best tells you you're worthless and stupid, that no one else would want you, that you're lucky to have him, that it's all your fault? When he escalates gradually from a shove to a slap to a punch and he's always got a reason to blame you that you can't entirely deny?" She drew an unsteady breath. "You can't have physical abuse without emotional abuse, and the emotional can be so much more devastating. When you destroy a person's self-esteem, her confidence, her hope, you can't be surprised when she finds a drastic solution to the problem."

"More research?" he asked quietly.

She shook her head. "I watch television. I read a lot."

"You would never stay in a relationship like that."

"No. The first time a man raised his hand to me, I'd be out the door. But I'd bet I'm a stronger person than your mother was when she met your father. Abusive men don't choose strong women. We're not malleable enough, vulnerable enough, fragile enough." She paused. "I don't mean to insult your mother."

He shook his head dismissively. "No, you're right. She was all that and more. Do you know she never stopped loving him? She never gave up believing that it was her fault, that if she could just be better, it would all stop and we would all live happily ever after. Not until he was dead."

"I don't understand that," she admitted. "But sometimes the way we feel is the way we feel, and logic and sense have nothing to do with it." Like Tyler not always believing that he was a good man when everyone around him knew he was. He had a reason for thinking that way, and whether it was logical to others was inconsequential. It made sense to him.

Feeling a tremendous urge to lighten the mood, she picked up the salad bowl and two bottles of dressing. "Our steaks aren't burning out there, are they?"

"Mine hasn't gone on yet. Yours should be done in a minute." He waited until she came even with him to move, but it wasn't toward the door. Lifting his hand, he brushed his fingers along her jaw, so gently she hardly felt it. Then he walked away.

Dinner was easy. They sat across from each other and talked about nothing important—the weather, the best time for planting flowers, the work they planned to do in Jayne's kitchen. Normal, everyday conversation that made Tyler feel like a normal, everyday person. How long had he waited to feel that way again? And how long would it last?

Until he told her everything about Angela.

Grimly he pushed the thought out of his mind. It would come out eventually, but damned if he was going to let it ruin the night. He needed this—needed Jayne—too much. Maybe later he would be strong enough, but not tonight.

He'd just risen to clear the dishes when the phone rang.

Setting his plate down again, he crossed to answer, then watched as Jayne took over the task. "Hello," he said absently.

"Hey, Tyler, guess who this is."

"Oh, gee, let me think…it wouldn't be Lucky, would it?"

She giggled. "Yep. Is my mom there? 'Cause I called our house and she wasn't there, and Miss Sarah said maybe she's at your house."

"Yes, she is."

"Tell her I'm gonna spend the night here, okay? And tell her we're gonna sleep in the tree house just to make her freak. Okay? So I won't be home until sometime tomorrow—"

"Whoa, Lucky. You need to talk to your mom."

"Aw, but, Tyler—"

"Hold on." He took the phone to Jayne in the kitchen, then removed everything else from the table. Bracing the receiver between her ear and shoulder, she started rinsing dishes while talking. "I don't know, babe….Of course I trust Sarah…But you haven't spent the night with anyone but Grandma and Grandpa in a long time….We-e-ell…okay."

Even from a distance Tyler heard the squeals of delight that made Jayne wince.

"I love you, sweetie. Have fun."

Since her hands were wet, Tyler removed the phone, then shut it off. "She'll be all right."

"Oh, I know." She smiled ruefully as she began loading the dishwasher. "Truth is, I'm thinking about myself. I haven't spent the night alone in, like, five years."

"You want me to send Diaz and Cameron home with you? They'll share your bed, but I'll warn you—they're both cowards. If someone tries to break in, they'll be under the bed whimpering."

"That's okay. I'll be under there with them." She closed the dishwasher door, then faced him. "I'd rather share my bed with you."

His throat went dry and his internal thermostat shot up somewhere past the red zone. She'd said the words so casually, but there was nothing casual about the fast, hot lust coursing through him.

Or the hesitant look in her brown eyes. She moistened her lips with the tip of her tongue, then shifted awkwardly. "Sorry. I, uh, don't do bold very well."

"I don't know. You got me hard with seven words."

Her gaze dropped to his groin. He half expected her to blush, but instead she responded with a sweet, sexy smile. "So you're interested."

"It's a little hard to hide."

"Well…" She glanced around, then laced her fingers together. "I guess we could, uh…maybe we should…"

"We don't have to jump into bed right this second." Not that he would mind. "Wait here a minute."

He cut through the living room, then down the hall to his bedroom and into the bath. A few years ago, when the loneliness had become too much, he'd bought a box of condoms, keeping them in his night stand drawer, intending to use at least a few. He hadn't, though, and they'd wound up nothing more than a reminder of what was missing from his life. He rifled through the bathroom drawers until he'd found them, stuffed a couple in his pocket, then returned to the kitchen. On the way past the woodstove, he picked up a block of waxy firestarter and a box of matches.

Circling the island, he caught Jayne's hand and pulled her through the French door to the deck. The grill was still warm when they passed it, but its heat didn't extend more than a few feet. At the center of the deck, he released her and knelt in front of the freestanding fire pit that had been Rebecca's house-warming gift. He rarely used it unless she came for dinner, but tonight seemed a very good time.

The wood stacked nearby was old and dry. It took only a minute to get a fire blazing. While Jayne warmed herself in front of it, he pulled a double-wide chaise closer, laid the back flat, then drew her down onto it with him.

She settled on the thick cushion, lying on her back, watching as he stretched out beside her. "Did you make this?"

"Yeah." It had been meant as a gift and had sat there on the deck for months. When he'd never decided who to give it to, he'd had the cushion made and kept it.

"It's nice."

"More stable than a hammock." The warmth from the fire drifted around them, the smell sweet and smoky, nearly over-powering Jayne's own scents. "Tell me something for real. How many times have you gotten out of a hammock without help?"

She smiled smugly. "Hundreds. My dad's had one in the backyard for as long as I can remember. He read me stories there, we took naps and he taught me everything I needed to know about living. It was our special place."

He nuzzled her hair from her ear and brushed his mouth across it, making her shiver. "Feel free to need help whenever I'm around."

"Like I said, it worked out well."

He nuzzled her ear again, and her fingers curled tightly around a handful of his shirtfront. Everything in him wanted him to hurry—to go straight for her mouth, her clothes, her body—but his control was rigid. He'd waited a long time for this, and for all he knew, this could be his only chance. He could let the truth spill about Angela, or Rebecca could decide to tell her tomorrow, or she could decide he wasn't worth the effort. He might not measure up to Greg, might not satisfy her, might not—

She caught a handful of his hair and tugged his mouth to hers, gliding her tongue inside. Her fingers were gentle and strong and touched him in just the right way to make him burn. His blood was hot, searing his skin, heating his breath. He wanted to shuck his clothes and hers and see just how much hotter he could get and survive.

His shirt slid from his shoulders, down his arms, the night

air a cool shock against his back, and her hands were touching him, moving restlessly across his stomach, his chest, his throat, his jaw. Bracing himself on one arm, he blindly reached for her hand but got distracted by her skin, soft, silken, feverish. Ending the kiss, he gazed down at her and stroked her from cheek to jaw, from throat to the swell of her breasts, from shoulder to fingertips, making her lashes flutter, her breath catch. She grasped his fingers with hers and slid them back up, molding his hand to her breast, gasping, whispering his name.

It was the most erotic thing he'd ever heard.

Her dress buttoned down the front, and each button opened easily, revealing her pale lacy bra, gold-tinged skin stretching across her rib cage, the delicate dip of her navel, lacy barely-there panties. Muscles clenched, hand trembling, he stroked her. Her breathing hitched, her flesh quivered, and she made the softest, hottest little sounds deep in her throat.

He couldn't fill his lungs. Couldn't think clearly for the haze clouding his brain. Couldn't stop shaking. Couldn't stand too much more. But through sheer will, he forced himself to do all those things. To take his time, to press his lips to all that smooth golden skin, to tease and arouse her, to mouth her nipple through the delicate lace, to unfasten the small hook and uncover her breasts, to ignore the throbbing and the hunger and the desperate need and the incredible ache.

"P-please," she whispered when he drew her nipple into his mouth.

He knew what she wanted. When he slid his fingers under the elastic of her panties, she instinctively lifted her hips. When he drew them down, she kicked them away, then reached for his jeans, fumbling over the button, rasping the zipper. Her delicate, strong fingers groped inside, wrapping around his erection, and she forgot about his clothes. He struggled out of them, his shirt hitting the cushion, dropping his jeans and briefs to the floor the instant he retrieved the condoms from the pocket.

"Do you have…?" Panting, she left the question unasked as

he pressed one of the packets into her hand. She ripped open the plastic and unrolled the sheath over him with such care that he gritted his teeth on a long, low moan. "Now," she pleaded, tugging at his hips, opening to him, guiding him.

He slid inside her, filling her, and came, the release so intense that bright light exploded on his eyelids. He shuddered against her, his breathing harsh, his cry guttural when she suckled his nipple between her teeth. But the orgasm was only the beginning. He was still stone-hard inside her, still craving, still needing. Though his body was so sensitized that every breath throbbed with pain, he began thrusting into her, and she met him, taking him long and deep.

He was in the middle of his third orgasm when she arched beneath him, her hips pumping in frantic little strokes, her breath reduced to nothing more than desperate little pants. Tension shot through her body as she stiffened against him, and deep inside, her muscles convulsed around him, tightening, relaxing, tightening again, draining him.

Slowly, muscle by muscle, her body softened, even as he softened inside her. He rested his forehead on her shoulder as the rushing in his ears and the pounding in his chest slowly receded. When he could take a breath, he did, and when he could lift his head, he did that, too, to find her watching him with an expression he couldn't quite grasp. Solemn. Satisfied. Sweet. And something more, something serious and intimate and…hopeful. Something that could save him.

Or destroy him.

It seemed forever before he could look away—not until she shifted and he realized she bore the bulk of his weight. He moved to the side, disposed of the condom, then turned back to her. "What do you think? Do you still want to share a bed with me?"

Her stretch reminded him of a sleek, sensuous cat, and her smile was, at the same time, sweet and seductive. "Absolutely. Again and again and again…"

Chapter 11

Tyler's bedroom was exactly what Jayne had expected—masculine, utilitarian, filled with furniture of his own making and amazingly neat. The walls were a buff color, the ceiling tan and the drapes and bedding were coordinating patterns in tan and blue. The lodge-style bed was stained a deep mahogany, while the dresser and nightstands were dark blue with mahogany tops. There were few personal touches—a cut-glass dish on the dresser that held a watch, a wallet and a handful of coins; two dog beds, shoved into opposite corners; and a few family photos that she fully intended to study once she found the strength to move again.

The only thing out of place was the condom wrappers dropped to fall where they would.

And her?

She was sprawled on her stomach across the bed, a dark blue sheet pulled across her torso, a matching pillowcase against her cheek, her hair pushed up over her head to let her sweat-dampened skin cool. She was so very tired, but not the least bit sleepy.

She gazed at Tyler, also sprawling, except he lay on his back, one arm folded over his eyes to block the overhead light. He looked magnificent, all smooth brown skin and muscle. He could give any cover model she'd ever seen a run for his money. Sweet and considerate, handsome as sin, an impressive body and incredible energy. What more could a woman ask for?

Unable to resist, she laid her hand on his rib cage, gliding her fingers over satiny skin, sinewy muscle and bone. She had half expected to see scars, courtesy of his worthless father, but the only ones she'd found were small and could as easily have been the result of typical child's play, work on the farm or hazards of his job.

Del Lewis had given his oldest son plenty of scars, though—on the inside, where no one could see them but he could feel them.

She tapped her fingertips on his rock-hard abs to get his attention. "How long?"

Moving his arm, he opened one eye to squint at her. "How long what?"

"Over at my house, when I started to touch your—" shyly, slyly, she glanced at his penis, soft now, and grinned when even that caused a slight twitch "—you said it had been too damn long. How long?"

He opened both eyes but gazed at the ceiling instead of her. "A couple years. Maybe…five."

She tried to imagine Greg—or any other man she knew—voluntarily going five years without sex, but it was impossible. Greg had resented those few weeks of abstinence before and after Lucy was born—eight, no more than nine. Five years…wow.

And *she* was the one he'd chosen to end it with.

"Because of—what is her name?"

"Angela. And no, not because of…well, maybe in a round-about way."

She turned onto her side, adjusting the sheet so it covered everything vital. She lacked the confidence to lie there totally exposed, not unless he was doing something about it. Besides, a conversation with the man she was falling in love with about the woman he'd once loved—maybe still did love—was best done with protection. "Because she broke your heart."

"No," he said quietly. Firmly. "She didn't."

"But you loved her."

Finally he turned just his head to offer her a wry grin. "Are all you romance writers so hung up on love?"

"You can't have happily ever after without it," she replied. "Did you love her?"

"I did."

Jayne swallowed hard. Never ask a question unless you're prepared for the answer—advice she'd picked up from someone long ago but remembered too late. She'd known he'd loved Angela. She just hadn't been ready to hear him say it. She certainly wasn't ready to hear him say he still did.

"For a time I loved her and then I didn't. We reached a point where all we were doing was fighting and having sex. I hated the fighting. I'd spent my whole life around it. The sex was still good, but you can't base your future on good sex."

That was better. Past loves that were entirely in the past were okay. "You must have been hurt when it ended."

He gave her another of those wry looks. "I *must* have been?"

"You moved up here. You isolated yourself from the rest of the world. You stopped having sex. Breaking up with her had one hell of an effect on you. If it wasn't hurt, then what was it?"

He turned onto his side to face her, tugged one side of the sheet free and covered himself. "It wasn't hurt. It was just…she showed me some things about myself that I didn't like."

"What kind of things?"

For a long time he looked at her, then he quietly, deliberately answered, "Private things."

Jayne swallowed, hoping the pain didn't show on her face. "There's an awful lot about you that I do like."

After another long silence, he said, "You shouldn't."

Yes, she should, although she didn't like the fact that he was probably going to break her heart. And it was probably too late to do anything about it.

"Do you want me to go home?" she whispered.

For a moment he was so still, so solemn, that she thought he might say yes, but then he slid his arm around her and pulled her across the bed until she was tucked snugly against him. His chin pressed to the top of her head, his muscular leg insinuated between hers, he answered with the same quiet certainty.

"No, Jayne. I want you to stay. For as long as you will."

She awoke reluctantly Saturday morning, wishing for a few more hours' sleep. But the sun was full-force in her face and Lucy would be up before long, wanting breakfast and adventure and—

Her bedroom windows faced north and west, she realized, so the only way the sun could hit her was if it was midafternoon or the world had turned on its axis. She eased her eyes open and saw unfamiliar linens and furnishings and abruptly remembered the night before. Oh, yeah, the world *had* turned on its axis.

She didn't need to look behind her to know that she was alone in the bed. Tyler had held her close long into the night. Every time she'd moved, even in her sleep, she had felt him, smelled him, been surrounded and protected by him. She listened quietly but didn't hear any sound from him.

As the sunlight advanced, she threw back the covers and sat up. There was no sign of her clothes in the bedroom or the attached bath. She combed her fingers through her hair, rinsed her mouth with mouthwash while wishing for her toothbrush, then located a chambray shirt in his closet. It smelled of fabric softener and, more subtly, of Tyler, as if the very essence of him was woven into the fibers. Sliding her arms into the long sleeves, she buttoned up the front, then opened the door and cautiously stepped out.

No barks from Cameron and Diaz greeted her. No television. No Tyler. On a meandering journey through the house, she located her sandals by the back door and found her dress and underwear draped over the washing machine and dryer, the fabric damp from the morning dew, but still no sign of Tyler. His pickup was parked out back, though, so he couldn't have gone far. Then she noticed the open workshop doors.

Maybe he'd wanted her to go home, a twinge of morning-after uneasiness suggested. But maybe he was as much out of practice with morning-after etiquette as she was.

Stepping into the shoes, she went outside and headed for the barn. Off in the distance, the dogs barked. Nearer, the birds sang unseen in the trees. Those were the only sounds—peaceful, natural—until the whine of a power saw sliced through the air. She stopped in the doorway and watched Tyler a moment. He wore jeans that rode low on his narrow hips, a pair of battered work boots, safety glasses and nothing else. He measured, made another cut, then measured again before he noticed her.

Laying the glasses aside, he faced her, one hand on the saw table, the other on his hip. He'd stood that way in the kitchen last night just before he'd told her that his mother had killed his father, but all that tension was gone this morning. He looked relaxed. At peace. "Good morning."

Now that she'd tracked him down, wearing only his shirt, she got a full-blown case of the morning-after nerves. "I…good morning."

"I didn't expect you to be up for a while. I told you I was coming out here, and you said, 'Uh-huh,' without missing a snore."

"I snored?" she asked, dismayed by the notion.

"Delicately. About like Cameron," he said with a grin. Picking up the extra-large mug on a nearby table, he brought it to her before returning to stack the cut boards together.

The mug and its contents were warm and smelled heavenly of coffee beans, cream and caffeine. Just a deep breath was enough to raise her level of awareness, and a sip warmed her all the way to her toes. "Ooh, you make the real stuff."

He gestured to the coffeemaker near the sink. "Don't you?"

Taking another drink, she answered with a shake of her head. She was enjoying her coffee when something he'd said earlier sank into her brain. *I told you I was coming out here...* He *hadn't* wanted her to go home. The relief banished the morning-afters completely as she moved farther into the room. "What are you doing?"

"We're building a pantry today, remember?"

"Oh, yeah. I thought I was going to help with that."

"There's plenty left for you to do. Did you find your clothes?"

She nodded.

"We're lucky some critter didn't carry them off for nesting material."

"I'd track down any critter that ran off with my favorite Victoria's Secret bra. It's the prettiest and sexiest one I own."

"I didn't notice," he remarked as he lifted a sheet of plywood onto the cutting table. "I was more interested in getting you out of it."

"Which you did quite well." She stopped beside him. "Can I help?"

"Yeah. Put these on."

She set the coffee aside, then put on the safety glasses he offered. He pulled her over to the saw, right between the table and his body, and gave her a quick lesson on the tool, but truthfully she was more than a little distracted. His voice was pitched low and occasionally turned a bit husky, and heat fairly radiated off his body. He brushed her breast more than once while reaching to show her something, and the one time she stepped back unexpectedly, she found in an intimate way that he was as fully aroused as she was.

"Tyler?"

"Hmm." He nuzzled her ear, and her head instinctively rolled to one side, giving him better access.

"Can this wait a while?" She reached back to stroke him through the faded denim, then gasped as he slid both hands under her shirt to cup her breasts. She turned, rising onto her toes, wrapping both arms around him, kissing him fiercely, greedily. His hands were between them, making short work of the buttons. Then the shirt was open, exposing her to the morning air, to his hands, to his mouth as he suckled first one breast, then the other.

Pulling his mouth back to hers for another claiming kiss, she opened his jeans, released his hard, heated length and arched her hips against it, whimpering with the pure raw need to feel him inside her. For one instant she thought of the box of condoms on his nightstand, then he braced her against the table and all thought fled her mind. Knees bent, he filled her with one long thrust before wordlessly coaxing her to wrap her legs around him. Blindly he carried her to another table, this one lower, its height perfect to accommodate them, its surface smoother.

Sunlight streamed in the windows, and the air was cool against her flushed skin, smelling of wood and Tyler and raw sex. He stroked into her, hard and deep, while his tongue mimicked the action in her mouth and his hands teased and caressed her breasts, her nipples, her belly, between her legs. Sensation was building, gathering, sweet and ragged and sharp, making her muscles quiver and her heart race.

"Hey, Bubba, I—" Rebecca's voice came from the door behind Jayne, sounding distant through the rushing in her ears. "Oh, my God— I'll go—"

Jayne knew she should stop, should be embarrassed, should be mortified, but all she could do was plead, with kisses, with words, with touches, for release. An instant later, with one more thrust deep inside her, with one more tormenting stroke from his fingers, she came, and so did he, emptying himself, filling her.

As soon as the intensity waned, as soon as the fever started to fall and the shuddering began to ease, she lifted her head from Tyler's shoulder. "Please tell me Rebecca didn't walk in on us."

A thin sheen of sweat coated his face and trickled down his throat as he dragged in a breath to slow his pants. "Sorry. I didn't think I needed to lock the door at seven-thirty on a Saturday morning."

Now she was mortified. As he pulled out of her, she gathered the edges of the shirt and quickly refastened the buttons from the neck all the way to the hem. He left, going to the sink against the far wall, then came back, his jeans done up, with a handful of paper towels for her. Politely he turned his back while she cleaned up.

"We, uh, forgot the condoms," he remarked.

"I didn't forget. I just wanted you too much to wait."

A muscle flexed along his spine. "You do pretty damn good with bold. You trying to get me hard again before we have to go out there and face her?"

She slid to the floor and he turned once again. "Why don't you go? I'll just huddle right there." She gestured to a large cubbyhole underneath the adjoining worktable.

Tilting his head to one side, he studied her a moment before gently unfastening the top two buttons on the shirt. "Are you embarrassed?"

"That your sister walked in on us having sex?" Jeez, what kind of question was that? She wrote about steamy, wild, superorgasmic sex, but she didn't, as a general rule, experience it, and she certainly didn't get caught experiencing it. Of course she was embarrassed!

"That you were having sex with *me*." His eyes were shadowed, his expression hard. He looked so tough and so vulnerable that she wanted to close the distance between them and hug him tightly until those looks were long gone.

Instead she remained where she was and gave a straightforward, no-room-for-misunderstanding answer. "There's not another man in the world I'd rather be with, Tyler."

After another long moment, he nodded and the vulnerability disappeared. "Do you want to wait here while I send her home?"

It would be easier for her, though eventually she would have to see Rebecca and putting it off would just make it unnecessarily awkward. Besides, so what if Rebecca had walked in on them? It wasn't as if they'd both been naked and howling, though they'd been close, she admitted. She'd been wearing Tyler's shirt, and he hadn't shucked his jeans. Rebecca couldn't have seen much. Not that she'd needed to see any more than she had, obviously, to know what was going on.

Abruptly a giggle escaped Jayne. "This is the kind of thing you expect to happen when you're young and sneaking around behind your parents' or your roommate's back. Not when you're grown up and have two houses with four bedrooms with locking doors at your disposal."

He gently tucked a strand of hair behind her ear. "Aw, what's the fun of bedrooms with locking doors?"

"Hey, I wasn't the only one having fun in that bedroom last night."

"No, you weren't. And just for the record, Jayne, there's not another woman I'd rather be with."

She swallowed over the lump in her throat and turned away, making a show of looking for her shoes, to hide the sudden dampness in her eyes. "Do you know where I lost my sandals? I had them on when you picked me up."

"You seem to have a tough time keeping track of your clothing." He bent to pull one out from beneath the table saw and offered it to her.

"Only around you, sweetheart." She located the other one, slid her feet into them, then gave him a bright, tight smile. "Let's go say hello to your sister."

"Well, this is a big change," Rebecca announced after Jayne had said hello, then escaped inside to get dressed. "Not a surprise, mind you. After you brought her to the farm last week and everyone saw the way you two looked at each other, it was no longer a question of *if* but *when*. Frankly you got to the *when* quicker than I expected."

Tyler leaned against the deck rail but didn't say anything. He didn't want to encourage her to continue talking about his personal life.

Not that she needed encouragement. "Have you told her…?"

"About what?"

She shrugged. "About us. About Mom and…"

"Yeah."

That earned him some surprise. He'd never told anyone voluntarily—not even Angela. She'd heard the gossip in town and confronted him, and he'd only confirmed it. "Wow. What about Angela?"

His fingers clenched the railing tighter as he made a conscious effort to keep the tension out of his voice. "She knows some of it."

"How it ended?"

"No." Guilt nagged at him. He should have told her everything before going to bed with her; it was only fair. But if she'd known everything, she wouldn't have let him touch her. She wouldn't have kissed him. Wouldn't have looked at him as if he *meant* something to her. "I couldn't…we're just…we're not…"

Rebecca left the chair to stand beside him, laying her hand over his. "You don't have to tell her, Tyler. It was an aberration. A one-time thing. It's never going to happen again."

He wanted to believe that—wanted to point to the five years he'd spent alone as proof. But he'd been *alone*. That didn't prove anything except that when he didn't have anyone in his life, he couldn't do anything to hurt them.

"She has a right to know," he said quietly.

"Why?"

He scowled down at her. "Because it *could* happen again. Because I could—"

"No, you couldn't. It's in the past. It doesn't matter anymore."

Neither of them could even bring themselves to put his actions five years ago into words, and she wanted to believe it didn't matter anymore? It. How it ended. What he'd done. What happened. It was a part of him, a sin he had to do penance for forever, and it carried too much importance in Rebecca's life, as well, but they were both too afraid to say it.

He had hit Angela.

Had lifted his hand in anger against a woman, just as Del had so often done.

He had turned out just like his father.

"Can you imagine in your worst nightmare ever hitting Jayne?" Rebecca demanded.

"No. But I couldn't have imagined hitting Angela, either." It had been the furthest thing from his mind. They'd been fighting, as they so often had. She was yelling and he'd yelled back and suddenly he'd acted on instinct. He hadn't thought, hadn't planned, hadn't considered it. He'd just done it, as if it was the most natural thing in the world.

Because he was Del's son—the angry one, the one most like him—maybe it *had* been natural. No, it hadn't happened again since then, but his life had been anything but natural since then.

"You've punished yourself enough for it," Rebecca said. "It was one instant of anger, and you've paid for *five years*. If anyone deserves a good life, it's you. Don't let what happened with Angela ruin what you've got with Jayne."

"What I've got… She thinks I'm some kind of good guy. She lets me spend time with her kid, for God's sake. And she doesn't have a clue. She was horrified when I told her about…" He shrugged rather than name his father. "She thought he deserved a more painful death. She doesn't even know how much like him I am."

"You're nothing like him! He was a mean, selfish, violent drunk who got off on hurting people who were weaker and more vulnerable. You've never deliberately hurt anyone in your life!"

Her convenient memory lapse made his smile thin and bitter. It was the fights he'd gotten into, blackening more eyes and bloodying more noses than anyone else in the history of Sweetwater schools, that had led to Daniel taking him in hand. "You think Angela accidentally ran into my hand with her face?"

Rebecca couldn't come up with a suitable response to that because she knew there had been nothing accidental about it.

"I look like him, Rebecca. I sound like him. I have his temper. I have his blood. Everyone agrees I'm just like him."

Once more she couldn't argue, so she hugged him instead. "It was *one time,*" she said fiercely against his chest.

"But that's how it starts, isn't it? One time, and I was sorry as hell. I would have begged her on my knees to forgive me if she hadn't left. And if she had forgiven me, the next time I wouldn't have been quite so sorry, and before long it would have been all her fault." He didn't need to feel her shiver to remember that she'd already put the blame on Angela.

"You can't give up your life because of that one moment."

"If it's a choice between that and hurting someone else…"

"You don't think Jayne's going to be hurt when you break up with her? You don't think Lucy's little heart will be broken?"

"Better to break her heart than something else."

She held him a moment longer, then stepped back and wiped at her eyes. "Just remember one thing before you go breaking hearts, Tyler. Emotional hurts can be a whole lot more damaging than physical ones. You and I are living proof of that."

Returning to the chair where she'd waited, she picked up a paper bag from the floor. "I brought breakfast for you and came to tell you that I'm on my way to Knoxville. I'll be back in time for the family thing tomorrow."

He took the bag with a quiet thanks.

Halfway to the steps she turned back. "You're right about one thing, Bubba. Jayne does think you're a very good guy.

Maybe if you thought as much of her, you'd give her a chance."
Spinning around, she crossed the deck in a few strides, took the
steps two at a time, then disappeared around the corner of the
house.

Give Jayne a chance. What kind of woman, knowing his
family history, knowing his own history, would give *him* a
chance? All the experts had predicted that he was the one most
likely to turn out like his father. The court had ordered him into
therapy; he'd seen a psychologist on a weekly basis from the
time he was fourteen until he was twenty-one. He'd been
warned, watched, treated, analyzed and watched some more.
And none of their precautions had prevented exactly what
they'd feared most from happening.

As Angela had said afterward with a malicious smile, *Blood
will tell.*

He didn't have many options. He could tell Jayne the truth
and see the affection and the respect disappear from her eyes.
He could watch fear and revulsion replace the liking and he
would lose something he could never get back.

Or he could just end it with her—*Hey, it's been fun, you've
been convenient, but I've had enough.* Let her think he'd used
her the way her ex had. Let her hate him for being a callous
bastard.

As long as she didn't hate him for truly being his father's
son.

But what if he told her the truth and the affection and respect
didn't disappear? She did give him credit for being a better man
than he was. What if she, like Rebecca, viewed it as an aberration? What if she was still willing to let him come around her
and Lucy? What if she still let him touch her?

The little voice that sounded so much like his father stopped
the hope cold. *And what if it does happen again?*

He had tried so damn hard to prove all those experts
wrong—to show everyone that he was *nothing* like Del. That
he'd inherited nothing more than the shade of his hair, his eyes,

his skin from him. That he despised the man more than any of them ever could. He had been one of Del's victims. The very last thing in the world he'd wanted was to create his own victim.

But he had, and it had been so easy. He hadn't even had to think about it. He'd just done it. And in that moment afterward, before the shock set in, before the reality sank in, he'd thought—

"Where's Rebecca?"

Starting, he turned to find Jayne approaching. She'd gone home to change clothes and pull her hair back in a ponytail. She looked beautiful and sweet and sexy as hell.

She looked like the best part of his life.

How the hell was he going to find the strength to let her go?

"She, uh, was on her way somewhere. We'll see her tomorrow at the farm."

She stopped in front of him, her brow wrinkled into a frown, then reached out to touch him as if she had the right. As if she felt the need. "Are you okay?"

He gazed at her fingers resting lightly on his wrist. Slender, nails trimmed neatly, painted pale pink. Small contact, but it chased the chill from his skin and made his breath come easier.

He would find the strength, but not just yet. *If anyone deserves a good life, it's you,* Rebecca had said. She was wrong. If he deserved it, he would grab it with both hands and never let go, but surely he deserved more time. More friendship. More sex. More Jayne. *More.*

Just a little.

And then he would do what he had to do.

From somewhere he summoned a smile as he caught her hand and drew her over to a pair of Adirondack chairs. "Yeah. I'm better than okay. Ready for breakfast?"

It was amazing how quickly things could progress. Little more than a week ago, Jayne had been elated by her first real kiss with Tyler. Now, for all practical purposes, he was living with them. He went to his house only to shower and change after work, then he joined them for quiet evenings with Lucy and quieter nights with Jayne before slipping out the next morning to get ready for work while Lucy still slept. Cameron and Diaz had moved in, as well, their food in the new pantry, their dishes in a corner of the dining room. They kept Jayne and Lucy company while Tyler was working and slept next to Lucy's bed at night.

There wasn't anything permanent about it. He hadn't moved any of his clothing or toiletries from his house. It wasn't even something they'd talked about. After the first few nights that she'd asked him to stay, it had just become habit.

A habit she loved.

With a man she was well on the way to loving.

It was Saturday morning, and she was supposed to be catching up on e-mail while Tyler and Lucy covered her little room with orange paint. She was having trouble concentrating, though, when they were having so much more fun down the hall. Tyler's voice was a low rumble, his words indistinct, but clearly he was showing his usual patience and respect to Lucy's ten thousand questions. *Why did you paint around the edges first? Why did you put tape all over? Why do you make a* W *with the brush?*

Greg would have snapped at her after the third question, thrown down the roller and stormed off. No, Greg never would have *picked up* the roller. That was too much like work, and if there was one thing he avoided, it was work. Along with responsibility. Dependability. Acting like a grown-up.

Tyler embodied those things. He was the kind of man Greg had promised to become, and she'd been foolish enough to believe him. But now she had that man for real. Had the sweet kind of family life she'd always wanted.

For the time being. Whether Tyler would want to make it permanent was anyone's guess. If he didn't...

It wouldn't be the first time she'd been disappointed. But it would be the worst.

She answered a few notes from readers—it seemed so pretentious to call them fans—then scanned the digests from a few of the writers' loops she subscribed to before Lucy's giggles drew her attention down the hall again. Unable to resist, she signed off, then went to stand in the bedroom door.

Lucy, wearing her oldest shorts and T-shirt along with a too-big ball cap to protect her hair, was liberally smeared with orange paint—her own doing, Jayne was sure. While Greg didn't like work in general and messy work in particular, Lucy delighted in it. In fact, those two lines painted across each pudgy cheek couldn't possibly be anything but deliberate.

"Hey, Mom. How's it look?" She extended both arms, roller included, to encompass the room. Paint dripped in a thin line onto the dropcloth that covered everything in the room.

"It's…orange." And bright enough to hurt their eyes once the afternoon sun hit the west-facing window. "Are you sure you're not going to go blind in here?"

"Oh, Mom."

"Watch the roller, Lucky." Tyler, also wearing paint-spattered clothes, had finished painting three of the walls while Lucy, apparently, had talked and rolled *W*'s everywhere she could reach on the fourth wall. He looked remarkably neat for having spent an hour in a room with her daughter and a paint roller. "It's not bad once your eyes adjust."

"No, it's not bad," she agreed. "It's just really…orange."

"When she gets tired of it, we can repaint."

"I'll never get tired. I love it!" Lucy insisted, doing a little twirl for emphasis. "I bet I've got the only orange bedroom in the world!"

"I'll bet she doesn't," Tyler murmured. "Did she mention she wants black sheets?"

"I'm not surprised. I'll have to think about that." Jayne hesitated, then brushed a strand of his hair back. "When you're done here, you want to go into town and get something to eat?"

"Okay. Why don't you start cleaning her up and let me finish that last wall?"

"All right." Raising her voice, she said, "Luce, let's hose you down and get ready for lunch."

With a roll of her eyes, Lucy obeyed. Once she'd reached the door, Jayne checked the soles of her shoes, found wet paint on both and pulled them off, then gave her a push toward the bathroom. "I'll be right there. Don't touch anything."

As Lucy skipped off, Jayne turned back to Tyler. "Thank you."

"For what?"

"Letting her help. Not getting onto her for being a mess."

He shrugged. "She can't learn if she doesn't try."

He acted as if it was nothing any other man wouldn't have done, but she knew better. Greg wasn't the only father of her acquaintance who didn't have the patience to deal with an exuberant, inquisitive child.

"You know—" she tugged the hem of his T-shirt sleeve to dry a drop of paint on his arm "—I like an awful lot about Tennessee, but, far and away, Tyler, you've been the best part of moving here." Rising onto her toes, she pressed a quick kiss to his mouth, then went to the bathroom.

By the time Lucy was bathed, dried and dressed, Tyler had painted the fourth wall, closed the paint can and rinsed the rollers. He went home to change clothes, then returned in his truck, idling out front while Jayne locked up. She'd taken advantage of his absence to change, as well, putting on a T-shirt, shorts and flip-flops. When she reached the pickup, she turned so he could see the back of the shirt. It was black, with a hot pink stick figure of a woman and the words *Romance—Read it!*

He read the text under the drawing with a grin. "Angryromancegrrl?"

"You bet. Because of all those obnoxious people who say obnoxious things about our books." She buckled her seat belt, then gazed out the window as he pulled away. Her house still needed a coat of paint, and the yard could use another go-round with the mower, but the place was looking pretty good. She was slowly making headway with the backyard, and it was about time, Tyler's grandmother had told her the Sunday before, to start planting flowers. With all that had been done, and all that still needed doing, it looked like home. It *felt* like home.

Then she glanced across the cab to Tyler. He felt like home, too.

For once, none of his family or friends were in the diner besides Rebecca, and *she* didn't notice them come in. She was sitting at a table for two near the bathrooms, talking with another woman and looking unusually somber.

Lucy climbed onto a bench in a booth, and Jayne and Tyler sat across from her. The waitress, Carla, brought glasses of water and menus and gave her and Tyler a speculative look that ended in a sly smile. "You need to look at the menus?"

"Nope. I'll have a hamburger and fries and a sticky bun," Lucy spoke up.

"Sorry, pumpkin." Carla scraped a bit of orange paint from Lucy's fine hair. "We're out of sticky buns this morning."

"Well, poop. But I'll still take the hamburger and fries."

"Me, too," Jayne decided. "With iced tea for me and milk for her."

"Chocolate milk."

"Of course chocolate," Carla said with a wink. "That's the only way to drink it. What about you, Tyler?"

"I'll have the same."

After she left with the menus, Jayne gestured toward the back. "Who is that with Rebecca?"

He glanced in their direction. "I don't know." No sooner than the words were out of his mouth, the woman looked over her shoulder at them, and he stiffened. "Oh. That's…" He looked down at the tabletop and mumbled the rest. "Someone we used to know."

The woman's hair was red, though artificially so. The blue of her eyes was artificial, as well, her skin fair, her features delicate. It was difficult to nail down her age. Somewhere between twenty-five and thirty-five, Jayne guessed. She was slender, not too tall and pretty in a very confident sort of way.

And just the sight of her had made every muscle in Tyler's body go taut.

She couldn't be...*please don't let her be Angela.* What were the odds of his old girlfriend showing up right after he'd found a new one? Minimal. But who else in his past would have that kind of effect on him?

"She's coming this way," Jayne said quietly. Rebecca had gone into the kitchen, and the redhead was making a beeline for them.

Tyler's tension level ratcheted even higher. By the time the woman stopped at their table, the stress was practically humming through him. "Hello, Tyler. It's been a long time."

How long? Jayne wanted to demand. And if the woman said five years, she'd probably grind her teeth to dust in an effort to keep her mouth shut.

After a moment, he pulled his gaze up, but he didn't smile. "Hey."

"How have you been?"

"Fine."

The woman included Jayne in her smile. "The only man I've ever known who could condense five years into one word."

Jayne's stomach knotted. This wasn't quite how she'd envisioned Angela. She had pictured someone very pretty, feminine, not too bright and spoiled—the kind of woman that men tripped over each other to do things for. The redhead looked intelligent and seemed quite capable of doing things for herself, less likely to trade on her looks because she had so much more to offer.

"Could I talk to you privately, Tyler?" the woman asked.

He wanted to say no—Jayne could tell by the way his fingers knotted. But with a glance her way that didn't reach her eyes, he pushed to his feet and started toward the door.

"We'll just be a minute," the woman said with an apologetic smile before following him.

"Who's she?" Lucy asked.

"I don't know. A friend of Tyler's."

"I don't think so. Friends are people you're happy to see, and he didn't look happy."

Jayne watched as they crossed the street to the courthouse square, then sat down on a bench there. She'd always thought jealousy was such a petty emotion. When a friend got a better contract or had better sales, sure, she wished the same good fortune for herself, but she didn't begrudge the friend the success. She was blessed in her own life—her daughter, her parents, her strength, her career and, for now, Tyler. The redhead was from his past. Jayne was his present—and hopefully his future.

But that ugly little feeling curling in her gut was undoubtedly jealousy mixed with concern. Even Lucy had noticed he wasn't happy to see the woman. Along with all that, too, was the need to protect him. She didn't want anything he'd thought was over and done coming up now to cause him more grief. He'd had enough of that in his life.

"Hey, Mom?"

She turned her attention back to her daughter. "What, sweetie?"

"Can Charley and me have a sleepover like you and Tyler have been doin'?"

Jayne blinked. "Like…" Lucy was sound asleep long before she and Tyler went to bed, and he was out of the house and gone for work an hour or more before she awoke. "How do you know he's been staying over?"

Lucy rolled her eyes. "I get up sometimes to pee, Mom, and Cameron Diaz are there all night, and sometimes I hear you."

Her cheeks burning, Jayne stammered. "H-hear us wh-what?"

"Talkin'," Lucy replied as if it was obvious. Before Jayne

could relax too much, she went on. "And sometimes breathin'
loud."

As in snoring? Or trying-to-be-quiet-but-their-lungs-were-
about-to-explode heavy breathing? "Oh," she said, and her
voice came out unnaturally high and small. She cleared her
throat and tried again. "Well."

"So when we go to the farm tomorrow, can I ask Charley to
spend the night sometime?"

"I don't even know if I've met Charley's mother."

"You haven't. They're divorced, and she doesn't come to the
farm on Sundays because it's Charley's dad's family, not hers.
But you met him. He's the one with the blond hair. And since
Tyler'll be there, too, it'll be okay."

Jayne spared a smile for Lucy's description. Half the men in
the Morris family had blond hair, while the rest had light brown
hair or were bald. Tyler was the exception. "Listen, Luce, let's not
go around telling everyone that Tyler spends the night with us,
okay?"

"Why? Is it wrong?"

"No, not at all. It's just personal. Like I don't tell people
how much money I make or how much taxes I pay because
that's personal."

"Okay." Then, with a grin she said, "How much money do
you make?"

"Enough."

"Enough to buy a pony?"

"Afraid not. I don't need another mouth to feed."

"But you wouldn't have to feed him. He'd eat the grass
around the house, and then you wouldn't have to mow, either."

"I don't think it's that easy, Luce. But you know what? You
can save your money and when you have enough to buy a horse
and take care of it, we'll talk, okay?"

"But that'll take foreevvver." Letting her eyes roll up, Lucy
collapsed in the booth, her head tilted to one side, her tongue
dangling from the corner of her mouth.

"What's that?" Tyler asked as he slid onto the bench.

With a quick glance outside, Jayne saw the redhead getting into a car parked down the block. She looked back at Tyler but couldn't read anything in his expression. He just looked…tough.

"She's showing me how she'll look by the time she saves enough money to buy a horse."

"That face would scare a horse into running off."

Lucy did her best to maintain the look, but her giggles chased it away. Sitting up, she asked, "Who was that lady?"

He gave the same answer with the same lack of enthusiasm. "Someone I used to know."

"But you don't know her no more?"

"Yeah, I still know her. I just hardly ever see her."

"Does she live here in town?" Jayne asked, hoping she achieved some measure of casual in her tone.

"No."

"Did she live here when you knew her?"

He rested his forearms on the table, gripping his hands, before briefly glancing her way. "Look, I don't want to talk about it, okay? It's personal."

Once before, when he'd told her about Angela, he'd cut her off with a similar line. It stung even more now than it had then. Biting the inside of her lip, she nodded once, then looked away.

"I know what personal means," Lucy announced. "It's something that's not wrong but that you shouldn't tell everyone. Like you having sleepovers with Mom is personal."

Again Tyler's gaze cut to her, though Jayne refused to meet it. It felt as sharp as his tone. "You told her?"

"She gets up sometimes to pee," she replied stiffly.

"Mom! That's personal!"

"Sorry, sweetie." She gave Lucy a tight smile, then turned her gaze out the window again. If the other women in Tyler's life were personal and private, what was she? Convenient? Handy? Easy? She certainly hadn't required any effort. Be a little nice to her and her kid, and she couldn't be any more willing.

Honesty forced her to admit that she wasn't being fair to Tyler. He hadn't taken advantage of her, hadn't coaxed her into anything she hadn't wholeheartedly wanted. So she was falling in love with a man who didn't trust her enough to open parts of his life to her. Just because she wanted to share everything with him didn't mean he wanted the same.

And if he couldn't trust her, then he couldn't love her. No matter that he treated her with affection and fondness and respect.

She'd been right about one thing that day.

This was going to be her worst disappointment ever.

Chapter 12

For once, the tables were turned. Instead of Jayne trying to draw Tyler into conversation, he was trying to do the same with her, but with lousy results. If he asked a question, she answered in as few words as possible. If he made a comment, she nodded or *hmm*ed. The rest of the time she gazed out the window as if there was something of great interest out there.

He'd lived half his life in Sweetwater. He knew there wasn't.

He ate his lunch without tasting much of it. The tension that had spread through him earlier was in the air now, creating a barrier between him and Jayne as real as if it were physical, and he didn't know how to pull it down.

When they got ready to leave, she reached for the check at the same time he did. "I'll pay," he said stiffly.

She refused to look at him. "No, I will. Consider it payment for painting Lucy's room."

He didn't want payment for painting Lucy's room—and if he did, a hamburger and fries at the diner wouldn't be near enough. But he let go of the check, watched her scoop it up and head toward the cash register before he lifted his gaze to the ceiling and sighed.

Lucy skipped ahead, shoved the heavy glass door open, then paused. "Come outside with me, Tyler."

With a glance at Jayne's unyielding profile, he obeyed.

Hopscotching over the lines in the sidewalk, Lucy tilted her head back. "So what do we do this afternoon?"

"I don't know." Before lunch, he'd been thinking that lying in the hammock with Jayne seemed a perfect way to spend a lazy hour or two on a warm Saturday. Now he doubted she would get near him in the hammock unless it was to dump him out, and he had only himself to blame.

Lucy hopped past the truck, then came back on one foot. As she came even with it, she jumped onto the running board, one arm wrapped around the rearview mirror for balance.

When she tilted the mirror, Tyler saw Jayne approaching behind him. Without turning, he caught her wrist and pulled her up short when she would have walked on by. "Okay. You want to know who that was? Her name is—"

"I couldn't care less who it was."

"Well, you have a funny way of showing it." When she tried to pull free, he held her, gently forcing her to face him. "Look, I'm sorry. I just didn't want to…"

Finally she looked at him, waiting, but when he didn't finish, she shook her head. "You didn't want to see her with us. You didn't want to explain us to her. You didn't want to share any part of your personal life with me. Not a problem. I understand now. Neighbors, convenience, secrecy—"

Gritting out a curse, he slid his hands into her hair and covered her mouth with his, hard, hot, hungry. She held herself stiff for a moment, two, then a tiny moan escaped her as she wrapped her arms around his neck and kissed him back. For a time he forgot that they stood on Main Street, in front of Rebecca's diner, there for anyone to see. All he knew was how good she felt, how sweet she tasted, how badly he needed her—

Until the blast of a horn, followed by a shrill whistle, split the air. Few people could whistle like his kid brother, sharp enough to bust eardrums and make wild critters run for cover, their grandfather said. Raucous calls in voices he dimly recognized grew louder as he ended the kiss, as the rushing in his ears receded.

Raising his head, he focused on the old farm truck idling in the middle of the street. Alex was behind the wheel, and a half dozen of his buddies filled the cab and the bed, all of them grinning ear to ear. They weren't the only ones watching, either. Old man Tennys and his wife were on the sidewalk across the street. Rebecca and Carla stood at the diner's plate-glass window. And a gaggle of his grandmother's church lady friends were paying close attention from down the block.

"Can I be next?" Alex called.

"You're not my type," Tyler replied. "Does Grandpa know you've got all those passengers in his truck?"

"I asked if I could borrow it to haul some stuff for Justin. He didn't ask what stuff."

Tyler scowled at him. "Pay attention to your driving. And be careful."

"Yeah, same to you, Bubba." With a laugh, Alex drove away.

As the sound of the engine faded, Tyler turned his attention back to Jayne. If he was any kind of man, he would spill out everything right there and beg her to understand, to forgive him, to give her a chance to prove that he deserved her and Lucy in his life.

But if he was any kind of man, he wouldn't have any secrets to spill.

Before he could find something he trusted himself to say, she spoke. "Just tell me one thing, will you?"

His throat tight, he nodded. One question, any question, and he'd answer truthfully.

"Was that Angela?"

"Good God, no." The words burst out of him in a rush of relief. She was *jealous?* The notion was as foreign to him as kissing a woman on Main Street. Angela had been too sure of him, too sure of herself, to even consider the idea that he could get involved with someone else, and there had never been anyone besides her. "Her name—"

Again Jayne interrupted him, but without anger this time. "I don't want to know, not until you *want* to tell me."

"I do—"

"No, you don't," she said with a rueful smile. "You just don't want me to be mad at you. And it's okay. I'm not mad."

But she was still a little hurt. It was in her eyes. He raised one hand to gently touch her face. "Just for the record, Jayne, you are the most *in*convenient woman I've ever known." She made him want things he couldn't have—made him want to be a man he couldn't be. He would try if he had the chance, would spend the rest of his life trying, but that chance could come only with the truth. With her trust and understanding. Even then...

It was too damn big a risk.

She rewarded him with a teasing smile. "Thank you. My goal in life is to be inconvenient." Rising onto her toes, she kissed his cheek, then pulled away. Catching his hand at the last instant, she drew him toward the truck, where Lucy was now making faces at herself in the mirror.

Tyler swung Lucy off the running board while Jayne opened the door. The kid grinned up at him. "I guess you do like kissin' and yucky stuff," she remarked.

"Like I told you, Lucky girl, when you get older, it won't seem so yucky." Not that he wanted to imagine Lucy old enough to kiss someone the way her mother had just kissed him. There couldn't possibly be a man out there good enough for her, not that Tyler would have any say in the matter.

The reminder renewed the ache in his gut.

They stopped at the grocery store, where they ran into

Charley and her mother, Ellen, and left a short while later with a week's worth of groceries and without Lucy. Since the middle section of the seat was empty, Jayne slid over to sit next to him. The simple act made him feel like the kid he'd never been.

Soon after passing the turnoff to Sassie Whitlaw's place, Jayne gestured into the woods on the right. "Look, there's a cemetery back there."

"Yeah." He wasn't surprised she'd never noticed it before. There was no sign, the trees grew thick and the dirt lane was barely wide enough for a regular car to get through, much less a hearse. "That's the original cemetery for Sweetwater. Edna's buried there."

"Can you show me her grave?"

He slowed to a stop, checked the rearview mirror, then shifted into reverse. Once he turned off the road, it was a bumpy quarter-mile drive to the clearing under the trees that passed for parking.

The cemetery was nothing fancy. The graves were dug in neat rows and overgrown with about an equal mix of grass and weeds. Straw from the pine trees towering overhead blanketed the ground, and long-faded plastic and silk flowers marked every site.

They walked between rows of headstones to Edna's plot, right next to her husband's. There were more Millers around, along with a half dozen Brauns, Edna's family.

"What a lovely place," Jayne remarked softly.

"It's a definite improvement over the newer one in town. There the grass is lush and the markers are flat so they don't interfere with the mowing."

"Is your father buried there?"

He pulled a weed from the base of Edna's tombstone. "I don't have any idea where he's buried."

Jayne looked up at him. "You didn't go to his funeral?" Two weeks ago she would have sounded stunned, but knowing what she did, she wasn't even surprised—merely asking for confirmation.

"Nah. His parents showed up in Nashville, claimed the body and left again." He gave her a sidelong look. "They blamed my mother for his death."

"They should have looked a lot closer to home."

He opened his mouth, then closed it again, but she didn't notice as she bent to touch Edna's marker, pressing her fingers against the warm concrete for a moment, before straightening. "We'd better get the groceries home."

Sure. They could talk at home.

They returned to the truck, and once again she slid over to sit beside him, her hand resting lightly on his thigh. Steering with his left hand, he slid his right arm around her shoulders and pulled her closer. "You know, there are lots of places in these hills where people go parking."

She rested her head on his shoulder. "Remember? Two houses? Four bedrooms?" After a moment, she sheepishly added, "A chaise longue? A worktable?"

"Aw, where's your sense of adventure?"

"You must have mistaken me for someone who has a sense of adventure. I write about it. I don't live it."

"I don't know. You packed up, moved to a new place where you didn't know anyone and started over. That seems pretty adventurous to me."

"Lucy thinks so, too," she said with a satisfied smile. "It's been A Good Thing…though I have to admit, I had my doubts that first day. All that snow and the house was such a disappointment and we had no power or firewood. If we hadn't had such a neighborly neighbor, Lucy and I probably would have frozen to death."

"I'm not neighborly," he said automatically as he turned into her driveway.

She gave him a sly look before she slid across the seat. "You go ahead and tell yourself that. The rest of us know the truth."

They put the groceries away, then went to the bedroom down the hall and made love. Neither of them suggested it or made the first move. They just did it, as if it was the only thing on both their minds.

Afterward, Tyler lay on his back, all the pillows stuffed behind him. Jayne sprawled half over him, her hair tickling where it had come out of its braid. Their skin was slick with sweat where they touched, but he didn't mind. He'd gone so long without this kind of touching—and would again. He wanted to enjoy it while he could.

The windows were open, and a box fan balanced in one was turned to low, blowing cool air across them and scenting the room with the wildflowers that grew just outside. Though he rarely slept during the day, he could manage a nap if he lay there long enough, quietly enough.

He didn't. "Her name is Gail Gennaro," he said and felt Jayne tense, then relax. Though she didn't look at him, she was barely breathing. "Outside of my family and Angela, she's been the most important woman in my life. She's my shrink."

Finally Jayne tilted her head so she could see him. Her gaze was steady, carefully composed, but he identified the faint signs of relief in her eyes.

"You watch television. You read. You know a lot about abusive relationships. You know that daughters raised in that environment are more likely to find themselves in the same situation when they're grown."

She nodded once.

"And sons raised in that environment—" he swallowed hard "—are more likely to become abusive themselves when they're grown."

Another small nod. "Without intervention."

His chest was tight, his muscles on the verge of trembling. He tried to force a breath, but it didn't help. "Dr. Gennaro was—is our intervention. When our grandparents got custody of me and the kids, they were ordered to seek counseling for us. We did the first four years with Dr. Gennaro's partner. When he retired, she took over. I quit going in regularly when

I turned twenty-one, though I've seen her from time to time since then."

"Until you began seeing Angela."

It was actually when he'd stopped seeing Angela that he'd also stopped seeing Dr. Gennaro. He'd gone in one last time and told her what had happened—how all their work had been for nothing, how he'd disappointed her and proven everyone right. She had tried to reason with him, but he hadn't been in a place where he could accept reason. All he'd known was that if he isolated himself, everyone else would be safe.

Jayne's delicate fingers rubbed in a soothing motion across his chest. "There's nothing wrong with seeing a psychologist. Your father abused you. He put you through some traumatic times. It would have been wrong if you *hadn't* seen someone."

In theory, he agreed with her. Getting them into counseling had been the smart thing to do, and it seemed to have worked with Aaron and Josh and to some extent with Rebecca. But it hadn't seemed smart at the time. Everyone in town had known, providing the kids who'd teased them mercilessly with one more piece of ammunition. That weekly hour, talking about the worst times in his life, had been torture. It had been proof that he was as flawed as his father, that the whispers and worries were on target; otherwise, why did the judge insist he go?

"It was something I had to do—I had no choice—but it's over," he said flatly. "I hated every moment of it, I'm not proud of it and I don't like thinking about it."

She cocked her head to one side. "You think you should have been strong enough to get through it without help?"

No, but with all the help the shrinks had provided, he should have been strong enough to get through it without hitting Angela. He shouldn't have been such a failure.

But the only response he gave her was a shrug.

"You were a *child*, Tyler, who experienced things that would have given any full-grown adult nightmares. Needing help to deal with it wasn't a sign of weakness. It just showed how normal you were. Look how well you've turned out, how you've succeeded in spite of what your father did."

Okay. This is the time. Take a breath and tell her you didn't succeed. Tell her you hit the woman you were practically living with.

And lose her.

He couldn't do it. God help him, he couldn't let her go just yet.

He was feeling pretty damn hopeless when Jayne spoke again, her voice drowsy. "What did she want—Dr. Gennaro? Did she come here to see you or was that just good luck for her?"

"She was just passing through and stopped to say hello to Rebecca."

"And she got to say hello to you, too."

"Yeah." She had asked how he'd been and whether he'd dealt with what had happened. She was a psychologist and even she didn't want to say the words. She had wanted to know about Jayne and how much she knew, and she'd encouraged him to tell her everything. Easy advice for the doc to give when she didn't have to live with the consequences.

Give her a chance to understand, Tyler, she'd said. *If you love each other—*

He'd stopped her there. He hadn't said anything about love. Whatever they felt didn't matter. All that mattered was that he would die before hurting either her or Lucy the way his father had hurt them.

Dr. Gennaro had been disappointed. She'd tried to reason with him, but he'd said goodbye and returned to the diner. Funny—five years had passed, and he still wasn't in a place where reason could overcome fear.

Jayne snuggled closer, her eyes drifting shut. "I'm sorry I was upset. Tell me what Angela looks like so it doesn't happen again."

He stroked through her hair, undoing what was left of the

braid, sliding his fingers beneath the silky cool curtain. "I told you—I don't remember."

"Hair? Eyes?"

"Blond. Blue."

Her yawn crinkled her entire face. "Hair can be dyed. Even if I'd known, I probably would have gotten jealous anyway because—" another huge yawn "—I lo'…you." She was asleep before the last sounds of her voice faded.

She did not say *I love you*. Couldn't have. Shouldn't have. The last thing he wanted, the last thing he could bear… *No*. He'd misunderstood. She hadn't known what she was saying. She wouldn't remember when she woke up.

He wouldn't forget.

He settled her more comfortably against him, earning a soft sigh before her breathing resumed its slow, steady rhythm. He watched her a moment, then brushed a kiss to her forehead. "I love you, too," he whispered without sound.

It was the first time he'd ever said those words to a woman.

It would also be the last.

Visiting with Greg's parents had usually ranked somewhere between tedious and excruciating. Depending on their moods, Jayne had found herself trying to keep the conversation civil or refereeing verbal sparring matches. Regardless of their moods, she'd always gone away from the encounter with a headache.

Tyler's family was nothing like the Millers. Jayne had spent each of the past three Sundays with them, and they were starting to feel very much like her own family. They were nice people who worked hard, went to church, loved their families, their country and their God, though not necessarily in that order.

Though he'd been cheated of a decent father, Tyler couldn't ask for a better family.

A woman couldn't ask to marry into a better family.

Jayne rolled her eyes at that thought as she grabbed a lawn

chair and carried it from the dessert table to the shade of an old oak. She'd just settled in when Tyler's mother approached carrying a tote bag and a chair of her own. "Mind if I join you?"

"Please do." Sipping her tea, Jayne glanced across the yard. The women were scattered in small groups, some watching babies and toddlers while they slept, others talking. Kids played everywhere—in the yard, around the barn, in the nearby woods—and all the younger men, including Tyler, had gone off to tinker with Dutch's ailing tractor while the older men talked about weather and crops. With a little change in clothing, the scene could have easily taken place in the fifties or even earlier. It was peaceful. Soothing.

Carrie removed a pair of half-glasses from the bag, along with a sandwich of fabric and batting, a needle and a thimble. The fabric was a quilt square in shades of peach, coral and green, the colors delicately hued, the pattern complex.

"That's beautiful," Jayne remarked.

Carrie's cheeks turned pink. "Thank you. I just started it. Do you quilt?"

Jayne shook her head. "I've written characters who do," she admitted with a grin, "so I've researched it, but I've never actually tried. It seems very complicated."

"Oh, no, not at all. Believe me, if I can do it, anyone can." Carrie took a few stitches before glancing at Jayne. "I could help you make your first one, if you'd like. If you'll be staying long enough."

There was a hint of a question in her last words. Would she be relieved to hear that Jayne wanted to never leave Sweetwater? There was only one way to find out. "I plan to stay forever if things work out."

"What things?" Carrie asked with another quick peek, as if she wasn't comfortable with straight-on looks.

"My career, mostly. I have to be able to make enough to support Lucy and me or find a job to supplement my income. Sweetwater doesn't seem to have a lot of job openings."

"No, but if you need something, you'll find it." Carrie did seem relieved. Was she worried about someone coming into her son's life, then leaving again?

Probably, because she didn't ask what, besides Jayne's career, had to work out. If Tyler broke her heart, she would have no choice but to move again. She couldn't live across the road from him, knowing that he didn't care enough to want her forever.

If that happened, maybe she would just move into town. As isolated as he kept himself, there would be little chance of running into him unless she wanted to.

But that wouldn't be fair to him. After all, her friends were his friends, his family.

Not that she had to be fair when a man broke her heart.

Which he hadn't even done yet. Things were good between them. The sex was great. They weren't arguing. They'd settled into a sweet, satisfying relationship. She was happy. He was happy.

And a little bit distant.

There. She'd said it—or at least thought it. Even though they'd made love the afternoon before, lazed in the hammock before Lucy came home and spent the night as if they'd shared a bed forever, even though they'd laughed over breakfast and come here to the farm just like a family, he'd been a little preoccupied. She'd caught a look in his eyes a time or two—withdrawn, regretful, sad. It had disappeared the instant he'd caught her looking, but it still troubled her.

Carrie quilted neat diamonds in a section of the block before laying it on her lap. "I'm guessing you know about my husband and me."

"Tyler told me."

Toying with the thimble, Carrie gazed off across the yard. "I knew raising kids in a home like that wasn't the best thing, but I thought it was okay. As long as he left them pretty much alone, it wouldn't hurt them. I didn't know until years later that he was hitting Tyler, too. He never told me. He lied to protect his daddy, just like I taught him, only I never imagined him lying to me."

Wishing for a quilt block to occupy her hands, Jayne gazed off, too, her focus on the cluster of men and boys around the tractor. Tyler was easy to pick out of the group. His blue jeans and T-shirt blended in with the others as surely as his dark hair gave him away.

"I didn't know how seeing things like they saw could affect kids," Carrie went on. "Josh—he doesn't have more than the faintest memory. He was only three when… Aaron was six, so he remembers more, but it doesn't bother him so much. Tyler, though…he kept the kids from the worst of it when he could. He looked out for them. He fed them, bathed them, dried their tears. He was more of a parent to them than either me or their daddy. He never got to be a kid himself, and that's my fault. I regret that more than anything else."

"I don't think he regrets it," Jayne remarked as Tyler slid his arm around Alex's shoulders. "It helped him to become what he is today—a strong, compassionate, kind man."

Carrie's smile was thin. "No matter how he denies it." After a moment, she picked up her quilting again. "You've been good for him."

"I like to think so," Jayne said, then laughed to take the smugness out of the words. "Lucy adores him."

"And you?"

I love you, she'd told him Saturday afternoon. Was that the reason for the distancing she'd seen in him? Or had she merely dreamed the words? The only way to know for sure was to ask him. Or to say them again. If he pulled away, she would know.

And regret.

Turning to Carrie, she quietly replied, "I adore him, too."

"Then it's unanimous." With a satisfied smile, Carrie returned to her quilting.

Jayne didn't ask what she meant by that. She knew Tyler

cared for them. Hadn't he kissed her right in the middle of Sweetwater the day before? For a man as private as he was, that was an amazing gesture that meant the world to her.

But would he ever love her? Would he ever fully trust her?

Maybe. She was a hopeless romantic—one of the requirements for her job. She had to believe that maybe someday he would. She could wait. She wasn't going anywhere—not, at least, for seventeen months or so.

"Lucy's such a sweet girl," Carrie said as she snipped a thread, then rethreaded the needle. "I know how hard it is being a single mother. You should be proud."

Jayne's gaze sought out her daughter, walking carefully along the top of the board fence, one hand clutching Tyler's for balance. "I think Lucy could raise herself. She's easygoing, doesn't have a temper and doesn't pout very often. She's a good kid."

"Because she's got a good mother." Carrie held the tail of the thread against the needle, wrapped the thread around the needle a few times, then pulled it through the circle of thread, forming a perfect knot. "For so many years, being a mom was all I could think about—doing the best I could, making up for all I did wrong, for all their daddy did, trying to raise good, happy, healthy kids. I loved it, but it was a job. Now that the kids are all grown and I'm getting older, I find myself wanting to be a grandma. Being a mom is work. Being a grandma is fun. Being a grandma to a little doll like Lucy…" Carrie shook her head with an indulgent smile.

Before Jayne could do more than wonder if she'd just been given Carrie's seal of approval, pounding footsteps interrupted. Lucy was on the ground now, and she and Tyler were racing toward them. She skidded to a stop between the two chairs, her face flushed, her hair on end and her grin brighter than the sun.

"You won," Carrie said.

"Yup. But only 'cause he let me. He had to 'cause he's big and I'm little. What're you making?"

"A quilt."

"It's pretty. Charley has a quilt with horses on it."

"I know. I made it for her. Would you like me to make you one when I'm finished with this?"

Lucy's eyes widened. "Would you? In my favorite colors? With horses?"

"Sure. What are your favorite colors?"

A choked-back snort drew Jayne's attention to Tyler. He knew what Lucy was going to say as surely as she did. She rolled her gaze as her daughter boldly replied, "Orange and black."

To her credit, Carrie didn't so much as blink. "Okay. We'll add some shades of brown and white, and it'll be beautiful."

As Lucy beamed with pleasure, Jayne looked slowly around the group. Tyler really couldn't have asked for a better family.

Neither could Lucy.

And neither could she.

Chapter 13

By six o'clock almost everyone had left the farm. Tyler, Jayne and Lucy stayed to help clean up—carrying dishes and chairs into the house, gathering trash, folding tables and returning them to the small shed out back. It was easy work that Tyler didn't mind at all. He liked the farm when it was quiet, when the loudest sound was the chickens clucking as they scratched in the dirt around their coop.

He carried two wood chairs through the kitchen and slid them into place at the dining table, then lifted his mother's quilt bag off one. She was in the kitchen, dividing up leftovers to send some home with him. The portions were three times what she normally gave him. "Where do you want your quilt stuff?"

"Just leave it there on the counter."

He set the bag down, then leaned against the counter, arms crossed. "Can you do an orange-and-black quilt for Lucy that won't look like Halloween?"

Carrie's smile was sweet and just a little bit sly. "I didn't say how *much* orange and black I would put in it. It'll be fine."

He nodded toward the bag. "Who is this one for?"

"Oh…I haven't really…where is that lid? I thought I put it right here, but…"

It wasn't like his mother to get flustered over nothing or to change the subject to avoid answering a question. As she made a show of searching for a lid to the bowl she'd just filled with fruit salad, Tyler suspiciously pulled the square from the bag and studied it. It was one twelve-inch square, a fraction of the whole, but he didn't need anything more to recognize the pattern—pieced circles that overlapped to form interlocking rings.

As in wedding rings.

His gut knotted. "Mom—"

She looked guilty for a moment or two, then shook it off. "A mother likes to be prepared."

"How many double wedding ring quilts have you already made trying to be prepared?"

"Two for Rebecca and one for you." Carrie shrugged as if it didn't matter that five times she'd thought one of her children was going to get married and five times she'd been disappointed. Did she even suspect that number six was coming up fast? "Someone is always getting married. They make wonderful gifts."

Then give it to someone else. Marriage wasn't in his future— not with Jayne, not with anyone—and he couldn't even tell Carrie why. She would be so disappointed and she would blame herself for staying with Del all those years. She'd carried too much blame for too long. He wouldn't add to it.

"Go ahead and make the quilt," he said quietly. "Just don't get your hopes up." Don't hope that it could be a wedding gift for him and Jayne. That it would become a Lewis family heirloom. That Jayne would become family.

Carrie packed the plastic containers and foil-wrapped

packages in a grocery bag, then came to stand in front of him. "I know you never saw anything in my marriage to recommend it, but you need a family of your own, Tyler, and Jayne and Lucy need to be that family. You love them and they love you and that's all that really matters. Everything else is just details."

She said it as if the details weren't important. But the difference was in the details, Daniel had taught him. And according to Jayne, *It's all in the details.*

He slid his arm around her and hugged her close. "Make the quilt, Mom, and give it to her. Just don't hope…."

She squeezed him tightly for a moment, then tilted her head back to look at him. "I always hope, Tyler. Without it, what's the point of living?"

He held her a moment longer, then pressed a kiss to her forehead. "I'd better get going."

They walked out front, where Jayne was talking with his grandparents. Lucy was braced on one hip, her eyes closed, her mouth open in a soft snore. Carrie smoothed a strand of damp hair back from Lucy's face. "She's like that bunny on the TV commercials. She just keeps going and going."

"And when she finally stops, she's dead to the world," Jayne replied.

"Want me to take her?" Tyler offered, and Jayne gratefully handed her over, taking the paper bag in trade.

"Thank you for having us again," Jayne said to his mother and grandparents. "It was wonderful."

"Thank you for coming." Carrie stepped forward and, to Tyler's surprise, drew Jayne into a hug. She was very demonstrative with the family but not at all outside it. *You need a family of your own,* she'd said, and she was treating Jayne and Lucy like that family.

That made one more person he'd be hurting before too long.

But there were degrees of pain. Some hurts could be borne a lot easier than others.

After saying goodbye, he carried Lucy out to his truck parked a few hundred yards down the road. Her arms wrapped around the paper bag, Jayne walked at his side, wearing a satisfied smile. He half expected one of those big, lazy, contented sighs from her any moment now.

He settled Lucy in the center seat, fastening the belt around her as she sank to the side to lean against Jayne. He was buckled in his own seat and maneuvering the truck in a tight turn when Jayne spoke. "Your mother's a sweetheart."

"Hmm."

"Someone should have killed your father the very first time he laid a hand on her. If he wasn't stopped then, it was practically guaranteed it would happen again."

Despite the warm air coming through the windows, a chill spread through Tyler. He wanted to protest that just because a man screwed up once didn't mean he would screw up again.

But wasn't that exactly what he was afraid of?

From the day the story of Del's death had gotten out, everyone had waited for him to prove he was his father's son. It had taken nine years, but he'd done it. Would it happen again? Rebecca swore it wouldn't. Dr. Gennaro thought it was highly unlikely. But his opinion was the only one that mattered. He was the one who had to maintain control, who had to live with the consequences, and he honestly didn't know.

He needed someone to gaze into his future, from that day until the moment of his death, to see that he would never lose control again. He needed a promise, a one hundred percent guarantee.

But nobody could give him that.

Which meant he had to continue living as he had since Angela—alone. If there was no one in his life, he couldn't hurt anyone.

"I'm sorry." Jayne gently touched his forearm. "I shouldn't have brought that up."

He forced something of a smile. "At least there's no question where you stand on the matter." In her book, a man got one chance, no more.

And he'd blown his five years before he'd even met her.

"I'm not shy about stating my opinion on anything." Her smile was full and warm and sexy. "Want to hear what I think of you?"

No. Because she was wrong. Too generous. She didn't know everything she needed to know to form an accurate opinion.

He was saved from answering by the appearance of a vehicle coming toward them. It was a bright red SUV, and Zachary Adams was behind the wheel. He slowed to a stop and so did Tyler, exchanging greetings and small talk. By the time they both drove on, Tyler hoped she'd forgotten her question.

She hadn't, but she was willing to let it slide. "Maybe I'll just show you instead when we get home."

Little words to send such a big response through him.

Some fifteen minutes later he parked behind her Tahoe, carried Lucy inside and laid her on their bed—on Jayne's bed, he corrected—since her room still smelled of paint, then went to the kitchen. She'd already put away the leftovers and was folding the paper bag into thirds.

"Do you mind if I go over to the workshop for a while?"

"You don't have to ask my permission, Tyler. You can just say, 'I'm going to the shop.'"

He made a dismissive gesture and waited.

"Go ahead. Have fun. What time do you want to have dinner?"

"I'm not really hungry. You guys go ahead and eat without me."

It would be the first time in nearly two weeks that he hadn't shared a meal with them, besides his workday lunches. Apparently realizing that, she studied him a long time, then smiled. It wasn't her brightest or happiest or steadiest smile, but it was a try. "Okay. You, uh…" The smile slipped away, replaced by uncertainty. "You'll be back before bedtime, won't you?"

He shouldn't give a definite answer. *Maybe, depending on how late I work. Probably. Let's see.* But instead he said, "Of course," and he meant it. He'd spent most of his life doing and being what other people needed, but for at least one more night he was going to do what he needed.

He would deal with tomorrow when it came.

Looking relieved—and making him feel like a bastard—she squeezed his hand. "I'll see you then." She brushed a kiss to his jaw, then slipped past him to lead the way into the living room. As he walked out the door, she was settling in at her desk, the computer booting up in front of her.

He spent the next three hours in the shop, working on a wall-hung display case for small collectibles. Since the only person he knew who collected small things was Great-aunt Hilda, he supposed it would be her wall it eventually hung on. It was a simple piece, not easy to ruin with inattentiveness, and if he did make a mistake, well, it wasn't as if he had hours of work in it.

He measured, cut, sanded and routed by rote and he thought of Jayne and Lucy, of his mother, Rebecca and Dr. Gennaro, of his brothers and his father. He thought about the way his life had been a month ago and wondered how hard it would be to go back to that.

It hadn't been so tough the first time. Everything had been so fresh—the shock that he'd hit Angela, the fury that he shared with his father the one thing he hated most about him, the disappointment that his best hadn't been good enough and the hopelessness….

He had never known such hopelessness.

Until now.

When he found himself standing motionlessly and staring into the distance for the tenth time, he decided to call it a night. He cleaned his work space, shook the sawdust from his T-shirt and washed up, then shut off the lights and stepped outside to lock the door. A pole light illuminated the area around the barn, and another light on the deck shone on the furniture and grill there. Everything was quiet and still. After the chaos of the first half of his life, he'd learned to value quiet and solitude.

Somehow he had to forget that quiet and solitude could be far more satisfying with three than alone.

He walked down the driveway, passing from light into shadow before reaching the openness of the road, where the moonlight shone. His porch light was a faint yellow glow to his left, and ahead on the right the light from Jayne's living room spilled out the windows and open door like a beacon. His stride lengthened and his pace increased. He crossed the yard, took the steps two at a time, then came to an abrupt stop on the porch.

"Hey, babe." Jayne was lying in the hammock, wearing the *Smart women read romance* T-shirt that she slept in most nights. He'd bet her long legs were bare, but would have to look under the sheet to see for sure. Her hair was down, her face washed free of makeup, and she looked beautiful. "Want to join me?"

She scooted over and offered a portion of the sheet, but he shook his head as he carefully stretched out beside her. His body temperature had just gone up enough to make him hot inside his own skin.

Turning onto her side, she rested her head on his shoulder, then brushed a bit of dust from his jaw. "You want to tell me what's wrong?"

He swallowed hard and her fingers bobbed with the action. "Nothing's wrong."

"You know, you don't have to spend every free minute with us. You're still entitled to time on your own. I'm a big girl. I can entertain myself for hours at a time."

He bent his free arm to pillow his head and gazed up at the sky. He couldn't insist again that nothing was wrong. He'd already lied to her once; he wouldn't repeat it. Instead he changed the subject. "Do the men in your books like to talk about things? Is that some sort of female fantasy?"

Though his tone was snide—something he really hadn't intended—she didn't take offense. "I guess it is. Small problems left unresolved grow into big ones, when all that's usually needed to resolve them is an honest conversation."

Then he blew the subject change. "You think we have small problems?"

Her gaze was so steady and intent that he could have felt it in pitch-black darkness. "I think you do."

"Oh, jeez, there's a news flash. I told you about my father beating my mother and me, about her killing him and the court ordering me into therapy. And you think I have some small problems. Damn."

Her gaze didn't waver, and she didn't show even the slightest urge to give him a well-deserved smack for that response. Instead her fingers rubbed gently over his skin. "Tyler, I know you'd dealt with more trauma by the time you were fifteen than most people face in a lifetime and I know it's left its mark. But it doesn't change who you are. It doesn't change the way I feel about you. I lo—"

He grasped a handful of her shirt, lifted her on top of him and kissed her hard. He didn't want to hear those words from her—not tonight, not ever again. Hearing them made him want to believe, and he knew better. He hadn't believed in fairy tales when he was a kid, and it was too late to start now.

For an instant she remained stiff against him. Then, with a husky groan, she kissed him back—with heat, hunger, passion. In the small part of his brain capable of rational thought, he suspected she believed his kiss was meant to convey with actions what he couldn't put into words—that he loved her, too—and the knowledge stirred the guilt inside him. But he didn't push her away, didn't stop kissing, touching, caressing her until they were both naked enough for a quick, hot, hard orgasm.

Finally she collapsed on top of him, their breathing ragged, their skin wet with sweat. Her panties were somewhere on the floor. His shirt was bunched halfway up his chest, and his jeans were halfway down his legs. He jerked the shirt off, then kicked off his jeans. As they hit the floor, the open living room windows registered somewhere in the fog that was his brain. "Where's Lucy?" With her room smelling strongly of paint fumes the night before, she'd slept on the sofa. If she was there again…

Stretching like a satisfied cat, Jayne rubbed against him and his breath caught in his chest. "Bit late to ask, isn't it?" Her voice was throaty and affected him as surely as a touch, making his taut muscles tremble. "She's in her room. I turned the fan around backward in the window so it sucks the smell out." Ducking her head, she dragged her tongue across his nipple, and his entire body reacted, twitching, quivering.

Rising onto her knees, she peeled her shirt over her head and dropped it. Her skin took on a golden glow in the soft light. He studied her a moment, from head to—well, knees—then touched her. Silky hair, silken skin. Long, elegant throat. Nice breasts, full, the nipples rosy and taut. Narrow waist. Sweetly flared hips. Soft curls. Strong, long thighs.

Just looking made him hard again. Touching made him hurt, but it was a good pain, a welcome pain. He'd had too little of it in his life and faced even less in the future, but for now it was enough.

And that was more than he had any right to hope for.

Jayne gave up trying to sleep sometime around dawn and slipped from the bed, pulling on a robe and fuzzy slippers. Tyler lay on his stomach, covers pulled to his waist, arm flung out across her side of the bed. It had been a comforting touch through a restless night—one she doubted he would have offered if he'd been awake.

He'd distracted her the night before, she acknowledged as she nuked a cup of water for instant coffee. She'd wanted just a hint of what was going wrong between them, because no matter how he denied it, something *was* wrong, and she desperately wanted it to be fixable. She desperately wanted them to work, to last forever.

Maybe the answer was simple: he wasn't as involved in the relationship as she was. The possibility made her lungs tighten and her stomach hurt. Other problems—too much us time, feeling suffocated, being put off by some annoying habit— could be dealt with. But if he didn't feel as strongly as she did, if the "real thing" to her had merely been a short-term affair to him…what could she do? She couldn't *make* him love her. She could only deal with it.

Unlocking the front door, she went out onto the porch. Cameron and Diaz darted after her and loped into the woods, disappearing into the thin morning light. They were easy to please—a little affection, a lot of food and the freedom to run wild for a portion of each day, and they were happy.

Sounded a lot like Greg.

The air was damp, just cool enough to make her velour robe comfortable. To the west, the sky was still dark, but soft light was creeping over Laurel Mountain in the east. Except for an occasional bark from the dogs or a nearer *chirrup* from some unknown creature, everything was silent. Peaceful.

Except *her.*

Forcing her worries from her mind, she focused on the sunrise. She couldn't remember the last time she'd seen it, had actually taken the time to watch it, admire it, feel humbled by it. Probably when Lucy was a baby, waking at odd hours more for the company, Jayne had always believed, than for the bottle she usually got.

Back then, Jayne's life had been close to perfect. She'd had a beautiful child whom she loved more than life itself. Greg had still been in his trying-to-make-it-work phase and she'd still been in her pretending-it-was-going-to-work phase.

She wouldn't kid herself with Tyler. Every fear inside her insisted he was looking for a way out. She wished she was strong enough to make it easy for him. Any one of her heroines would kick him to the curb and make him do some serious groveling when he came to his senses, but she wasn't one of her heroines. She felt pretty damn weak.

The screen door creaked a moment before Tyler sat down beside her. The scant time was enough to take a cleansing breath and clear her expression. She smiled faintly and said a quiet, "Good morning."

"You're up early." As she watched, he tugged on his socks, shoved one foot into a boot and laced it, then did the same with the other. Then he rested his forearms on his knees and gazed off toward the east.

"I couldn't remember the last time I saw the sun rise."

"Happens every morning about this time."

"What a coincidence. I'm usually asleep every morning about this time."

He didn't ask why she couldn't sleep that morning. Afraid she might answer? Instead, he stared off into the distance as if watching the sky turn delicate shades of rose and gold required every bit of his attention.

"When Lucy was little, sometimes we would watch the sun set, and when it disappeared from sight, she would stand up and applaud," she remarked. "Once she asked me to rewind it so she could see it again."

He didn't even crack a smile. "Too bad life doesn't come with a rewind button—and a redo button."

"Yeah." She stifled the urge to ask him just how far back he would go if he could or what he would do differently. Let them shiver through their first night in their new home without heat? Rein in that unwelcome neighborly gene? Refuse any contact with them?

Maybe the do-over he wanted involved Angela or maybe it went even farther back. She couldn't begin to guess.

A single ray of bright sunlight pierced the sky as he heaved a sigh. "Guess I'd better get ready for work." He leaned across to kiss her, but she impulsively turned her face away so his lips brushed her cheek. The act startled her as much as him. He sort of hovered there a moment before finally straightening, then pushing to his feet.

Regretting the impulse, she set her coffee aside and stood, too, hands crammed into the deep pockets of her robe. "Sorry," she said with a wobbly smile. "I haven't brushed my teeth yet. Morning breath and coffee…" She wrinkled her nose as she fell silent.

He gave a halfhearted smile, as if he believed her. "I'll see you this evening."

"Be careful."

"Yeah."

With her stomach tying itself into a tight knot, she watched him walk a few feet before suddenly speaking again. "I love you, Tyler."

He stopped short, turned and just looked at her for a moment. His dark eyes grew shadowy and his mouth settled in a grim line. "Please stop saying that."

So it hadn't been a dream Saturday. She *had* said it. And he had deliberately stopped her from saying it again the night before. He didn't want to hear it. Didn't want to know it.

It wasn't fair. She wasn't supposed to fall in love with someone who didn't love her back. She wasn't supposed to want so much when he apparently wanted so damn little. They were supposed to be on the same page, wanting the same things, sharing the same dreams. He wasn't supposed to be destroying those dreams on a beautiful Monday morning.

Her fingers knotted inside the pockets, but she tried to keep the tension from her face. "Not saying it won't make it any less true."

"What will?" he demanded.

Her breath caught and the blood drained from her face. "The way you're behaving right now might be a good start."

He started to walk off, then swung around and came back toward her. "The way *I'm* behaving? Things aren't working out the way you wanted, and it's *my* fault? I didn't ask you to fall in love with me. I didn't want you to. All I wanted was to spend some time with someone, have a little fun. I never said a damn thing to make you think it was anything more than that."

Someone. Not her in particular. Anyone would have done. She just happened to have been convenient. "Have a little fun, a little sex," she said sarcastically.

His face flushed guiltily. "You started it, sweetheart."

It was the first time he'd called her by anything but her name, and he did it in such a snide tone that she wanted to shake him. Worse, she couldn't deny his words. All he'd done was kiss her a few times. She was the one who'd brought sex into the picture when she'd stood in his kitchen that Friday night and boldly told him she wanted to share her bed with him.

It had seemed so simple then. She'd wanted him. He'd wanted her. What could go wrong?

Obviously a lot.

"So…" She drew a breath to steady her voice. "Let me see if I've got it straight. This was just supposed to be a—a fling, an affair. You get a few meals that you don't have to cook yourself, spend a few hours where you don't have to entertain yourself, have sex so you don't have to—" His gaze narrowed, shades darker and degrees colder, and she finished with a jerky shrug. "And when you get tired or bored or you've had enough, you walk away. It's over. How was I supposed to know this? What were the signs I was supposed to pick up on so I'd know it wasn't *real?* Where were the rules for this game you forgot to tell me we were playing?"

The flush spread to the tips of his ears as he offered his own shrug. "Come on, Jayne. Do you really need everything spelled out for you? You're a grown woman. You've been walked away from before."

Tears burned her eyes, but she stubbornly forced them back. "You never said—"

"That I was interested in anything long-term." A chill swept over him, making him look as distant and frigid as a winter-shrouded mountain peak. "How could I be? You're a pretty woman, Jayne…but you're not Angela."

Her intake of breath was audible, the pain physical. Crossing her arms tightly to keep herself together, she took a step back, stumbling on the top step, then righting herself. He'd told her he no longer loved Angela, and she'd wanted so much to believe him. She'd been eager to accept his lies—hadn't even considered that he might be lying. Had never considered that he might have no more use for her than Greg had.

Cameron came tearing out of the woods, Diaz a few yards behind him. They were headed for Tyler's house when they abruptly shifted direction and came their way instead. She smiled thinly at the sight of them. "Before you came out this morning, I was thinking how much your dogs are like Greg. I guess they come by it honestly. You're both bastards." Fumbling for the screen door handle behind her, she opened the door, paused halfway through it and said flatly, "I'm not Angela and you're not the man I thought you were. Looks like we both got screwed."

Then she went inside, closed and locked the door, sank to the floor and cried. It was so unlike anything her heroines would have done. They were strong. They held their heads up and dealt with adversity calmly, capably. Not even a broken heart could keep them down.

But she was no heroine, and they'd never had a heartache like this, because she'd never had a broken heart. She'd relied on imagination to write those emotions, and it had failed her. She

hadn't known she could hurt like this. Hadn't known she might
literally break into pieces. Hadn't suspected that every breath
would burn, that every beat of her heart would ache, that
numbness would be slow to come and inadequate at blocking
the pain.

And she had no one to blame but herself. Tyler had been
right. He'd never asked for anything more than a little of her
time. Never talked about a future that included both of them.
Never implied he wanted more from her than companionship
and sex. He'd never even asked her out for one simple date.

Even Greg had wanted to go out with her from time to time.

But he'd treated her with liking and respect. Sometimes
he'd looked at her as if she *meant* something. He'd touched her
so tenderly and held her close even in his sleep. He'd taken her
to his family's get-togethers three Sundays in a row. He'd kissed
her on Main Street!

Even she had to admit that was a flimsy foundation for love
and forever.

Of course, it was easier to see now that she knew she had
just been a substitute—and a poor one at that—for the woman
he really wanted.

Long after she heard his pickup truck pass, she eased to her
feet. Her butt was sore from sitting on the hard floor, her eyes
were puffy and red, and her nose was runny. Those were the last
tears she would cry over Tyler, she promised as she blew into a
tissue.

She didn't believe it for a moment.

After a shower, she got dressed, then pulled her suitcase
from under her bed. One of the good things about her job—she
was free to travel pretty much when and where she wanted. She
could turn almost any trip into a business expense and could
write anywhere she could set her laptop or her legal pad.

She and Lucy and this book were going on a trip. She didn't
know where, though.

Just away from here.

* * *

When he reached the highway, Tyler eased the truck to a stop. There was no traffic in either direction, but still he sat there, his hands knotted around the steering wheel. It was the only way he knew to hold himself together. Rigid control. It had gotten him through the last five years. It would get him through this.

Please, God.

He scowled hard at the road. Daniel's house was to the left, but he couldn't bring himself to make the turn. He felt frozen from the inside out. Sick. Despairing.

He had been strong his entire damn life, but he wasn't strong enough for this. He wanted to turn the truck around, go back to Jayne's and tell her everything. He wanted to beg her to give him another chance. He wanted...

Her. And Lucy. Forever.

A honk sounded behind him, and he looked into the rearview mirror to see Sassie Whitlaw's beat-up old Ford. She steered into the other lane, pulled up beside him and leaned over to crank down the window. "You all right, son?"

He'd never been further from all right in his life. But he managed to unclench his jaw long enough to say, "Yeah. I was just thinking...."

The old woman grinned. "Well, think all you want. Once I'm gone, the morning rush hour is over. You take care." With a wave, she turned onto the highway headed for town.

Take care. He'd always tried—with Rebecca and the boys, his mother, his grandparents. He'd tried to be the best man he could be, but he'd failed repeatedly. He'd spent his first years in Sweetwater in constant trouble. He'd done the unforgivable with Angela. He'd disappointed Rebecca and Carrie. And now he'd hurt the one woman he loved most. Rebecca and Carrie would forgive him, and Angela had probably forgotten him, but Jayne...

She was going to hate him forever for his ugly lies.

Better to be hated for that, though, than for his ugly secret, right? She wasn't the forgiving type when it came to little things like a man hitting a woman. *One strike, and you're out.* If she knew that he'd hit Angela, she would look at him with such disgust. She would be afraid to let him near her or Lucy.

He knew, because he'd looked at his father with disgust, and had been afraid to let him near Carrie or the kids.

This was for the best. He *knew* that in his head. But he still wanted to go back. To apologize. Explain. Beg. Plead. Promise.

His jaw clenched because he couldn't let himself be weak. He forced one hand loose and flipped on the left-turn signal. He checked traffic in both directions, pivoted his foot from the brake to the accelerator, pulled away from the stop sign and turned right. Away from Daniel's. Away from Jayne.

For a time he let himself believe he was driving aimlessly, but the pretense was hard to keep up when he found himself in Munroe on the block that housed Dr. Gennaro's office. She was just getting out of her car when he parked beside it. She walked around to his side of the truck, looked at him for a moment, then smiled sympathetically. "Come on in."

Her office filled the bottom left half of an old house converted to commercial use. The waiting room had once been a parlor and still looked the part with cabbage-rose wallpaper, old-fashioned and uncomfortable furniture and crocheted doilies on every flat surface.

Dr. Gennaro put her purse and briefcase away, removed her jacket, then went next door to start a pot of coffee. When she returned, she leaned against the edge of the desk and gestured for him to sit down. He did. "You look like hell."

"Thanks," he said drily.

In jeans and a green shirt, with her red hair held back by a band, she didn't much look like a psychologist. She'd been just out of school when he'd met her, and in the years since, she'd gotten older, married, had two babies and put on a few pounds.

All he'd gotten was older and more lost.

She watched him for a few moments before leaving the room again. When she returned with two mugs of coffee, she gave him one, then sat behind the desk. "I know you didn't drive all this way for a cup of my coffee, because it's not that good. You need to talk?"

He did. He just didn't know where or how to start.

"Okay. I'm guessing this has something to do with the woman you were with Saturday. Jayne? Is that her name?"

He nodded.

"I'm about as sure as can be that you didn't lose your temper and hit her, so..." She tapped one red nail on her coffee mug for a moment. "She broke up with you? No. You broke up with her. Why?"

He gripped his own mug in both hands, barely noticing that the ceramic was only a few degrees cooler than scalding. "She wasn't supposed to..." *Fall in love with me.* It was hard to even think the words. The concept seemed so impossible. He'd spent five years convincing himself that no woman would ever love him, that he could never give her—or himself—that chance. It had taken Jayne only a month to prove him wrong. "To fall in love."

"Why not? You're both single. You have a lot in common. You're close to her daughter, who, Rebecca tells me, adores you. She likes you and you like her. Falling in love is the next normal step in the relationship, Tyler."

"Yeah, well, I don't get to have 'normal' because I'm not. Remember?"

She barely resisted rolling her eyes, though she did gaze at the ceiling for a deep breath before looking at him again. "So you broke up with her because you think it's safer for her. Better to break her heart than something else?"

He scowled at her. "Isn't it unethical for you and Rebecca to discuss me in your sessions?"

"Come on. How many times have you and I talked about her or the boys in our sessions? You're a family. Your problems all stem from the same source. You're kind of a package deal." After a sip of coffee, she went on. "You know what's stopping you from having a normal relationship, Tyler? You. Just you. Nobody else is blaming you for hitting Angela. Nobody else is waiting for it to happen again. Nobody else is afraid. Just you."

"Nobody else is waiting for it to happen again because nobody knows it happened the first time."

"Would it be so bad if they did? If you said, 'I made a mistake and I've learned from it and I'm going to do my best to see that it doesn't happen again'? People make mistakes, Tyler. Some make huge mistakes, and they deal with them and they get back to their lives."

He concentrated on pressing his fingers tighter against the mug. "My father beat my mother. My grandfather beat my grandmother. For all I know, *his* father beat *his* mother. It's who they are. It's a part of who I am."

"No." Her hair swung as she vigorously shook her head. "It's something you witnessed growing up. Violence isn't inherited, Tyler. It's a learned behavior. Your father learned it from his father, who was violent, and his mother, who never fought back. *You* didn't learn it, though. You never thought it was all right. You hated it when he hit your mother. You wanted it to stop even if it meant your father's death."

"But…" He swallowed hard. "It's been drummed into me since I was fourteen that I'm just like him and that I can't be. I have to be better, I have to be in control, I have to make up for looking like him and sounding like him and acting like him."

"Looking and sounding like him—that's superficial. It's genetics and it doesn't mean a damn thing. As for acting like him…do you get drunk every chance you get? Do you squander every penny you make on booze and women and good times while your family goes hungry? Do you get angry if someone looks at you the wrong way? Do you believe that women were put on this earth to please you, to do your cooking and cleaning and to be your punching bag? Do you believe you have the right to punish Jayne if you don't like what she cooks for dinner or if she folds your socks the wrong way or if her daughter gets cranky when she's tired?"

"Of course not," he said impatiently.

"So besides the superficial, how exactly are you like your father?"

"The worst way. He hit my mother." His jaw clenched along with every muscle in his body, but he didn't let the words go unsaid. He didn't spare himself. "I hit Angela."

"How many times did he hit your mother? The abuse was an ongoing thing for fifteen years, so it must have been a lot. A hundred times? A thousand? Ten thousand? And you hit Angela once. Forgive me if I don't see a huge, significant, unforgivable connection here."

"Angela wasn't like my mother. She left. But if she had stayed, if she'd acted like it was just a mistake, it would have happened again." As he'd reminded Rebecca, that was how it started—one punch, regret, apology, followed by another punch, with less regret and a less sincere apology, until it was a regular thing.

"Let me tell you something, Tyler," Dr. Gennaro said, coming around to sit in the chair a few feet from his. "If you were that kind of man, it would have already happened again. You wouldn't be able to control yourself through sheer will. You wouldn't be willing to live life alone. Can you imagine your father voluntarily removing himself from society? From your mother's life, from your and your siblings' lives?"

For a time he sat motionless, fifteen, sixteen years in the

past. In a flash of rare courage, Carrie had once stood up to Del, had told him she was going to take the kids and leave him. *You can't live without me,* Del had replied. *You're too stupid and worthless. Besides, I'd kill you.* And then he'd proceeded to damn near do it with his fists.

Numbly Tyler shook his head.

"These men can't bear to lose their victims. It has nothing to do with love or the marriage and everything to do with control and the need to dominate. They need that outlet for their rage, and it's easier to terrorize the target they've already got into staying than to find a new one. When a woman does leave, that's when he's most likely to kill her. If she's successful in escaping him, then he has no choice but to find a new victim. But look at you. Did you try to stop Angela from leaving?"

"No." He had already realized the relationship was ending. He hadn't been in love with her anymore. He would have helped her pack and made the move for her if she'd wanted.

"Afterward, you came to see me. What would it have taken to get Del to seek help?" She paused, not expecting him to answer, and smiled thinly. "Probably handcuffs and a gun, because *he didn't believe he was doing anything wrong.*"

Everything in Del's life had always been someone else's fault. He'd never accepted responsibility for a damn thing. Why should he? Everyone else had been willing to take the blame for him.

"Once Angela was gone, did you go looking for someone else to take her place? No. You isolated yourself up on your mountaintop and kept your distance from all women—from everybody—for five years. *Five years,* Tyler. If she had gone to the police and you'd been arrested and convicted, you never would have gotten so harsh a sentence." She shook her head stubbornly. "You're *not* like your father. You don't fit the profile of an abuser. You never have."

"But…" Tyler breathed deeply. He'd hit a woman once and

had been sickened by it. Violent aggression had been an everyday part of Del's life, and he'd enjoyed it. How many times had he laughed while punching Tyler or kicking Carrie? How many times had they seen that gleam in his eyes—excitement, anticipation—just before he started hitting? Often enough for Josh, who'd been only three when Del died, to recognize it and run to hide.

"You lost your temper," Dr. Gennaro said quietly. "You reacted instinctively but wrongly. You apologized to Angela. You punished yourself for it. It's way past time to let go and move on. Quit—pardon the term—beating yourself up. Forgive yourself and live."

Live. Have a future instead of taking it one grim day at a time. Spite his father and have a normal life with a wife and kids. Be happy and contented like Daniel and Sarah, Zachary and Beth, Jayne's parents and his grandparents. Spend the next fifty years with someone who loved him. Have hope.

Without hope, according to his mother, what was the point of living?

Jayne and Lucy were his hope.

"What if it happens again?" That was his fear, and he was much more accustomed to fearing than hoping.

"I don't believe it will."

He rubbed his chest where a strange sensation fluttered, then eased. Was that how hope felt? "She's never going to speak to me again."

"Did a good job of breaking up with her, did you?" She reached across to squeeze his hand. "Tell her everything, Tyler. It'll help her understand."

"Or give her more reasons to stay away from me."

She smiled. "Never underestimate a woman in love. Give her a chance. Give yourself a chance. Live well and be happy. It really is the best revenge."

Rising, he set his coffee cup on the desk. "Be happy—

there's a foreign concept." Except for the past few weeks. Though he'd been dreading the inevitable end, he had been happy. If it wasn't too late to get that back again… "Thanks, Doc."

"You're welcome, Tyler."

Jayne had said that to him once—and he'd truly *felt* welcome. He wasn't likely to feel it the next time he saw her, but with luck…

The drive back to Sweetwater seemed to take twice as long. Why not? When he'd left, he'd been running away. The bands in his chest tightened when he turned at Sassie's chicken, and by the time he'd jolted over the next few miles of road, his gut was tied in knots.

All for nothing.

Jayne was gone.

"Where are we going?"

As she eased the Tahoe forward a few feet in the drive-up lane at the bank, Jayne glanced at Lucy in the rearview mirror. "I told you—on a trip."

"A trip where?"

"I'm not sure yet." Her first impulse had been to head north to Chicago, but the idea of being thirty years old and running home to Mama and Daddy because some mean man had broken her heart had seemed so immature. So she'd decided to head southeast instead. There were plenty of places to explore in Georgia and South Carolina, historical places that might give her a new book idea.

However, considering that every time she thought of her work-in-progress, all her heroine Arabella wanted to do with her hero Jake was stake him out naked on an anthill and watch the vicious little creatures finish him off, she wasn't too hopeful.

"How long are we gonna be gone?"

That question was a repeat, too. Jayne gave the same answer as before. "I don't know. A few days." Maybe forever.

"Nobody asked *me* if I wanted to go on a trip," Lucy said grumpily, kicking the seat with one sneakered foot. "'Cause if anyone *had* asked, I would've told 'em no. Charley was gonna call today to see if I could come visit, and Tyler and me was gonna paint the trim in my room."

Reaching between the seats, Jayne grabbed Lucy's foot and gave it a warning squeeze. This was *not* going to be a fun day. They hadn't even made it out of Sweetwater yet, and already her head was aching and her patience was wearing thin. She tried to mask it with a breezy tone. "Well, honey, that's one of the tough things about being a kid. You have to do what your parents tell you to."

"Yeah, like go on a stupid trip. Why didn't Tyler come?"

"He had to work."

"He could've taken time off. It's called vacation."

"Watch your tone, Lucky girl."

"Don't call me that. That's Tyler's name. I bet he didn't want us to take this trip, either. He'll be all alone without us. Why don't you just let me stay with him?"

Because he doesn't want you any more than he wants me. But Jayne would bite her tongue in half before saying the words out loud. The next few weeks or months were going to be hard for Lucy, much harder than when Greg had left. Tyler had been more a father to her than Greg ever had. Though they shared one important thing in common—in the end, neither of them had wanted to be a permanent part of her life.

How could she have been so wrong? Had she been so needy after Greg that she'd let emotion blind her to reality? Had she been out of the dating world for so long that she no longer knew the game?

She'd been too easy, too gullible, and now she *and* Lucy were paying for it. She was so sorry, but she'd honestly thought Tyler cared for them. And she wasn't the only one he'd fooled. Rebecca had believed it, too, and Carrie, and they knew him better than anyone.

Her mother had tried to warn her. *It's too soon,* she'd said right after meeting Tyler.

Yeah, and a few days later she'd been hugging him, saying, *Take care of my girls.* He'd fooled her, too.

The tap of a horn behind them drew Jayne's gaze to the rearview mirror, then to the lane ahead of her. The car that had been there was gone, so she pulled forward, passed a check to the teller inside and drummed her fingers on the steering wheel. She had so many decisions to make, when all she really wanted to do was crawl into bed, pull the covers over her head and cry. Where would they go? What would she do with the house? How could she make this awful ache go away? When would she stop loving Tyler?

Never, a malicious little voice whispered. He was the happily-ever-after one, the forever-and-ever one.

Just as Angela was *his* happily-ever-after, forever-and-ever one.

"Ma'am?"

She blinked back the moisture in her eyes and saw that the teller had opened the drawer so she could take her cash. She scooped it up and slid it into her purse without counting it, smiled tautly at the young man and started to pull away from the window. Before she'd gone more than a few feet, a pickup squealed to a stop in front of her, forcing her to stomp on the brakes to avoid hitting it. "Damn it—"

It was Tyler.

"Mom!" Lucy admonished her for swearing, then she exclaimed, "Hey, there's Tyler. You said he was working."

Ignoring Lucy's suspicious tone, Jayne checked the rearview mirror, but the car behind her was just inches off her bumper. She was trapped, and panic turned the fresh ache growing inside her to welcome anger.

She slid to the ground as he jumped out of his truck. There wasn't enough room to move between the vehicles so she faced him over the hood. "Get out of my way."

"Going somewhere?" He gestured to the rear of the Tahoe, where their suitcases were clearly visible.

"That's none of your business."

"The hell it isn't. You're running away, aren't you?"

She glared at him. "As of this morning, nothing I do is any of your business. Now move your damn truck before I move it for you."

Taking the few steps to the passenger door, he leaned inside, snagged the keys from the ignition and dangled them from his index finger. "We need to talk."

Her stomach knotted at his nerve. A few hours ago he'd broken her heart, and now he wanted to *talk?* Had he thought of more reasons why he didn't want her? More ways she didn't measure up to his precious Angela? "You couldn't possibly say anything that I want to hear."

"How about 'I'm sorry'?"

"The two most meaningless words in the English language. You think you can do anything, say anything, then say I'm sorry, and I'll forget about it?" She snorted. "You're more like Greg than I thought."

Tyler rested his hands on the SUV's hood and stared at her across the narrow space. "How about 'I love you'?"

Her breath caught in her chest, increasing the ache there. How could he…*why* would he… "You bastard," she whispered.

His eyes closed briefly, then he opened them again. In them she recognized regret. Guilt. Pain. So much pain. "I don't blame you for being mad at me. I screwed up. I hurt you and I'm damned sorry. But I love you, Jayne, and if you'll give me a chance…"

She stared at him until she couldn't bear his pain a second longer. Gazing away, she saw they had an audience—the bank teller, who'd no doubt turned the speaker to its loudest volume; a man and a woman, both watching from the cars behind her; a few customers who'd come out of the bank lobby; a few more people who'd stopped on the sidewalk; and Rebecca and Carla, who'd come outside from the diner across the street.

More importantly Tyler knew they had an audience and he didn't care. He'd apologized in front of them all.

The private man who'd isolated himself for so many years, who'd hated the attention just being seen with her and Lucy had brought, had just said *I love you* in front of all these people.

It made her believe him in a way nothing else could have.

"Go on, honey," called the elderly man in the car behind her. "Talk to him and get out of my way."

She gazed back at Tyler, his cheeks flushed, his dark eyes shadowed. He looked as if he hadn't even gotten to the hard part, and that was probably true. Now he had to tell her why he'd said such hurtful things that morning. But there was a hint of hope in his eyes, and she felt a corresponding flare inside her. She was a hopeless romantic—or, as some old movie had better put it, a hope*ful* romantic.

He glanced around, his gaze skimming over all the curious faces, then looked at her again. "Please, Jayne…"

She wanted to say no. Wanted to run away and hide. Wanted to close her eyes and plug her ears with her fingers. Wanted to never hurt so badly again as long as she lived.

But this was her life, her heart, her future on the line. How could she run away? How could she refuse to hear what he needed to say? How could she pass up a chance to make things right? To stop this ache?

She raised her gaze to the sky, then looked around again. Another teller had joined the man at the drive-up window. More customers had come out of the bank. Rebecca, standing some twenty feet behind Tyler, wore a fearful expression. She knew what the public declaration had cost her brother and didn't want him hurt. When her gaze met Jayne's, though, she offered a tiny smile and an encouraging nod. Only Lucy, still strapped in her seat, appeared disinterested. She'd turned on her portable DVD player, and the sounds of *Angelina Ballerina* drifted through the open window.

"All right," Jayne agreed grimly. "Give me my keys."

She stuck out her hand, and for a moment Tyler hesitated. Afraid he couldn't trust her? That she would get in the Tahoe and drive off without hearing his apology? Tempting as it was, she wouldn't. She deserved an explanation, and after the past few minutes, he deserved to give it.

Reluctantly he leaned across and dropped the keys into her palm. She wrapped her fingers tightly around them. "Rebecca, would you mind if Lucy stayed with you at the diner for a bit?"

Rebecca didn't even try to hide her relief as she came forward. "Of course not. I'd love the help. Come on, kiddo. We've got work to do." She helped Lucy out of the seat belt, then lifted her to the ground.

Immediately the little traitor ran to Tyler and extended her arms for him to pick her up. When he did so, she cupped his face in her palms. "We're not divorcin' you," she said firmly. "We was just goin' on a little trip, then coming back. You and me have got painting to finish."

He murmured something in her ear, and with a grin, she whispered back to him. After pressing a loud, smacking kiss to his forehead, she wriggled down, took Rebecca's hand and skipped off.

Jayne swallowed the lump in her throat. Her five-year-old daughter shouldn't even know the word *divorce,* much less the pain it meant. She shouldn't face saying goodbye to the most important man in her life.

Maybe she wouldn't have to.

"Where do you want to have this talk?"

Tyler swallowed hard, too. It didn't clear the hoarseness from his voice. "Follow me." He didn't say anything else, but his gaze did. *Please...*

She climbed into her truck. As their audience began turning away, the tension in her eased a bit. Much of it remained, though. Obviously his reason for dumping her had been important enough to him that he'd deliberately hurt her. What if it was too important to overcome? Saying *I'm sorry* and *I love you* didn't guarantee they could work things out.

But it was a good start.

He led her to a park on the edge of town, an odd-shaped space with no parking besides the gravel strip that edged the street. There wasn't much in the way of playground equipment—a swing set, a merry-go-round, a jungle gym—but plenty of open space allowed room for soccer, football or baseball games, and there were picnic tables under the trees.

She parked next to his truck, stepped over the low pipe railing that kept cars off the grass and walked with him to the nearest table. It was made of concrete, pitted and rough, and already held warmth from the morning sun. He sat on one bench. She sat on the other and waited.

He laced his fingers together, working them back and forth before looking at her. "You were leaving, weren't you?"

She started to shake her head, then to nod, then settled for a shrug. "Probably."

"I would have found you."

"After the things you said this morning, I thought you'd be glad to see us gone."

Heat flushed his face. "I'm an idiot."

"At least we agree on something." She smiled and so did he, but both were pathetic gestures. "You want to explain to me how three hours ago you just wanted a little fun but nothing permanent because I couldn't measure up to Angela and now you're saying you love me?"

His face reddened again, and he rubbed one hand over his unshaven jaw. "I've never had a lot of experience with women—with relationships. For a long time, I was too angry. For the past five years I was too…afraid."

"Because of Angela. Because she hurt you."

"No." He drew a breath and looked as if he would rather die than say the words he was about to say. "Because *I* hurt *her.*"

Jayne was puzzled. *He* broke Angela's heart? That didn't make sense. Why did he exile himself to the mountain unless he was the one nursing a broken heart? Why did he cut himself off from women, from practically everybody? Why did he give up even meaningless sex with one-night strangers? Unless…

There were different ways to hurt someone. Emotionally. Verbally. Physically. His father had covered them all, destroying Carrie's self-esteem, confidence and self-worth, along with bruising and breaking her. He'd damaged his children, especially Tyler, with his words and his fists.

And sons raised by abusive fathers were more likely than the average boy to become abusive themselves.

Her stomach knotted, and she pressed one hand there to ease the nausea. She didn't want to say the words either, but she forced herself. "You…hit…her."

He nodded, his expression so bleak, so lost. He was sickened by what he'd done.

She felt sick, too. Because after seeing how his mother had suffered at his father's hands, he'd hit a woman himself? Or because after trying so hard to not be like his father, he'd failed?

"What happened?"

He drew a deep breath, then glanced around, as if making sure no one else was close enough to hear. With a look of utter misery, he finally looked back in her general direction but not directly at her. "We were fighting one day. By that time, it was all we did. She was saying stuff about my mother and my father and me, and I was pissed off. I just wanted her to shut up." He closed his eyes for a moment, then corrected himself. "I just wanted to shut her up. And I did. I backhanded her. I didn't think about it. I didn't know I was going to do it. I just did it. Instinctively. Naturally. The way my father hit my mother and me all those years."

The bands around her lungs eased. "Was that the only time?"

He nodded.

One backhanded slap. One moment of anger, one loss of control. "And you thought that single incident proved that you were just like your father."

He lifted his hands in a helpless gesture. "I looked like him, walked like him, talked like him. I had his temper. I was the one everyone worried about. I was the one they all expected to *become* him. And that day, I did."

What was that like? Jayne wondered. Knowing from the time he was an impressionable kid that everyone in his world expected him to turn out just like the violent father he hated? What kind of pressure had that put on a boy whose biggest concerns should have been school and girls? Unbearable. As if he hadn't lived through enough already, those worries and expectations had made a normal life impossible for him. No doubt, their intentions had been good—the court, the psychologist, his family and friends—but the result...

She tried to imagine him using his physical strength to hurt someone, but the image wouldn't form. With his mother killing his father and going to prison and the intense scrutiny he'd been under, he'd probably had more than his share of fights in school. But to strike a woman, when it went against everything he'd experienced and believed in, the provocation must have been significant.

She could easily imagine just how nasty Angela had been. She could see the angry, frightened boy inside Tyler who'd guarded his brothers and sister, who'd defended his mother, who'd taken beatings in silence to protect his family, coming to the fore and reacting instinctively.

And she could so easily imagine the resulting revulsion of the man he'd become.

"That's why you asked me that evening in the woods if I was afraid Lucy would turn out like her father—if she was genetically programmed to that."

He nodded once more.

She couldn't remember thinking anything of the question at the time—that it was odd or that he might be asking for a reason. It made perfect sense now. "Why didn't you tell me sooner?"

His hands were clenched into white-knuckled fists, his gaze directed away from her. "I never told anyone but Rebecca and Dr. Gennaro. Even Mom doesn't know. I couldn't bear people knowing they'd been right to worry about me, that I *was* just like Del. I thought if you knew the truth, you wouldn't want me around you or especially Lucy, and I really needed to be with you."

The truth. That he'd been human. That he'd done something he wasn't proud of. That he'd made a mistake and paid for it.

She gazed across the park to where the grass gave way to woods. A few miles through those woods was her little house, where she'd been happier than anywhere else, and his house, where he'd lived alone and lonely because that was all he thought he deserved. "What does this have to do with you breaking up with me?" she asked, though she already knew. He'd never told anyone. He'd been too ashamed, too disgusted, too convinced that he was a horrible person.

His doubts that he was a good man were more understandable in light of this. Wrong, but understandable.

"I thought I could spend time with you and Lucy and not be so alone for a while. I never intended to fall in love with you. I didn't deserve that, not without guarantees that I—that it wouldn't happen again. Then, after a while it was too late. You'd made clear what you thought of men like my father and me. One strike, and you're out. I didn't want you to hate me for that, so I thought…"

Better for her to think he just didn't want her than to know that he'd lived up to everyone's worst expectations. Better for *him*. Not so good for her.

Her smile was thin, unsteady. "You didn't trust me. You didn't give me a chance."

For a moment his fingers unclenched as if he might reach for her. But after that moment, they slowly knotted again. Was he afraid to touch her? Afraid she would reject him? "You said someone should have killed my father the first time he hit my mother, that the first time a man raised a hand to you, you would leave. I had my first time five years before I met you. I didn't think I had a chance."

Heat warmed her face. "I was talking about your father and men like him—not you. One incident doesn't make you an abuser, Tyler. I would never judge you by his example."

Finally he met her gaze. His eyes were dark, filled with pain and made her want to gather him close and just hold him. "You would be one of the first who didn't."

The truth of that statement made her ache. Del Lewis had been dead fourteen years, but he was still influencing his son's life, affecting the way others viewed him, the way he saw himself. She hoped the bastard burned in hell for eternity.

But Tyler had suffered enough.

"I judged myself against my father," he went on. "I thought, with our background, with my history, that no woman would want me—that I didn't even deserve to be wanted. I thought I had to live alone so I wouldn't destroy people the way he did. But I was wrong. I'm not like him. Violence isn't a part of my life. It's not my nature, even though I've always been afraid it was." His voice hitched, and he dragged in a noisy breath to settle it. "I just want to be normal, Jayne. I want to have a home with you and Lucy. I want to be a family. I want to be the man you thought I was."

She'd told him he wasn't that man, but she'd lied. He had been through so much—abuse, horror, dangerous rages, torment, murder, great loss, suspicion, terrible expectations. And yet he'd grown into a kind, compassionate, decent man. It was a testament to how incredibly strong he was.

She drew a deep breath, and all the tension left her chest. Laying her hand over his, she gently worked his fisted fingers loose, then twined her fingers with his. "You're the best man I know, Tyler, and you'll always have a home with Lucy and me. There's just one condition. You have to marry me and you have to trust me and you have to accept that there's nothing you could tell me that would make me stop loving you. I'll always love you."

Still holding her hand, he moved around the table to sit beside her. He brought his free hand up to her face, gently tucking a strand of hair behind her ear before grazing his fingers across her cheek. "That's three conditions," he said, his voice low, the stress gone from his face. "Will you marry me?"

Slowly she smiled. "I don't think I have any choice. In my books, my heroine always marries her hero. Since you're my hero…"

The intensity of his dark gaze was diminished by the blush that turned his cheeks bronze. "I've never been anyone's hero before."

"Of course you have. You're Rebecca's hero. And Carrie's. And Lucy's. Everyone thinks you're a hero, Tyler, except you."

He smiled faintly, then grew serious again. "I swear on my life, I'll never hurt you or Lucy." There was something in his voice that made the words not so much a promise but a statement of fact. He would always deeply regret what had happened with Angela—Jayne knew that—but he'd put it into perspective and he was leaving it where it belonged. In the past.

"I know you won't." Her words were a statement, too. She knew him. She loved him. She had faith in him.

Rebecca had once said she believed Jayne was destined to rescue Tyler from his past and from himself. At the time Jayne hadn't given any thought to how she was meant to rescue him. Now she knew: with love and faith. The most powerful gifts she could give him.

He faced her on the bench, his fingers gently gripping hers. "I love you, Jayne."

"I love you more."

With a wry grin, he shook his head. "Not possible." Then he leaned closer to kiss her, his mouth brushing across hers before settling over it. His tongue slipped inside, and his free hand slid over her shoulder, coaxing her closer. He kissed her hungrily, needily, until they were both short of breath, until their body temperatures exceeded the morning's heat, until she trembled and so did he.

Finally he ended the kiss and gazed down at her solemnly. "It was all worth it."

"What was?"

"My life. My father. Everything that happened. I'd go through it all again to end up with you."

Blinking away the tears that filled her eyes, she rested her head on his chest. It was better than one of her books. They would marry, make a family for Lucy, have babies of their own, live and love and argue and make up, grow old together, grow contented together.

They would live happily ever after.

Silhouette Desire

Introducing an exciting appearance
by legendary
New York Times bestselling author

DIANA PALMER
HEARTBREAKER

He's the ultimate bachelor...
but he may have just met
the one woman to change his ways!

Join the drama in the story of a confirmed
bachelor, an amnesiac beauty and their
unexpected passionate romance.

"Diana Palmer is a mesmerizing storyteller
who captures the essence of what
a romance should be."—*Affaire de Coeur*

Heartbreaker *is available from Silhouette Desire
in September 2006.*

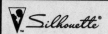

SPECIAL EDITION™

COMING IN SEPTEMBER FROM
USA TODAY **BESTSELLING AUTHOR**

SUSAN MALLERY

THE LADIES' MAN

Rachel Harper wondered how she'd tell
Carter Brockett the news—their spontaneous
night of passion had left her pregnant!
What would he think of the naive
schoolteacher who'd lost control? After
all, the man had a legion of exes who'd
been unable to snare a commitment, and
here she had a forever-binding one!

Then she remembered.
He'd lost control, too....

positively
+pregnant

**Sometimes the unexpected
is the best news of all...**

COMING NEXT MONTH